D0458726

RING OF FIRE

CENTURY
QUARTET
BOOK I

RING OF FIRE

CENTURY
QUARTET
BOOK I

By Pierdomenico Baccalario

Translated by Leah D. Janeczko

Illustrations by Iacopo Bruno

Random House New York

Published in the United States by Random House Children's Books, a division of Random House, Inc., New York. Originally published as *L'Anello di Fuoco* by Edizione Piemme S.p.A., Casale Monferrato, Italy, in 2006. Copyright © 2006 by Edizione Piemme S.p.A. This translation is the property of Atlantyca S.p.A., www.atlantyca.com. All rights reserved. All other international rights © Atlantyca S.p.A., foreignrights@atlantyca.it.

Color insert: original photos by Walter Menegazzi, with art by Iacopo Bruno, copyright © 2006 Edizioni Piemme.

Random House and the colophon are registered trademarks of Random House, Inc.

Visit us on the Web!
www.randomhouse.com/kids
www.century.it

Educators and librarians, for a variety of teaching tools, visit us at
www.randomhouse.com/teachers

Library of Congress Cataloging-in-Publication Data
Baccalario, Pierdomenico.
[Anello di fuoco]
Ring of fire / by Pierdomenico Baccalario ; translated by Leah D.
Janeczko. — 1st American ed.
p.   cm. — (Century ; [bk. 1])
Summary: Four seemingly unrelated children are brought together in a
Rome hotel where they discover that they are destined to become
involved in a deep and ancient mystery involving a briefcase full of
artifacts that expose them to great danger.
ISBN 978-0-375-85895-6 (trade) — ISBN 978-0-375-95895-3 (lib. bdg.)—
ISBN 978-0-375-89226-4 (e-book)
[1. Good and evil—Fiction. 2. Rome (Italy)—Fiction. 3. Italy—Fiction.]
I. Janeczko, Leah. II. Title.
PZ7.B131358Ri 2009   [Fic]—dc22   2009008204

Printed in the United States of America
10 9 8 7 6 5 4 3 2 1
First American Edition

Random House Children's Books supports the First Amendment
and celebrates the right to read.

This book is for my grandmother,
who sees the stars from very close up.

CONTENTS

I know that I am mortal.
But when I explore the winding circles of the stars,
my feet no longer rest on earth, but, standing beside Zeus,
I take my fill of ambrosia, the food of the gods.
—Ptolemy, astronomer

Nature loves to hide.
—Heraclitus, philosopher called the Dark One

THE BEGINNING

THE STARS OF URSA MAJOR ARE PERFECTLY STILL IN THE SKY.

The time has come for them as well.

Inside the shelter surrounded by ice is the sound of fingers drumming nervously on the table. Then a question, which hangs at length in the smoke-filled air.

"Do you think she'll come?"

There's no reply. The aluminum windows are bitter cold. It's snowing outside. The glacier gleams with a bluish glow.

"I think I hear wolves . . . ," one of the two men murmurs, scratching his beard. "Don't you?"

"Let's start," the other man suggests. He's gray and gaunt, like a tree that's been through a fire. "We don't have much time."

The woman stops drumming her fingers on the table, checks her watch and nods. "He's right. Let's start."

The two men open their notepads and start to leaf through them.

"How are the children?" asks the man with the beard.

"They're still growing," she answers. "And soon we'll have to choose."

She has around twenty photographs with her. She shows them to her companions. The pictures are passed along swiftly from hand to hand.

"How old are they?" the gaunt man asks.

"Eight."

The bearded man is clearly nervous. He anxiously springs up from the table, draws his face up to the window and looks outside, as if he could make out anything through the massive blizzard. "I heard them again. The wolves, I mean."

The gaunt man croaks out a laugh. "We're surrounded by thirty kilometers of ice. How could you be hearing wolves?"

The bearded man stands there at the window until the pane has completely fogged over. Then he goes back to his chair and checks his watch for the millionth time. "Maybe we should've met in a place that's easier to reach. A park, like last time."

"She wouldn't have come anyway. You know what she's like. In any case . . ." The gaunt man points at the photograph of a young girl. "Not her, we said."

The woman runs her finger along the rim of her teacup, then raises an eyebrow without revealing any other sign of what she's thinking.

"I've changed my mind," she says, sipping her tea.

"I don't think you can change your mind just like that."

"This is my task."

"But this girl . . ." A short, bony finger points at the face framed in dark, curly hair. "She's still your niece."

"She speaks two languages better than you do. What's it going to take to convince you?"

"You know the risks."

"And you know the reasons."

"Last time we said no."

"Last time she'd just been born."

There's a long moment of silence during which the only sounds are the kettle on the fire and the wind whooshing through the fireplace. The men stare grimly at the pictures on the table: Western faces, slanted eyes, blond hair, red hair, light skin, dark skin. Boys and girls all very different from each other, except for one fundamental detail. They'll soon learn what it is.

The shelter's walls groan under the weight of the snow. Overhead, the stars slowly follow along their course in the gelid nighttime sky.

"I wouldn't want you to be making a mistake," the gaunt man resumes.

"You've never made any before?"

"I try not to. Especially because I don't deal with nice people . . . You know that."

The man with the beard clears his throat to make the others stop arguing. Then he says, "Let's not be overconcerned right now. It's still too early to decide. I just need to know where I'll have to take the map."

"Where did you hide it?"

The bearded man shows the others an old briefcase. "This should pass unnoticed. . . ."

"I hope so. Also because if anyone realized—"

The gaunt man suddenly stops talking.

He hears something outside the shelter. Footsteps in the snow. Boots. The yelping of dogs. Furious howling.

Wolves.

The three spring to their feet.

"Now do you believe me?" shouts the bearded man, rushing back toward the window.

A moment before he manages to reach it, the door to the shelter is

3

flung open. The newcomer walks into the room, wearing boots complete with crampons. A thermal mask and a pair of gloves are thrown to the floor.

"Sorry I'm late . . . ," the person says with a disarming smile. Long, thick black hair tumbles out of her hood. "But I had to find out where it's going to begin."

She removes the crampons from her boots with a snap.

She closes the door, shutting out the sled drawn by wolves.

And she says, "It's going to begin in Rome."

1
THE TRAP

Perfectly still in the darkness, twelve-year-old Elettra waits.

Her legs crossed, her hands holding the string that will set off the trap, she's sitting stock-still. As motionless as the old wardrobes lined up around her in a series of shadows, one darker than the next.

Elettra breathes slowly, silently. She ignores the dust, letting it settle on her.

Come out, come out . . . , she thinks, only moving her lips.

Shrouded in the darkness, her fingers clutching the string, she listens. The boilers hum in the distance, pumping hot water through the pipes in the hotel rooms. The meters tick away softly, each one at its own pace. A dusty silence reigns over the basement.

The hotel, the city, the whole world seems incredibly far away.
It isn't cold.
It's the twenty-ninth of December.
It's the beginning. But Elettra doesn't know that yet.

* * *

A little noise tells her the mouse is approaching. Tick-tack.

The sound of tiny paws on the floor, coming from somewhere in the darkness.

Elettra slowly raises the string with a satisfied smile, thinking, *The irresistible appeal of pecorino Romano cheese.*

"No one can resist pecorino Romano," her aunt Linda always says when she's cooking.

Tick-tack. And then silence. Tick-tack. Then silence once again.

The mouse sniffs the air, warily following the aroma's path.

He's almost in my trap, thinks Elettra, rubbing her thumb against the string. Then, in her mind, she asks, *How long is this going to take you, stupid mouse?*

She's built a simple trap: a piece of pecorino placed under a shoe box, which she's suspended from an old umbrella shaft. A single tug will make it drop down on the mouse. The only difficult thing is figuring out, in the dark, when the mouse has reached the cheese.

She needs to follow her instinct. And instinct tells her it's not time yet.

Elettra waits.

A little bit longer.

Tick-tack goes the mouse. And then silence.

Elettra loves moments like this. The very last moments of a perfect plan, when everything is about to end in triumph.

She can already imagine her father's look of admiration when he gets back from his trip in the minibus. And her aunt Linda's shrieks when Elettra shows her the mouse, stone-cold dead, held up by the tail, as is fitting for a stone-cold dead mouse.

Her other aunt, Irene, would simply say, "You shouldn't go down to play in the basement. It's a very dangerous maze down there." And then she'd add, with a flash of cunning, "No one knows where that maze leads."

Elettra hasn't come down here to play. She's on a mission to catch the mouse.

That's not playing.

Tick-tack goes the mouse.

And then . . .

Then the basement ceiling suddenly starts quaking, rattled by a series of booms that make the bottles shake in their wooden racks.

It can't be! thinks Elettra, looking up. *No, not now!*

But the quaking doesn't stop. The dust starts to stir restlessly. The pounding on the floor grows stronger, turning into a series of furious footsteps accompanied by a voice that grows louder. In the end, it sounds like a siren.

"EEELEEEEEETTRAAAAAA!" the siren howls, throwing open the door to the basement.

A flood of light drenches the stairs, the stacked-up furniture, the bottles of wine, the wardrobes and the statues. Elettra's eyes dart straight out in front of her. The little gray mouse is standing there, on its hind legs, barely a centimeter inside the shoe box.

"You're not getting away from me!" she says, tugging the string.

The box falls, but not on the mouse.

"No!" she cries.

At the top of the stairs, Aunt Linda's hand gropes around for the light switches and flicks them all on. A dozen bulbs blink on, their blinding light driving away all traces of darkness. They're hanging from the ceiling inside round lampshades made out of old bottles.

"Elettra! Were you in the dark?"

"Darn it!" she shouts, jumping to her feet. "He got away again!"

"Who got away?" her aunt asks, baffled.

Elettra glares at her threateningly, the umbrella shaft in her hand. "What do you want now?"

At the top of the stairs, her aunt looks around at the basement as if she were seeing it for the first time. "Oh, what a mess!" she grumbles. "One of these days your father and I will just have to come tidy it all up. It's just not possible, I tell you, to have a basement in this condition!"

It's as though she has completely forgotten the reason she came down in the first place.

Looking at her, Elettra feels anger blazing up inside. Her aunt gracefully runs her hand over her thick gray hair, without understanding the damage she's done. The shoe box is lying on the floor, useless, and the vast stone basement is hiding a mouse who's still in perfectly good health. The whole maze of hallways and rooms packed with things now looks dingy in the harsh light of the bulbs.

"What do you want, Aunt Linda?" Elettra shouts a second time. And then, as the woman makes no sign of replying, she adds, *"Aunt Linda!"*

Her aunt stares at her with her big, clear eyes. "Elettra, dear," she says, perfectly calm. "Your father called from the airport. He says there's a problem with the rooms. A serious problem."

"What's wrong?"

"He didn't want to tell me."

"So where is he now?"

Aunt Linda smiles. "At the airport, naturally."

* * *

Fernando Melodia snaps his cell phone shut. The recorded voice of an operator has just informed him that he's out of credit.

"Oh, no," he groans beneath his perfectly trimmed mustache. "Now what do I do?"

Beside him are the Millers, an American couple with an angry-looking boy. They're standing tranquilly beside the sign for terminal A, watching over a pile of giant suitcases.

They're shorter than their son, a lean, tall beanpole with messy hair who's looking around as if he were expecting to be taken away and hanged. Maybe he's embarrassed about how his parents are dressed: an otter-gray checked jacket and polka-dot bow tie for him, a khaki-colored suit for her.

There they are, the Millers. They've arrived. They're pleased.

They've reserved the hotel's last available room to spend New Year's in Rome. The professor's also here to attend an important convention on the climate. His wife is clearly the type who loves shopping sprees. Their son, on the other hand, seems to have been dragged here against his will.

Fernando sighs.

So that he can be recognized as the owner of the hotel, tucked under his arm is a sign on which he's written:

HOTEL

DOMUS QUINTILIA

WELCOME!

That was Elettra's idea. An excellent idea, although for a few long moments, Fernando had regretted bringing it. He'd simply held it up and the Millers had walked right over to him, smiling. The two adults, at least.

Handshake.

"It was so kind of you to come get us," Mr. Miller had thanked him, leaving behind his pile of luggage carts for a moment.

Fernando returned a sheepish smile and from that point on, that smile hasn't left his face for a moment.

A smile in which he'd gladly bury himself.

The reason for his embarrassment is that he's at Fiumicino Airport to pick up two people. Not three. Two French ladies by the name of Blanchard and not three Americans by the name of Miller. He's expecting a mother and daughter flying in from Paris Charles de Gaulle, flight 808, arriving at terminal B. The young perfume designer Cecile Blanchard and her daughter, Mistral. He planned to greet them, have them get into the hotel's minibus, and give them the keys to room number four, the one painted lavender, complete with bathroom, shower and a delightful terrace overlooking the side lane.

The last free room in the hotel.

The hotel doesn't have another free room for the three Americans. Looking at them, they're happy and calm, which shows they're convinced of the opposite. And that Fernando's made some kind of mistake with the reservations.

A tough situation, with very few ways out of it.

He clutches his creditless cell phone in his pants pocket and hopes Elettra will call him.

"Is there a problem?" the American professor asks him. He adjusts his bow tie, something he does incessantly.

"No, no problem at all," Fernando says reassuringly as he tries to come up with a quick solution and forces himself not to think about the fact that it's the holiday season and Rome's swarming with tourists. "We just need to wait for two other guests to arrive." He points up at the arrivals board listing the flight from Paris. "They'll be here any minute now."

Delving into the confused jumble of people and luggage carts, Fernando tries to calm down. *This can be solved,* he thinks. It isn't the first time he's gotten a reservation wrong since his wife passed away. But this is the first time the entire hotel has been full. And he's got the feeling that the rest of the city's booked solid, too.

Then he thinks about the Internet. Ever since he started allowing people to make online reservations, things have become incredibly complicated. Before, all you had to do was answer the phone. Now you need to start up the computer, download the e-mail, record the reservation, copy the name down into the register and make a note of a sixteen-digit credit card number.

It's turned into a job for bookkeepers.

A wave of people push their way out of the international arrivals exit, which means that the flight from Paris has landed. Fernando raises the sign over his head with a certain sense of doom.

Maybe the two Parisians missed their flight. Maybe they changed their minds. Or maybe there's a free room he's forgotten about. But that's highly unlikely in a hotel that only has four guest rooms.

He glances over at the American boy, who looks like the only person in the world gloomier than he is.

The phone continues to stubbornly refuse to ring. How long is it going to take Elettra to call back?

"Are you from the Domus Quintilia?" a man's voice asks him just then.

Fernando looks down and sees two small Chinese people: a man wearing a shiny silk suit and a cheerful boy with blue eyes and a pageboy haircut.

"I beg your pardon?" Fernando replies mechanically. And as he does, he feels the characteristic shiver of the unexpected crawl up his spine.

The man wearing the silk suit waves a paper printout at the height of his belly button.

"I am Mr. See-Young Wan Ho," he says, introducing himself, "and this is my son, Sheng Young Wan Ho. You were very kind to come pick us up."

"I'm . . . I'm sorry?" Fernando stammers. And while he's stammering, out of the corner of his eye he spots a French woman walking up to him, accompanied by a girl who clearly appears to be her daughter.

Mr. See-Young Wan Whatever waves his piece of paper for the second time at belly-button height. His son, Sheng, smiles happily. "We booked room number four at your hotel. It was very kind of you to come pick us up."

Fernando Melodia's sheepish smile completely freezes on his face.

Meanwhile, the French woman, the perfume designer, the only party he'd been expecting that evening, is telling her daughter, "Look, Mistral. That's the man from our hotel."

Fernando stands there, stock-still, not knowing what to do.

Maybe that's why he doesn't notice the man dressed in black who passes by him, leaving behind the lingering scent of violets.

2
THE DUST

THE HOTEL'S COURTYARD IS IRON-COLORED, STILL AND SILENT. Elettra zips across it in the blink of an eye, passing by the well and the twisted trunks of the vines, which majestically rise up to the balcony. Peering out from the balustrade of the terrace are four statues with indecipherable expressions.

Elettra reaches the foot of the stairs and sticks her tongue out at the stone mask over the arched entranceway. Then she takes the steps two at a time and reaches the room of her other aunt, Irene.

She knocks on the door but opens it without waiting for an answer. The room is bathed in a soft light coming in from the large French doors that lead out onto the terrace. The ceiling is frescoed in green and the floor is covered with black and white checkerboard tiles.

"Aunt Irene?" Elettra cries out. "We've got a problem with the rooms again!"

Sitting in her wheelchair at the far end of the room, Aunt Irene is reading by the light of a heron-shaped lamp. She rests the book on her lap and looks at Elettra over her glasses, tilting her head slightly. She's a very thin woman, her gray hair held back in an elegant tortoiseshell hairpin. When she was young, and before the accident that paralyzed her, she was very beautiful.

"You don't say!" she replies, as if she already knew about the problem. "Your father did it again, did he?"

Elettra bounces across the room in a characteristic little trot. She kneels down on the rug in front of her aunt, making her smile with a grimace. "It sure sounds like it. But this time he did it big time."

"Meaning . . . ?"

"A triple-booked room," explains Elettra. "He's coming back from the airport with two French women, three Americans and two Chinese . . . all convinced they've got reservations for room four."

"Tell me you're joking," the old woman groans.

"No! I just talked to him on the phone."

"It can't be!" exclaims Irene, letting her book fall to the floor. "Is it so difficult for him to write down three reservations? If only your mother were here! She'd tell him a thing or two!"

"Aunt Irene . . ."

The woman slaps the palms of her hands against the arms of her wheelchair. "The fact is, your father's always had his head in the clouds. If my sister and I weren't here to look after him, this hotel would already have gone out of business!"

"Dad doesn't want to run the hotel," Elettra says in his defense. "He's writing—"

"He's writing!" her aunt laughs nervously. "Of course! His legendary spy novel. How many years has he been 'finishing' it? Five? Ten?"

Elettra doesn't let herself get caught up in the old debate.

Instead, she checks the time. "We've got less than twenty minutes to come up with a solution."

Aunt Irene sighs. "Which would be . . . ?"

Elettra shrugs her shoulders. "General panic?"

"Call Aunt Linda up here," the old woman decides. "It'll take the brains of three women to compensate for a man's!"

"Well, it's simple!" Linda decides a few minutes later, perfectly calm. "We tell them we don't have room and we turn them away."

"We can't do that!" protests Elettra.

"Then we find them alternative accommodation at our expense."

"Right. That's the first thing we need to try," says Irene, backing her up.

Elettra gets straight to work, but after a few fruitless attempts she hangs up the phone glumly. "This isn't going to be easy. Even the Astoria's booked solid."

Aunt Irene thumbs through the list of hotels and bed and breakfasts resting on her lap. She reads out the next number to her niece, muttering, "Blast New Year's Eve and all these tourists."

Linda paces her sister's room with long strides. She pauses beside a collection of snow globes, picks one up and passes her finger beneath it.

"Dust mites," she declares, examining her fingertip. "Your room needs a good cleaning. It's not healthy for you to live in the middle of all this dust. Especially given your condition."

"Linda!" snaps Irene, sensing she's about to launch into one of her rants about hygiene. "My legs are paralyzed, not my brain! A little dust has never killed anybody."

Totally unconvinced, Linda turns the glass ball upside down, her lip curling with disgust. Delicate white snowflakes begin to whirl around inside the globe. "Horrible," she proclaims, putting it back in its place after a few seconds. "This is just the kind of thing that only helps create clutter."

"You don't have to like them! Besides, this is my room and I'll keep whatever I want in it."

"And all these horrible old pictures?" her sister goes on relentlessly. "And those old dressers, with the unmistakable smell of mildew that old dressers have? They'll ruin all your clothes, I tell you! You should get yourself some new dressers, like the ones in my room. And put vanilla potpourri in them. One sachet for each drawer and all your clothes will smell like—"

"Like vanilla! Yes, I can imagine!" Aunt Irene practically howls. "Linda, would you mind trying to focus on our problem with the rooms rather than thinking about sterilizing my life?"

Elettra hangs up the phone for the fifth time.

"No luck. Not even at the Milton. It looks like the whole city's full, as stuffed as a Christmas goose."

"Oh, that's right!" exclaims Linda. "Speaking of food, what should we eat tonight? I could make a few slices of polenta with a little lard, or . . . or some amberjack. We could bake it with a few potatoes and fresh parsley. . . ."

Elettra ignores her and makes a sixth attempt. But this call, as well as the following one, is no use. "Everything's full," she finally summarizes.

"Well then . . . ," sighs Aunt Irene. "That only leaves plan B."

"Don't even think about it!" Aunt Linda says, holding out her hands. "I'm not giving my room to strangers!"

"Linda, we don't have any other—"

"Besides, it's a mess, a total mess. And you know what they'd do! They'd go in there with shoes on! You know perfectly well no one goes into my room with shoes on! Oh, no! And the bathroom? It needs disinfecting. And once they're gone? I'd never be able to use it again! There would be strange germs, viruses I don't have antibodies for. Or you two, for that matter! There are illnesses that can survive steam at a hundred degrees Celsius! They said so on TV! Like the man who brought the bird flu virus back with him to Turkey. Did you read about that?"

"Linda!" Irene grabs her wrist, cutting her off. "Listen carefully. In your room we can put the two ladies. The French woman and her daughter. Look at me: women. She's a perfume designer. Clean, sweet-smelling. And she'll only be sleeping here a couple of nights."

Her sister grunts, not very convinced. "And where would we put the Chinese man?"

"In Fernando's room."

"And Fernando?"

"On the sofa in the sitting room."

"The sofa in the sitting room is fragile!" Aunt Linda protests. "You know perfectly well that Fernando breaks everything he touches. Besides that, he sleepwalks!"

"Look who's talking . . . ," breaks in Elettra. "You're a sleepwalker, too."

"I am not," exclaims the aunt. "Once in a while I just happen to . . . to talk in my sleep a little, that's all."

17

"A little?" her niece teases.

Irene tries to bring the argument to an end. "Let's keep the Americans in room four. The French ladies go in your room, you come here to sleep in my room," she summarizes, "and the Chinese man goes in Fernando's room."

"Fernando can't sleep on that sofa," insists Linda.

"Then he'll sleep under the sofa!"

"He can't sleep on the floor. It's dirty."

"Listen, Linda," her sister interjects. "One of the reasons our hotel is always so full is that there's no place cleaner or more sweet-smelling on the whole planet. Therefore . . . Fernando will sleep on the floor, and right now you and Elettra need to get all the rooms ready for our guests."

Convinced, the two turn to leave. But then Linda has a nagging doubt. "Sorry, but . . . even if we do it this way we're still three beds short. One for the Chinese man's son, one for—"

"Then here's what we'll do: we'll put all the kids in the bunk beds in Elettra's room."

"Are you joking?"

"No. They'll have a world of fun. Elettra speaks English better than all of us put together. And her room's perfect."

"Yes, but—"

"But what?" the girl says, cutting her off with a shake of her thick black curls. "It's a great idea. And maybe the only solution. Come on, Auntie! We can do it!"

"Mr. Mahler?" asks the young woman at the airport.

She's standing in front of the international arrivals exit. Around her is the orange glow from a streetlight. She's thin, with

18

long eyebrows and the slender hands of a photographer. She's wearing a pin-striped jacket, tight-fitting jeans and a pair of tall green leather boots.

The man she's just asked the question doesn't stop. He passes right by her and pretends to check out the line for taxis. He's thin, dressed in black, and has straight gray hair, high cheekbones and a nose as pointy as an ice pick. He has tiny eyes and a mouth so thin it looks like a slit. He's wheeling behind him an anonymous black carry-on bag and is holding an unusual violin case.

"Are you Mr. Mahler?" the young woman repeats, walking up to him.

The first snowflakes begin to fall.

Without shifting his gaze, the man murmurs, "Possibly."

"Beatrice," she says, introducing herself. "I've come to pick you up."

"Obviously."

The young woman bites her lip. "Would you care to follow me?"

"You came here by car?"

"Obviously," she replies, peeved.

Only then does the man turn around. His gaze is cold and distant. "Fine," he says. "I know the airport is far from downtown. And I'm extremely tired."

"Joe Vinile asked me to take you over for something to eat—"

"Not tonight," the man objects. "All I need are a bed and a bathtub."

Beatrice leads the way down the sidewalk. "Nice violin," she remarks, opening the door to her yellow Mini.

"It's not a violin," he replies, slightly intensifying his hold on the case.

3

THE FOUR

It's snowing when Fernando Melodia's minibus reaches the courtyard inside the Domus Quintilia, in the old heart of the Trastevere district. His guests step out into the densely falling snow and scurry over to the shelter of the old wood-covered terrace. Their host quickly disappears into the reception lounge. And as they begin to unload the first suitcases, he returns to the minibus, nervously explains what's happened with the reservations, describes the emergency solution that the ladies of the house have come up with and, without waiting for their response, disappears once again into the hotel.

A heated dispute breaks out among the guests. Swirling down around them, the snow grows thicker and thicker.

The American professor is standing stock-still beside the entrance to the hotel, a furious look on his face.

"This is an outrage!" he thunders. "I've never been treated in such a manner!"

His wife has grabbed one of his lapels and occasionally yanks on it like a leash. "George . . . Calm down. . . ."

"Calm down?" he sputters, pointing first at the ancient courtyard of the Domus Quintilia and then at the stairs leading up to the reception lounge. "How can I calm down? We reserved a triple room and now we're being given a double! Where will our poor Harvey sleep?"

Hearing he's been caught up in the middle of something, "poor Harvey" looks around, disgusted. "Let's get out of here," he grunts. He steps aside to avoid the giant Scottish suitcases of Mr. See-Young Wan Ho.

The man from China is also frowning, and his shiny silk suit isn't enough to improve his mood. "Well, what about me, then? I reserved a double, the one that's being given to you . . . and now I wind up in a single room! And I have a son here, too."

But unlike "poor Harvey," the Chinese boy is running and jumping around wildly in the snow, commenting on everything he can see: the wooden terrace, the four statues peering down from the balustrade, the bleak-looking stairway of the entrance with the jeering mask, the well in the middle of the courtyard, the hotel's minibus.

The two French guests have remained off to the side and don't seem to have any intention of taking part in the dispute. They perfectly resemble each other, like two peas in a pod, and are dressed identically. Thin, delicate clothing in a color as indeterminate as their straight hair. When Mr. Miller asks for their opinion, Mrs. Blanchard limits herself to pointing out, "Evidently a mistake's been made with the reservations."

"This is an outrage!" the American man thunders out again, not at all pleased with such acquiescence.

"Let's get out of here," his son repeats grouchily.

"Wait . . . ," Mr. See-Young Wan Ho says, looking over at the hotel entrance. "Something might be happening."

Hey, his son thinks, stopping in his tracks in the snow.

Elettra has appeared.

She has an oval-shaped face; dark, determined eyes; and a cascade of curly black hair. At her side is an equally beautiful woman with a fresh appearance, light eyes and silvery shoulder-length hair. Both of them are smiling and reassuring, like those who have the solution to any problem.

"We're so very sorry . . . ," the woman begins to say. "But everything can be worked out. You'll see."

"In any case, we can talk this over where it's warm, if you like," says Elettra, inviting them in.

Captivated by Linda's eyes, the American professor radically changes expression. He frees his jacket lapel from his wife's grip and replies with an unexpected and conciliatory, "Of course."

Even "poor Harvey" seems to show a glimmer of interest in what's going on. Mr. See-Young Wan Ho accepts the invitation with a little bow. The two French ladies allow a very sheepish-looking Fernando to slip past them so he can take care of the luggage, and they follow Elettra into a beautiful dining room with a low ceiling, where there are five little freshly set tables and bright, cheery paintings hung on the walls.

Waiting for them is an elderly woman in a wheelchair.

"My name is Irene," the woman begins, smiling at them calmly. "And I'm tremendously sorry about what's happened."

The American professor seems ready to protest, but then, as if something has just dawned on him, he promptly decides to hear her out.

"There are no excuses for the mistake we've made," the woman continues. "But we believe our proposal is reasonable. The city's full of people and it would be impossible to find you better accommodation. Believe me, the rooms you'll be staying in might just be the most comfortable ones in the hotel."

"But mine is missing a bed for my daughter . . . ," the French woman adds.

"We can solve that problem, too," Elettra then replies. "My room has two bunk beds. If . . . Mistral, right?"

The French girl nods shyly.

"If Mistral wants, she can sleep in my room. The boys can share the other bunk bed. That way, everyone will have a place to sleep."

Mistral looks over at her mother, awaiting a nod of approval.

Sheng lets out a convinced *"Hao!"* He tries to catch Harvey's eye, but the American boy is staring down at the floor, embarrassed. His parents quickly discuss the situation. Mr. Wan Ho looks tranquilly at the elderly woman in the wheelchair.

The first person to decide is Mistral's mother, who shrugs her shoulders and concludes, "My daughter's used to being independent. If she's all right with it, then it's perfectly fine with me."

"Would you like to see my room, ma'am?" asks Elettra.

"No, no. Is it very far from mine?"

"Two flights of stairs."

Mistral and her mother exchange an amused smile and then accept the proposal.

"Very well," approves Aunt Irene, pleased.

"Well, it is getting late," Mr. Wan Ho breaks in, smoothing down his suit. "And we had a long flight. If my son agrees, I accept your proposal, too."

Aunt Irene then turns to the two Americans. "That just leaves you, Mr. and Mrs. Miller."

The man folds his arms across his chest with total composure. The woman leans over to brush a stray lock of hair from the forehead of her son, who promptly moves away from her. "Is it all right with you, Harvey? If not, we could—"

"Yeah, it's fine," he answers. For a brief instant, he looks up from his shoes and meets Elettra's eye. Shyly, he whirls around to get the suitcases.

After a few more awkward pleasantries, the dining room at the Domus Quintilia empties out.

Irene begins to wheel herself toward the elevator. A little door in the wall behind her opens up just a crack.

"You can come out now, Lionheart," she says, speaking to the dark crack in the door. "The coast is clear."

Fernando Melodia peeks into the room, makes sure all the guests have left and walks in. In his arms is a stack of clothes, towels and pajamas. "How did you know it was me?"

"I could sense your guilty conscience in the air."

"I . . ."

The wheels of the chair creak on the floor.

Outside the window, the gaunt silhouette of a statue stares at the pale sky.

"Just be careful with the sofa," the elderly aunt cackles.

"I'd rather sleep on the floor."

"I think you'd better, given how Linda might react if you don't."

"Darn it."

"Darn what?"

Fernando looks at the stairs he's just come down. "I left my novel up in my room. Maybe I should go back and get it. Tonight I could—"

"Leave it there, Fernando," the old woman sighs. "I don't think our Chinese friend wants to steal your masterpiece. Why don't you give me a hand with this chair instead?"

Fernando puts his pile of clothes down on an armchair and wheels Irene up to the black gate of the elevator. "Was it hard to convince them?" he asks.

"No more than usual," she answers sharply.

The iron doors open up with a metallic groan. Fernando Melodia tilts the rubber wheels up slightly and then, with a gentle push, wheels the chair into the elevator. "It's snowing," he sighs. "That hasn't happened in Rome for a long time."

"Let's go up to the roof, then," Aunt Irene suggests. "We can't miss seeing the city mantled in white."

The yellow Mini zips through the traffic on the city's ring road, called the Grande Raccordo Anulare. Its little wipers battle against the snow sticking to the windshield. A graceful symphony is playing on the radio. Swinging from the rearview mirror is a stuffed skull-shaped toy.

"I've heard a lot of stories about you, Mr. Mahler," says Beatrice, passing a hotel's white minibus, whose red taillights glimmer through the snowflakes like butterflies.

"And what were the stories like?"

"They all ended the same way," says the young woman with a smile, edging the Mini into a gap between two cars.

"And did you enjoy them?"

"Very much."

"You like sad stories."

"Sometimes sadness can be fascinating."

"More often than that, it's just plain sad."

For a few moments the two remain in silence, which is interrupted only by the rhythmic swish of the windshield wipers.

"I don't think you've fully understood the nature of my work," the man with the violin says.

"Joe Vinile talks about you like you're some kind of legend."

"I've never met Joe Vinile. A legend at what?"

"At crime."

The gray-haired man shakes his head slightly. "Exactly. What did I tell you? He got it wrong."

"So it's not true?"

"Actually, I'd say my job is to efficiently satisfy other people's expectations," the man affirms.

"That's a matter of one's point of view."

"Points of view don't exist."

"Then what does exist?"

"What you know how to do. And what you don't."

"Right. Work, then." Beatrice keeps both hands on the steering wheel of the Mini. "Joe told me this mission is being done for—"

Jacob Mahler's hand darts out as fast as a lightning bolt. His finger is already in front of Beatrice's nose when a low, threatening hiss comes out of his lips. "Shhh . . . Never say that name."

26

She keeps both hands on the steering wheel. She pretends she doesn't see his finger in front of her nose. She lets out a faint laugh of surprise. "Why shouldn't I? It's just you and me here in the car."

"Never say that name," the man with the violin repeats, pulling his hand away dramatically. "That's a friendly tip."

"So we're friends?"

"Want another tip? Ask fewer questions."

Beatrice shrugs.

For an instant, she rests her right hand on the stick shift. Then she turns up the volume on the radio.

Her yellow Mini splashes across the glistening asphalt.

It's snowing harder and harder.

4

THE COINCIDENCE

"COME IN!" ELETTRA CALLS OUT, SWITCHING OFF THE FAUCET. SHE thought she heard someone knocking. "Come on in!" she repeats, this time louder.

Her room is shrouded in darkness, with the exception of the light coming in from the street, through the window grating. It's a soft, warm light made vibrant by the falling snow.

The door leading out to the hallway opens up just enough for Mistral, the French girl, to slip inside. Elettra gives her a little wave and points at the bunk bed. "It'd be best if you took that one, over mine," she suggests, her mouth still messy with toothpaste. "That way we can leave the other one to Harvey and . . ." She can't remember the Chinese boy's name.

"Sheng," Mistral says, finishing her sentence. She's brought a large lilac-colored bag with her. Pajamas, a change of clothes, a toothbrush and toothpaste. She's very tall, taller than Elettra, and she's pretty, dainty, with straight-cut hair and very large eyes, which are perfectly round and perfectly blue. Perched on a slender neck, her triangle-shaped face looks like that of a wading bird, a watchful, tranquil stork. The girl moves with careful slowness, not touching anything, her timidity verging on utter stillness.

Elettra looks at her with the critical eye of someone who's accustomed to forming an opinion about others based on very few details. A typical defect among those who see dozens and dozens of people pass through their lives, people who only appear different from each other. Her initial verdict is: hopeless. Mistral's slow. The two of them could never get along. Elettra's used to rushing around self-confidently, while Mistral, to be mean, looks wimpy. And that's no good. Especially for a pretty girl who's much taller than Elettra is.

"Your room is beautiful," says Mistral. Her English has a peculiar cadence.

The tone of her voice and the look on her face make Elettra immediately reconsider her first impression. "You really think so?" she asks.

"Yes. It's wonderful." Mistral rests her flowered, lilac-colored bag on the bed, opens it up and takes out a pair of cloth slippers and a white towel. "It smells very nice. And it's so tidy."

"Basic survival, believe me," jokes Elettra. "Aunt Linda forces me to keep everything in its place. It's all got to be perfect, right down to the last millimeter. Come with me. I'll show you the bathroom."

Mistral is captivated by the mirror surrounded by little lights. She brushes her hand over the lit lightbulbs and murmurs, "I've always wanted a mirror like this." She stares at it with a dreamy look on her face. Standing at the door, Elettra watches her and smiles, happy to be able to share in that little emotion.

"And just think, I almost never use it . . . ," she says.

"Why not?"

"I've got sort of a problem with mirrors," Elettra says with a sheepish smile. "The more I use them, the more . . . the more they lose their shininess and turn dull."

Mistral laughs. "You're joking, right?"

"No. And that's not all. I burn out lightbulbs and all kinds of electrical devices. So for me, a mirror surrounded by lightbulbs is a sort of . . . minefield."

Her curiosity piqued, Mistral asks her a few questions, laughing with amusement at this oddity. Her triangular face reflected amid the lightbulbs is a portrait of tranquility itself. And so, as Elettra answers her questions, she's very happy to gradually do away with her label of wimp, replacing it with a more positive one: romantic dreamer.

"What are you thinking?" the French girl asks her, resting her hands on the edge of the sink.

Elettra snaps out of it. "Huh?"

"It's like you were looking at me through a magnifying glass . . . or am I wrong?"

"Oh, no, sorry. It's just been a long time since . . ." Elettra gathers her hair in both hands and lets it tumble back down onto her shoulders. "Since I shared this room with a friend."

Mistral smiles in reply, making a vague gesture with her hand. "I'm the one who's sorry. Because of my mother's job, I'm alone a lot, too. And as soon as I'm around other people, I get the feeling I'm being ripped apart and judged."

"I wasn't ripping you apart, believe me. Quite the opposite."

"Just pretend I didn't even say it."

"Okay," Elettra says, changing the subject, "so what does your mother do?"

"She works with perfume," Mistral explains. "That is, she makes it."

"She makes perfume? How?"

"Oh, hopefully I'll learn that when I'm older. You need to go to a special school. The one I want to go to is called International Flavors and Fragrances."

"You mean there are perfume schools?"

"In France, yes."

"And where's the one you like?"

"In Grasse, a town on the Côte d'Azur. They've been making perfume there for hundreds of years. It's not easy, believe me. To become a perfumer you need to study a lot. You need to know how to tell the difference between the various fragrances in the right categories. There are perfumes that affect the mind, the heart, the spirit, which are light and soft, and then there are earthy ones, which last the longest. Perfumes can be sharp, sweet, sandy, natural, chemical. . . . It's enough to make your head spin!"

"Wow," murmurs Elettra, fascinated. "I didn't know there were people who . . . who were actually trained to make perfumes."

As the two girls are talking about the smell of lavender and the large copper stills used to distill rose water, there is a second knock on the door.

It's Sheng, already in his pajamas. The Chinese boy with a pageboy haircut that looks like it was cut with a bowl is sporting cheerful, blue-striped, two-piece pj's and a pair of cumbersome red gym shoes.

"I forgot my slippers at home," he explains at once, noticing the girls' bafflement.

Elettra goes to shut the door, but Sheng tells her that Harvey, the American, is on his way down, too. "I heard footsteps in the hall behind me."

And, in fact, a few moments later, Harvey appears in the doorway. Despite his height, he's all hunched over, as though he has a world of problems hanging from his neck. And his hair is over his eyes, as though he doesn't want to see anything except his feet. "I haven't got any pajamas," he says, looking at Sheng's striped pj's. "Is that okay?"

"How are you going to sleep without them?"

"I'll just stay in my undershirt and boxers," he answers, turning beet red, his back to the girls.

"We aren't scandalized," replies Elettra, winking at the French girl. "Are we?"

Mistral lets out a little peal of laughter, which is interrupted by Harvey's stomping over to his bed. "I'll sleep up on top, okay?"

"Okay, *hao*," says Sheng in a soft voice. "I've always dreamed of getting the bottom bunk. . . ."

Harvey stiffens, as if he heard a hint of irony in Sheng's reply. "Did I say something wrong? You want the top bunk? Whatever." And without waiting for an answer, he grabs his gym bag and tosses it onto the lower bunk. "I'll take the bottom one."

"Hey! What are you doing?" Sheng asks calmly.

"Bedtime," Harvey announces, disappearing into the darkness of the bottom bunk. Standing there in his gym shoes, Sheng looks at the girls with amusement, his face plainly showing how

32

surprised he is by all this. Harvey seems like a pretty bullheaded guy. The kind who wants to act tough.

Elettra senses a challenge in the air, which she readily accepts. She rests her hand on the boys' bunk bed, and, leaning over to look at the jeans and tennis shoes that the American boy is still wearing, she asks him, "Do you always sleep with your shoes on?"

Harvey opens his eyes wide with alarm. "Huh?"

Elettra repeats, "I asked if, over in America, you sleep in your shirt, boxers, jeans and shoes."

Only then does Harvey realize he's still completely dressed.

Embarrassed, he stares at Elettra's pajamas, then at Mistral's and finally at the striped outfit worn by Sheng, who starts undoing his gym shoes, explaining, "I forgot my slippers. But I always take these off before I go to bed."

Outside of the room, the snow drifts down slowly. The two girls are sitting cross-legged on the floor. Harvey's in the bathroom and Sheng's brushing his hand over the dandelion-shaped lamp on Elettra's nightstand. It's a bundle of countless tiny wisps of glowing glass. "My father?" repeats Sheng in impeccable English. "He works in tourism."

"Does he have a travel agency?"

"Kind of. He organizes cultural exchanges. A Chinese boy goes to live with a European family for a month and a European boy goes to live with a Chinese family for a month. It's a sort of student exchange."

"Sounds interesting."

"I'll let you know in a month," Sheng mutters. And then he explains. "Basically, I'm going to act as a guinea pig in Rome, although my father really wanted to send me to London."

"Why not Paris?" breaks in Mistral.

"Because I like *Gladiator* more than *The Da Vinci Code?*" quips Sheng.

"Paris is Paris."

"And Rome is a beautiful city," Elettra replies in its defense. "It's old and new at the same time."

"And with the snow, it looks . . . magical," adds Sheng, peeking out the window.

"You guys are lucky. It almost never snows in Rome."

"Have you already met the family you're going to live with?" Mistral asks the Chinese boy.

Sheng shakes his head.

"No. I'll meet them next year—that is, in a few days."

"Do you know if you'll end up in a house with a boy or a girl?"

"I haven't got the slightest idea."

The bathroom door opens up and is instantly snapped shut again. Harvey walks up to them, dragging his bare feet on the floor. "Done. If you want, we can go to sleep now."

None of the other three kids seems to want to answer him.

Elettra hugs her knees in her arms and says, "It sure must be strange, living away from home for a whole month. I don't know if I'd like it."

"A month where?" asks Harvey. When they explain, he sneers, "I'd never want a stranger in my house."

"I'm not the least bit surprised," replies Elettra.

"Um, why's that?"

34

"Because you obviously don't like company. You've barely said a word since you walked into the room. Except 'Bedtime.'"

"Well, what was I supposed to say? I'm exhausted."

"You could've said something like, 'Guys, I'm exhausted. How about you?' It's called 'pleasant conversation.'"

"I didn't know what to talk about."

"Well, how about your favorite movie, the last book you read, when your birthday is . . . ," Sheng blurts out, running his fingers through the lampshade's tiny wisps of light. "In fact, I'm tempted to tell you guys when I was born—"

Harvey cuts him off with a hoarse laugh. "Actually, my birthday's pretty funny."

"Not as funny as mine," Mistral adds.

"Believe me. Mine's the worst," Sheng insists.

"I don't think so," Harvey shoots back, clasping his hands behind his neck. "I was born on February twenty-ninth. Can you believe it?"

A sort of electric charge fills the room. Elettra can clearly feel it surging down to her fingertips. It's a shock that comes from outside, from the street, or maybe from much higher up. As if in the sky, at an infinite altitude, some ancient mechanism made of stars and ancient mysteries has switched on.

The air echoes with silence and then suddenly becomes still and cold.

Sheng's hand grabs on to the dandelion lamp's wisps. Mistral, sitting at the foot of the bed, gasps.

Realizing he's said something strange, Harvey sits up and asks, "Weird, isn't it?" But there's a note of uneasiness in his voice. "Don't you think it's strange? February twenty-ninth!"

"I was born on February twenty-ninth, too," Sheng whispers, turning to stare at him.

The room grows even colder. And the electrical charge in Elettra's hands grows stronger.

"I don't believe it," says Mistral. "It can't be!" Her blue eyes are gleaming with amazement. "Me too."

Sheng's hands freeze completely amid the lamp's wisps.

"Man . . . ," he murmurs. "What . . . what a bizarre coincidence."

"Go figure . . . ," muses Harvey, sitting on the edge of the bed.

Elettra needs to move. She's boiling hot. Inside of her is a seething volcano. She walks up to the window and throws it open, letting in the chilly nighttime air. *How could it be?* she wonders.

She looks up. The sky is overcast. No stars can be seen.

But that doesn't mean they aren't there.

She shuts her eyes and lets a few snowflakes land on her face. They melt into tiny teardrops. Her hands are so hot her fingertips are aching.

When she opens her eyes again to look at the three people in her room, she notices that none of them has said a word.

Grouchy Harvey.

Dreamy Mistral.

Cheerful Sheng.

"I don't believe in coincidences," Elettra says, her voice trembling.

She's logical, rational, perfectly organized. She understands people at a single glance. She categorizes them, classifies them and always has an explanation for everything.

Except for when she winds up burning out lightbulbs or

ruining mirrors. Except for when a printer goes haywire or a tele-vision screen changes colors when she walks by.

She doesn't believe in coincidences. Not ones like this, at least.

Because Elettra was also born on February twenty-ninth.

When she tells the others this, she feels the need to lean against someone. Her hand barely touches Sheng's shoulder, and all the tension and heat she's been keeping inside of her instantly surges out like a flooded river.

"Aaahh!" cries the Chinese boy, feeling a burning sensation.

The dandelion lamp in his hands lets out a burst of blinding light and shatters into a thousand pieces.

5

THE CALL

MANTLED IN WHITE, THE TRAFFIC IN ROME SLOWS DOWN TO A HALT like a weary animal. All alone in her yellow Mini, Beatrice tries to cancel out everything around her as she sits in the protective comfort of her car. She turns up the volume of her CD player full blast and lets the music carry her thoughts far, far away. She's surrounded by endless lanes of cars, honking horns and glaring headlights. The statues guarding the bridges of the Tiber River stare at her sternly.

She dropped Jacob Mahler off outside the small house she'd rented for him in the Coppedè district, near Corso Trieste. It was Mahler himself who'd requested it. He wanted to sleep in one of those bizarre, menacing-looking buildings full of strange faces, masks, crenellations, turrets, lilies, roses and vines intertwined beneath the pointed rooftops.

Well, if that's what he wants. . . .

Beatrice rests her head against the car window. She's tired. The cold glass feels good against her cheek. It freezes out her most troubling thoughts. She was expecting a lot from this day, and she has the feeling she didn't get much out of it. Not that she thought "the great Jacob Mahler" would be more easygoing, but she's disappointed by the man's pointless arrogance and by how she let her thoughts get muddled.

Jacob Mahler is tremendously self-confident and incredibly cold.

They say he's one of the very best professional killers in the whole world.

Inside the Mini is a lingering trace of his violet-scented cologne.

Beatrice shuts her eyes and thinks back to how they said goodbye.

"What should I tell Joe Vinile?" Beatrice asked, dropping him off outside the house. A wrought iron gate spiked with sharp points. Balconies resting on the backs of ancient mythological figures.

"Tell him we'll meet tomorrow at eleven past eleven."

"Here?" Snowflakes were clinging to her hair like little white spiders.

He shook his head, looking at her with his piercing, light-colored eyes. He nodded toward the house. "I'm not here. Nobody's here."

I'm such an idiot, thought Beatrice. *No one's supposed to know that Jacob Mahler's here in Rome.*

"We'll see you at Joe's restaurant, then?"

For the second time, Jacob Mahler shook his head, enjoying the chance to make her feel foolish.

"Where, then?"

"At the best café in Rome. At eleven past eleven." Having made this enigmatic statement, he turned around and walked through the gates.

"Mr. Mahler?" Beatrice called after him. "Mr. Mahler? The best café in Rome . . . Which one is that?"

A thick whirl of snow was carried in by the wind, forming a white curtain between her and Jacob Mahler.

When she looked again, he'd disappeared.

A honking horn suddenly snaps her back into the real world. Traffic has moved ahead a few meters. Beatrice puts her car into gear and creeps forward. It could take her hours to get home. And all she wants to do is crawl into bed and close her eyes.

She's gripped by the anguishing feeling of helplessness. She looks for her cell phone and scans down the list of names. She finds Joe Vinile's number, stares at the phone's glowing display but can't find the courage to hit the call button. Instead, she sends him a message: MEETING TOMORROW AT ELEVEN PAST ELEVEN, AT THE BEST CAFÉ IN ROME.

"What the heck!" she yells, tossing the cell phone over her shoulder. She clutches the steering wheel and counts the minutes it takes her to move one meter forward. Just then, the cell phone starts ringing.

Beatrice twists her arm back and finds it, checks the number and is relieved to see it's neither Joe nor any of her ex-boyfriends.

"Beatrice?"

It's Jacob Mahler.

Her mouth drops open slightly. Her stomach churns with worry while her brain wonders, *How'd he get my private number?*

"Yes, Jacob?" Beatrice bites her lip. She just called him by his first name.

"There's been a change of plans," Jacob Mahler continues.

"How so?"

"We need to do something tonight."

"Did you hear from Joe Vinile?"

"We need to go see a man."

"Where?"

"Under the Ponte Sisto. In half an hour."

"We can't," replies Beatrice. The cars around her aren't moving. The snow whirls down from the sky and gives no sign of letting up. "I'm in the middle of a traffic jam."

"Find a way. It's very important."

"It's impossible! Nobody's moving."

"That's why *we're* going to move. I'll wait for you here. I'm counting on you."

Beatrice is about to protest, but Jacob Mahler has already hung up.

Try to think, she tells herself.

To get back to the Coppedè district, Beatrice would need to reach the first traffic light and turn off on the street going up the hill, on the other side of the divider.

The cars are lined up in three lanes. An endless procession of white and red lights surrounded by snow. At this rate, just getting to the intersection might take her half an hour.

And she doesn't have half an hour.

Nobody's moving.

That's why *we're* going to move.

Find a way.

A crazy idea flashes through her mind. Her arm shoots back and grabs the jacket from the backseat. She clasps her fingers around the door handle, her hand trembling.

Nobody's moving.

That's why *we're* going to move.

Beatrice takes a deep breath. She switches off the engine, opens the door and gets out of the Mini, leaving it stranded in the middle of traffic.

"I've gone totally nuts," she says, starting to walk between the other cars. "I've gone totally nuts."

Horns are blaring out behind her, but Beatrice doesn't turn around. She starts running, reaches the traffic light and crosses the street. Just as she expected, cars are zooming down the road going up the hill.

"The mysteries of traffic in Rome," she murmurs with a smile.

Just past the intersection, she starts waving her arms. A dark car pulls up beside her. "Need some help?" the young driver asks, rolling down his window.

"Yes," Beatrice replies.

Suddenly, something strange happens.

Around them, all the lights in the city suddenly go out. The traffic lights go out. Then all the streetlights. Then the shop lights. The lights in all the houses.

Rome is plunged into darkness.

"What's going on?" the young man asks, looking around, astonished. Instinctively, he gets out of his car, leaving the door open.

To Beatrice, this is a sign of destiny.

"I'm stealing your car," she says.

Thinking she's joking, he plays along. "Oh, sure. Be my guest! What are you, a thief?"

"Maybe." Without giving him the chance to react, Beatrice dives down into the driver's seat, grabs hold of the steering wheel and peels out, splashing up a wave of slush behind her. The young man runs after her, shouting.

It's snowing.

Her yellow Mini is abandoned in the middle of traffic.

She's just stolen someone's car.

Rome is pitch-black.

But all she thinks about is getting to Jacob Mahler in time.

6
THE DARKNESS

IT'S PITCH-BLACK IN ELETTRA'S ROOM.

"Did you hurt yourself?" the girl asks Sheng, kneeling down beside him. The shattered dandelion lamp is lying on the floor in a thousand pieces.

"No, but—"

"Mistral?"

"Harvey?"

"I'm here."

"Me too."

"Is anybody hurt?"

"No."

"What happened?"

The kids move closer to each other, crawling on the floor.

"Watch out for the glass."

"It's everywhere," says Sheng.

Elettra feels around for the light switch. She flicks it, but nothing happens. She goes into the bathroom, but the light doesn't work there, either.

"No luck. We must've blown a fuse."

"A flame," says Harvey. "It was like a flame."

"I—I saw it come out of Sheng's hands," Mistral stammers. Her voice is quavering like a violin string.

"Man," repeats Sheng. "Man . . ." It's as though he is incapable of saying anything else.

The room is totally immersed in darkness. The only light coming in is the reflection of the snow falling in the courtyard. A dark courtyard, like the bottom of a black box.

"Where are you going?" asks Harvey, hearing Elettra move across the room. She sits down on the edge of the bed and slips on a pair of shoes.

"I'm going out to check the hallway."

"I'll go with you," the American boy offers, suddenly active.

Actually, Elettra's mind is somewhere else. She's thinking about the bolt of energy that surged through her. How she transmitted this to Sheng by touching his shoulder. How the energy made her aunt's lamp explode.

She's scared. She can feel her body trembling, right down to her bones.

The lamp exploded in a blinding flash of white light.

Harvey gropes around and finds his shoes at the foot of the bed. "I knew I shouldn't have taken these off," he jokes.

"You guys aren't leaving us here, are you?" asks Mistral.

Elettra makes her way toward the door. "I'm just going out to see if the light in the hallway works."

"I'm ready," says Harvey. Then he pats his legs, realizing he's still in his boxer shorts. "Um, just a sec." They hear a brief rustling of jeans. Elettra opens the door and tries flicking the switch in the hallway.

Clack. Clack.

Nothing.

"Man," murmurs Sheng for the millionth time.

"What do we do?"

"I'm going down to check the electrical meters," says Elettra.

"Have you got any candles?"

"In the kitchen, maybe," she replies.

"Where are you?" asks Harvey, groping around the bedroom. He trips over something, making a loud thud.

"My bag!" cries Sheng.

"Don't move, Harvey!" orders Elettra with a touch of agitation. "Everybody, stay right where you are! Let's let our eyes get used to the dark."

"I can't see a thing," says Sheng.

Neither can Harvey. He stays perfectly still.

They all remain in silence.

Elettra thinks, *Everything can't be as dark as this.*

A few moments later, Harvey says, "I'm starting to make things out a little. Elettra, I can see you near the door. I can see the beds, too."

"So can I," murmurs Mistral.

"I still can't see a thing!" Sheng insists.

Elettra nods. To her eyes, too, the glowing snow is helping her make out the blurry silhouettes of the furniture in the room. But beyond the door, toward the inner rooms of the hotel, the hallway is pitch-dark. "I can see a little bit . . . ," she says.

"Lucky you," replies Sheng. "Because I still can't see a thing. Maybe . . . the explosion blinded me. . . . Hey!"

Something's brushing up against his face. It's Mistral's hand. "Don't worry, Sheng. It's just me."

"What are you doing?" the Chinese boy asks her.

The girl's hands are caressing his face. "I don't think you were hurt, Sheng. It's just . . . well, maybe you should open your eyes."

Sheng gives an embarrassed start. "Huh? I *what* . . . ?"

"Your eyes are closed."

Sheng tries to calm down and slowly opens his eyes.

This time it's Mistral who gives a start. "Sheng!" she cries out. "Guys, look!"

"What is it?" he asks, suddenly nervous.

He sees Harvey and Elettra's shadows standing over him. A hunched beanpole and a wild mane of dark curls.

"Your eyes . . . ," whispers Mistral.

"What's wrong with them?" he asks, putting his hands up to his face.

Harvey shakes his head. "I must be dreaming."

"What?"

"They're yellow," says Harvey.

"They look like gold," whispers Elettra. "Like two precious little jewels . . ."

"You guys are kidding, right?"

Mistral shakes her head. "No, really! You've got two giant owl's eyes."

"Golden yellow."

"But it's going away," Harvey points out.

"What's going away?"

"The glow in your eyes. It's like they're . . . melting."

"Do they hurt?"

"No!"

"Can you see okay?"

"I see everything . . . yellow."

"But what can you see, exactly?"

Sheng gets up. "You guys, the beds, the door to the hallway, the bathroom . . ."

"You can see all the way to the bathroom?"

"Yeah. I mean . . . What, can't you guys?"

"Not me."

"Me neither."

"Everything's dark, Sheng. We can't see a thing."

"What's happened to me?"

"I'm going down to check the meters," decides Elettra, wheeling around.

"We're coming, too!" the other three shout out, almost in unison.

Moments later, the four kids are feeling their way down the hall leading to the dining room. "I'm seeing less and less yellow . . . and not so far away anymore," Sheng tells them.

He turns to look at Mistral, who says, "They're almost back to normal."

Sheng wipes his forehead with the back of his hand. "So whatever it was, it's going away, right?"

"That was pretty cool, though," comments Harvey. "A flame turning you into a nocturnal animal."

"Next time *you* do it, okay?" Sheng jokes.

Elettra leads the way. She knows the hallway by heart, but in the silent darkness, something is bothering her. And she's got the nagging feeling that somehow it's her fault.

They reach the dining room with its rows of little tables. The white tablecloths, in the near darkness, make them look like big, sleeping flowers. At the other end of the room, the elevator's emergency light is off.

"The whole power system must've shut down," Elettra says to herself.

She crosses the room, her hand brushing against the tables, making the porcelain cups rattle on their saucers.

"Does this happen often?" asks Sheng.

"Occasionally," Elettra lies.

"I can't see a thing," Sheng moans after a while. They're standing beside the big door leading out into the courtyard, at the bottom of the stairs that go up to the bedrooms.

"Auntie?" whispers Elettra, hearing a noise coming from the floor above.

Silence.

"I'd say they're all snoozing away."

"Actually, there's not much better to do during a blackout . . . ," Harvey points out.

"Could we open up the door to let a little light in?"

"Sure. Give me a hand," orders Elettra. She pushes on the heavy, well-oiled bolts, which slide across without making the faintest noise. The door opens up with a decisive clack, as if it were waking up from its silent slumber.

Outside, a mantle of white has covered everything. Soft

and light, compact and silent, it gives a graceful appearance to the square courtyard, the well, the awkward shape of the mini-bus. Over the terrace, the four statues have big heads of white hair.

"It's like being in *Lord of the Rings*," says Harvey.

"I wouldn't be surprised if Gandalf jumped out from somewhere," Sheng agrees.

Mistral bites her lip, remaining silent. The stone courtyard looks magical to her, too, but she was thinking of something far more poetic than a simple movie.

With the front door wide open, a glow now fills the hotel's atrium, allowing them to make out the stairway, the reception desk with its large copper umbrella stand and a thick cluster of garden plants.

"Elettra?" calls out Sheng when he notices that the girl of the house has disappeared.

"Coming!" a voice calls back from a distance. The kids hear a few drawers being opened and shut, and then Elettra's voice. "Great! I knew it!"

She reappears from behind the reception desk holding a pack of cigarettes.

"You smoke?" Harvey asks her, horrified.

Elettra smiles and her perfectly white teeth gleam with the reflection from the snow. "I don't. But my aunt Linda does. That is, she tries to make us believe she gave it up years ago, but I was sure she kept an emergency pack of cigarettes hidden around somewhere. And this is just what we need." She opens up the pack and takes out a green disposable lighter.

* * *

Harvey's thumb gives the lighter a flick, and a little flame lights up the stairs leading down into the basement. "Wow! Look at this place! It's like—" Mistral passes by him, cutting him off before he has a chance to ruin the fascinating effect of this place, too. It's an ancient stone basement, its stairs disappearing into a maze of rooms piled high with old things.

"It's magnificent . . . ," she remarks, taking in the atmosphere.

"*Hao!* Cool!" murmurs Sheng, admiring the stairs that disappear down belowground.

"The meters are right over here . . . ," Elettra says calmly, moving a few steps beyond the doorway. Harvey holds up the lighter so they can see the row of ugly black boxes, inside of which sparkle metal disks, which are perfectly still.

"It looks like they've stopped completely."

"There's an echo in here," Mistral points out, a few steps farther down.

"And a nasty old mouse, too," adds Elettra, checking the meters. "You're right, Harv. They've stopped."

The flame from the lighter flickers in the darkness. The American boy's eyes are big and deep. "Yep, Elly," he answers her, resting a hand on her shoulder.

Elettra blinks a couple of times. And she thinks, *Elly? No, no. That's no good.* She hates nicknames. And she's got to be the one who decides how friendly a boy can get with her.

"My name isn't Elly," she says, stepping away from him.

"Then my name isn't Harv," he replies stonily.

Then he lets the lighter's flame go out.

The basement is plunged into darkness.

I like this guy, thinks Elettra.

* * *

Covered with snow, the courtyard of the Domus Quintilia has a special charm of times gone by. Hearing a single, prolonged tolling of a bell, Elettra feels a cold shiver creep down her back beneath her pajamas.

"Maybe I should go wake up my dad. Or my aunt."

"But why?" Harvey asks her. "If the power's out, there's nothing they can do about it. Besides, unless I'm mistaken . . . that bell tower's out, too."

Mistral is beside them at the threshold of the front door. She points out the vertical silhouette of the Santa Cecilia bell tower to the others. "Harvey's right. It was lit up when we got here tonight."

"It's true!" cries Sheng, who adds, *"Hao!"*

"Why do you keep saying that?" Mistral asks.

"Hao? It's an exclamation. It's like saying 'cool' or 'great.'"

Elettra shakes her head, not listening to them. "It can't be. Nothing like this has ever happened before."

"The power of February twenty-ninth," remarks Harvey.

"What do you mean?"

"Four people born on February twenty-ninth wind up in the same city, at the same hotel. . . ."

"In the same room . . . ," Sheng specifies.

"And they make the lights go out all over Rome. It seems pretty normal to me. Or at least not very strange."

Elettra looks at the snow piling up on the well. She can feel her heart thumping in her chest and her thoughts whirling through her head. Harvey's right. The lights went out the moment she transmitted her energy to Sheng. And when she did, the lamp exploded and the boy's eyes turned into two golden nuggets.

52

"We could go take a look," she said, summarizing all her concerns.

"Where?" asks Sheng.

"Outside."

"Outside where?"

"Outside the hotel. We could take a walk down the street and find out if there's really a blackout everywhere. Or only here at our place."

"And once we find that out?"

"I don't know. We'll have found out. That's all."

"But why should we find out?"

"Because we're the only people in the hotel who are awake?"

Mistral shivers. "I'm not going. It's too cold."

They're all still in their pajamas, except for Harvey, who's already in his jeans.

"We'd all catch a cold," says Sheng.

"Your clothes are back in the room," replies Harvey, catching Elettra's eye. "We'll just put on something warm and then take a look around the city."

7

THE BRIDGE

THE TRASTEVERE DISTRICT LOOKS LIKE IT'S BEEN DRAWN WITH CHAR-
coal. Silent and still, it rises up over a white carpet of snow. Austere
buildings, sloping rooftops, dark porticoes, slanted gutters, tilted
chimneys.

Everything dark.

The kids warily leave the hotel, turn their backs to Santa
Cecilia and head toward the river. Their footsteps crunch down
gently into the compact layer of white snow.

Sheng is the only one of the four who hasn't stopped talking. To
keep his hair from getting wet, he's put on one of the hotel's shower
caps, and he's trying to convince the others to do the same.

"You look crazy with that thing on," Harvey remarks bluntly.
After the explosion and the blackout, his mood has radically
changed. He seems calmer, more self-confident.

The kids reach Piazza in Piscinula, where groups of people are
standing around talking about what's happened. They light up
their surroundings with their car headlights and point at the
buildings shrouded in darkness. There are men and women laughing and others complaining. A bartender's been unexpectedly left

without any music. A group of students have abandoned their backpacks in the snow to have a furious snowball fight. Elettra singles out two adults standing a bit off to the side and asks them what they know about the blackout.

"The lights are out in Trastevere," the woman replies. "And in the Parioli and Esquilino districts, too. But in some places, nothing happened."

"It's all because of that blasted underpass," grumbles the man, who then launches into a harsh assessment of the construction work being done. "Do you hear all that ruckus?" The kids listen and hear a constant, although distant, honking of horns. "Can you imagine what's going on in the roads, with all this snow and the traffic lights not working?"

Mistral dodges a snowball and packs one of her own, which she hurls randomly into the square. "Uh-oh. Bad idea," remarks Harvey.

"No, it isn't! It's a great idea!" cries out Sheng, standing beside Mistral. Soon they've started throwing and being hit by snowballs from every direction.

Without the streetlights or neon signs, the old quarter of Rome is an incredible sight, with its labyrinth of cobblestone streets and sleepy buildings. "Want to go see what the Tiber looks like in the dark?" asks Elettra when there's a lull in the snowball fight.

"Is it far from here?"

"No. It's right around the corner."

When they reach the river, the kids discover that the city's practically been divided into two parts. One side is lit up, but the other is shrouded in a thick mantle of silent darkness. Leaning against the parapet of the Ponte Garibaldi, Harvey, Elettra, Mistral and Sheng look out at the quarter on the other side of the Tiber, where the lights are still shining.

"So it isn't a total blackout!" remarks Elettra, a little reassured.

None of the others say a word. Admiring the glimmering reflection of the lights in the river and the lazy dance of the snowflakes, Mistral feels like she's been swept up in a daydream. "What's up there?" she asks, pointing over at Tiber Island, only half of which is lit up. It's as though the island marks the dividing line between electric light and darkness.

Elettra answers, "As far as I know, there's Fatebenefratelli hospital, a restaurant, a couple of churches and—" She stops short.

"What?"

Elettra lets out a strange laugh. "A Madonna statue called Our Lady of the Lights."

"A fitting name, I'd say," says Harvey. "Want to go take a look?"

"Oh, we can't. The Madonna's inside the church, which is closed at night."

"I meant the island," Harvey clarifies.

"If you guys want to."

The four kids head toward the oldest bridge in the city, which makes its way over the Tiber like a long, dark shadow. When they reach it, Elettra says, "This bridge is called Ponte Quattro Capi. It's named after a legend, naturally."

"What legend?"

"Halfway across the bridge there are four heads. They say they're the heads of the architects who built it. They were always arguing with each other, so they were beheaded once the work was finished. But their heads were sculpted on the bridge so they'd always be united, at least when they were dead."

"How horrible!" gasps Mistral.

"Actually, there are eight heads. Four plus four . . ." Elettra continues to explain as they make their way along the slippery, snowy bridge. "And they aren't really the heads of the architects; they're those of Giano Bifronte."

"Who's he?" asks Harvey.

"Janus, a god with two faces, one looking back on the past and one looking forward toward the future."

The Tiber drifts by lazily beneath the kids' feet. The snowflakes disappear in the river's dark, slow-moving water, while little gusts of wind dance beneath the bridge's curved vault.

"It's strange to see half the city lit up and half the city dark," murmurs Mistral. She wishes she had her paper and pencil with her so she could draw it. She tries to commit every little detail to memory. "I could stay here all night long looking at it."

"So are we going to the island or aren't we?" Sheng asks impatiently.

"Just a moment," says Elettra, standing beside the faces carved into the bridge. "Don't you guys feel hot?" she asks, almost without thinking.

"Hot?" Harvey asks, gawking at her. "Are you crazy? We're about to freeze!"

But Mistral walks up to her and asks, concerned, "Elettra? Everything okay?"

"Of course."

"Your hair looks strange. . . ."

When Mistral's hand touches her, a flame blazes up inside of Elettra, her hair turning into a thick tangle of long black snakes.

She looks up at the sky. Peeking out through the clouds are a few twinkling stars.

And on the other side of the bridge is a man running in their direction.

He's clearly exhausted. He staggers and looks behind him, frightened. He stops to catch his breath and then starts running again. When he's only a few meters away from the kids, the man falls silently down to the ground. He tries to get up but doesn't have the strength.

"Help!" he cries, sprawled out on the ground. He's clutching an old brown leather briefcase. Once again, he cries out, "Help!"

Elettra, Harvey, Sheng and Mistral stand there, stock-still, unable to move or take their eyes off the man. He must be sixty years old, maybe seventy, and he's wearing a very elegant raincoat.

"Whoa!" exclaims Sheng, stunned. "What's going on?"

Harvey takes a step back. "Let's get out of here. . . ."

Standing beside Elettra, Mistral tries to pull her friend back. "He looks drunk!" she whispers. But Elettra stands there, looking at him. The man has noticed her. He looks up at her. And . . .

I know him, thinks Elettra, although she's well aware it's not true.

He has a thin face with sunken features and a long white beard. There's something strangely familiar about him, although Elettra is positive she's never seen him before.

"Help! Help me!" repeats the man with new energy. He reaches out his hand. "Please . . . please . . ." His fingers are stiff and white from the cold. His face is imploring yet determined.

"Elettra . . . ," Mistral whispers behind her. "Don't get involved."

Lying on the ground, the man is clutching the briefcase to his chest. He doesn't stop staring at her for a single moment. It's as though he recognizes her, too.

"Who are you?" Elettra asks under her breath.

His lips purple from the cold, he begins to silently repeat a word.

"That's enough!" decides Harvey. "Let's get out of here!"

The man's lips obsessively continue to repeat the same word over and over.

"What . . . what's he saying?" whispers Elettra.

She's sweating. *It's hot. Doesn't anyone notice how hot it is?* she thinks.

"Guys!" Harvey insists.

"Let's go!" Sheng agrees.

Just when Mistral's almost managed to convince the girl to leave, Elettra finally understands what the man is repeating.

She bolts toward him.

"Come on!" she orders the other kids. "We've got to help him!"

When she gets near him, the man rolls over on his side, trying to stand up. Elettra grabs him by the arm and tries to help him to his feet, but he's too heavy. His clothes are dripping wet. And he's trembling. Shaking the snow from her hair, she waits for someone to help her.

Harvey reaches them. "You're crazy," he tells her. "Do you have any idea what you're doing?"

"No," Elettra admits. She grabs the man under one arm. Harvey does the same with the other. Together, the two manage to lift him up to his feet. He staggers, coughs and leans against the parapet. "Thank you . . . ," he says in a low voice. "You . . . you . . ." His hands are trembling constantly. His pants are torn at the knee.

"Who are you?" Elettra asks him. "And why were you saying that word to me?"

The man shakes his head. "It's begun! It's begun!" he shouts, pointing at something behind him. Because of the snow, it's impossible to make out what it is. All they can see is Tiber Island, half-lit-up and half-dark.

"What's begun?" Harvey asks him.

The man stares at him, a frantic look in his eyes. "You know. You all know! It's begun! They know. And they're coming!"

"Who's coming?" insists Elettra. "And who are you?"

The man looks back over his shoulder. "They're already too close." He clutches the briefcase to his chest tightly, as if he wants to crush it.

"Close to what?" asks Elettra.

"Let's go," Harvey decides categorically.

The man sees someone appear right behind the two kids and cries out, "Them!"

Elettra and Harvey whirl around, but it's only Mistral and Sheng, the latter with the ridiculous shower cap still covering his head. "Don't worry," Elettra tells him with a sigh. "There are just the four of us here."

"Four. Four. Four," the man begins to repeat.

"Guys . . . ," murmurs Sheng, drawing one step closer. "Are you sure everything's all right?"

"What does it look like?" Harvey replies sarcastically.

The man desperately tugs on his beard and hair.

Elettra asks him again, "Who are you? And why were you repeating that word?"

He stares at her with wide eyes. "I don't know," he murmurs, suddenly calm. "But you've got to help me before they get here."

"I don't understand."

"You don't have to understand. You just have to . . ." Trembling, the man holds the brown leather briefcase out to her. "Take this."

"I don't want it!" cries Elettra. "What is it? And why . . . ? I don't even know who you are!"

"Please," the man insists. "They're looking for me. I don't have time to explain. No one does. No one."

Elettra looks at Harvey, who shakes his head. Mistral is as pale as a ghost, and Sheng looks like he's ready to bolt. The white snow whirls around them, dancing. A strange energy makes her fingertips tremble.

There's nothing to understand. All that matters is instinct. And instinct tells her to accept the briefcase from the stranger. "What do you want me to do with it?" she asks him, taking it.

"Keep it in a safe place," the man orders. His face looks more relaxed, as if he's freed himself from an unbearable burden. "I'll come back for it as soon as I can."

Elettra nods. "When?"

The man raises his hand to caress her cheek and, although it's totally out of character for her, she lets him. "Soon. And thank you," He looks at Harvey, Mistral and Sheng with an odd, sad look. "Run," he adds. "Before they get here."

He looks over his shoulder.

And he starts running again.

* * *

The kids gather around Elettra and the leather briefcase.

"Is it heavy?" asks Sheng.

"No."

"Man!" he exclaims, pulling the shower cap off his head. "Does stuff like this happen often in Rome?"

Elettra tries to breathe calmly.

"Why'd you do that?" Harvey asks her, almost accusingly.

"I don't know," Elettra answers. "He needed help. He was scared. . . . And then . . . he kept repeating something."

"Huh?"

"He was lying on the ground. He was looking at me and he kept repeating it. . . . At first I didn't understand. But then, when I figured it out, it's like something . . . clicked."

"What was he saying?"

"A number," replies Elettra. The snowflakes are like thousands of little white insects. "Twenty-nine. Like our birthdays."

The man in the raincoat runs far away from Ponte Quattro Capi.

He runs.

And he keeps running.

He runs down a stairway leading to the bank of the Tiber and continues on swiftly, never looking behind him. Without the briefcase, he feels light and unusually pleased. He hasn't felt like this for days, weeks, months.

He laughs, stumbles by the riverbank, catches his balance and keeps laughing.

To his right, the black wall of the riverside street called Lungotevere rises up toward the clouds, seemingly without end.

To his left, less than a meter away, the river roars along, heavy with water. Everything else is distant, silent, unreal. It's as though the world consists only of that endless wall and that long, liquid snake of water.

He feels euphoric.

He stops to catch his breath and looks around. He's reached a series of dark arcades. Caught in the thorny branches of dark, low-lying bushes are shreds of cloth and plastic.

Mixed in with the sound of the river he thinks he hears some kind of music. A slow, incredibly painful melody. A dirge hiding something forgotten, dolefully distant. It drifts sweetly through the dark arcades and mingles with the sound of the falling snow. The music is soft. Warm. Inviting.

The man blinks his eyes several times, brushes his damp hair off his forehead and wonders if the music is really there or if it's only his thumping heart, his imagination. He pants, feeling the chilly air in his throat, takes a few steps, staggers and stops once again. Finally he's convinced that the melody is actually there. He's really hearing it. It's coming from the darkness, from the depths of the earth, from below the street, along which cars are crawling nervously, lined up in traffic.

Its sound is sharp and deep, alive and mournful.

"A violin." The man understands, drawing closer to the source of the music.

He rests his hand against the wall. He feels the slippery chill of the old bricks. He walks along, dragging his feet. He wanders into the darkness, led solely by the call of the violin.

He feels exhausted but he can't stop. He walks through the damp darkness of the arch like a bee trapped in a bottle. The farther he walks, the stronger and more captivating the melody becomes. It's calling out to him.

But just when its pitch reaches a peak, it stops entirely, suddenly.

The man looks around, disoriented.

Where am I? Why did I come down here? And where is "here"?

The river is still behind him, but it's immersed in a thick darkness.

Standing before him is a violinist with hair as gray as steel.

Jacob Mahler draws the bow away from his violin and lowers his arms to his sides. "Welcome, Alfred . . . ," he murmurs with icy calmness. "You aren't easy to find."

The man stands there like a pillar of salt. "What . . . ?"

" 'Gesang ist Dasein,' " Jacob Mahler recites, looking at his violin. " 'Song is existence.' Those aren't my words but those of Rilke, a German poet. He knew that no man could resist the call of music."

"What's going on here? What do you want?"

Jacob Mahler takes two steps toward him. The man he called Alfred teeters in the dark of night. "I want the Ring of Fire," Mahler whispers.

A long silence. The sound of dripping water. Rome echoing out in the distance.

"I don't know what you're talking about."

"You're the Guardian," whispers Jacob Mahler. "And a Guardian always has something to guard. I've come to get it."

"You're wrong. I'm not the Guardian."

"I know who you are. And I know all about the secret you're trying to protect. I flew twenty-nine thousand kilometers to come here."

The Guardian's eyes grow wide. "You're one of them."

Jacob Mahler's laugh is strident. "Of course I'm one of them. Whatever 'they' are, I am, too. Now tell me, Guardian . . . where is it? Where is the Ring of Fire?"

"I don't know what you're talking about."

The violin's bow hisses through the air like the gleaming blade of a knife.

"Look here!" Jacob Mahler cries out. "Don't fool with me!"

The Guardian swallows hard and then lets a faint smile flash across his face.

"What's so funny?"

"Nothing. I was just thinking. You flew twenty-nine thousand kilometers to come here to get something I don't have. And neither one of us knows what it is. Don't you find that . . . comical?"

"No. Where is the Ring of Fire?"

"Good question. But answering that would be like answering these: Is there order in the universe? Is there life after death?"

"Don't play games with me. Not now. Not tonight."

"Then I won't. Tell them they won't find the Ring of Fire. Because tonight it's all begun," the Guardian replies in a serious voice.

"Where is it?"

"I don't know."

Jacob Mahler grabs him by the shoulders. His grip is strong and firm. The violin bow slides a single time across the man's throat, just below his Adam's apple. He offers no resistance. He feels no pain.

He slides to the ground, drained.

Light.

The last thing he sees is a pair of women's boots. They're green.

The last thing he hears is the voice of the violinist, who orders, "Take his picture. And send it to the newspapers tonight. It's got to be on the front page."

Tonight.

White.

There's snow everywhere.

Everything's white.

After which everything goes dark.

FIRST STASIMON

"Hello?"

"Who is it?"

"It's me. I wanted news. . . ."

"The kids met each other."

"All four of them?"

"Yes."

"And then?"

"Then they went out together."

"What time is it?"

"It's nighttime. And it's snowing."

"Is everything going . . . as it should?"

"I think so. Alfred must've run into them by now."

"What are they like?"

"Curious enough. And, in case you're interested, Harvey's a lot like you."

"Let's hope not."

"Harvey will manage. The others will, too."

"You're optimistic."

"I need to be. Once they've opened the briefcase, I won't be able to help them anymore."

"And if they get it wrong—"

"They won't get it wrong. There won't be any more mistakes."

8

THE PAPER

"So he's dead?" Sheng whispers to Harvey.

The American boy takes a sip of his cappuccino with a dismal look on his face. "What do you think?"

"I don't know," replies Sheng, biting into his cream pastry. He silently waits for the others to show up. It's the morning of December 30, in the dining room of the Domus Quintilia. Aunt Linda has made a stunning assortment of pastries, including a chocolate and vanilla marble cake, an apple pie, orange tarts and a ring cake. She circles cheerfully around the tables, humming as she offers her guests boiling hot coffee as black as oil.

"Did you sleep well, kids?" she chirps happily, distractedly picking a hair off of Harvey's shirt.

"Very well, thank you."

The adults at the hotel are relaxed and calm. None of them seem to have any idea what happened last night.

Elettra's father is tranquilly reading today's edition of *La Gazzetta dello Sport*. Sheng's father is rubbing his eyes groggily. Harvey's parents, on the other hand, are looking over a brochure listing the current exhibits, after having uselessly tried to convince their son to go with them to visit the Capitoline Museums.

Elettra and Mistral are the last ones to walk into the dining room. Mistral's eyes show she's had a restless night, but she forces herself to smile and keep their promise that they won't say anything to anyone. Elettra walks beside her, far more carefree than her friend. They cross to the table where the boys are sitting alone and ask, "Any news?"

"I can't read Italian very well," replies Harvey, handing her the newspaper. "But I don't think it's good." On the front page is a photograph of a man lying on his back in the snow. His face is obscured by a dark stain spreading out from his elegant raincoat.

"Oh, no!" cries Elettra, raising her hand to her mouth.

"What does the article say?" Sheng asks her.

"That he was found . . . dead . . . by the side of the Tiber last night, during the snowstorm."

"How did he die?"

"They slit his throat."

Sheng's cream pastry plunks noisily into his latte.

"It doesn't say much more than that . . . ," says Elettra. "They're investigating to find out what happened, but they don't even know what his name was. They're asking anyone who has information to contact the carabinieri—the police, I mean. And . . ."

Elettra translates the whole article out loud to the other kids.

"They don't say anything else?" Harvey insists.

Elettra shakes her head. "It's breaking news. That's all they know."

"What about the blackout?"

70

"Oh, yeah . . ." She thumbs through a few pages. "They say it only affected certain parts of town. The electricity came back on at dawn and the problem seems to be solved. But they haven't figured out what caused it yet."

"Talk about a dark and stormy night . . . ," Sheng murmurs.

"Let's get moving," Elettra suggests.

The kids reluctantly finish their breakfast and speak briefly with their parents, asking if they can have the day to themselves. Sheng's father and Mistral's mother make no objections. Quite the opposite, in fact. The man from China decides to take the opportunity to sleep off his jet lag and the French woman says she has to do a little extra work for some of her key clients.

Harvey's parents, on the other hand, get into a lengthy debate with their son, which the boy survives at the price of a very bad mood. "It's no big deal," he grumbles when Elettra asks what it was all about. "Getting along with my parents is always kind of complicated." He seems ready to add something else, but then, with a shake of his head, he keeps it to himself.

Elettra doesn't press him for details.

She walks with him over to the door leading down to the basement, pushes aside the garden plants that Aunt Linda uses to try to hide it, and opens it up. They wait for Mistral and Sheng to join them, and then they all go down the stairs leading to the underground realm.

"We'll be nice and warm down here," Elettra points out, shutting the door behind her, "and nobody will bother us."

"Wishful thinking," grumbles Harvey. "You don't know my folks."

"They seem pretty interesting to me!" says Sheng.

"Yeah, sure . . ." Harvey's expression is as dark as a storm cloud. "Do they get on your case?"

"Yeah. That is . . . especially after they . . . Oh, never mind. My dad's always wondering how he could have such an ignorant son. My mom, on the other hand, never wants me to leave her side."

Little by little, as they make their way down the steps, the basement surrounds them with its maze of old furniture and empty picture frames. "Same thing here. My mother cried for a week when she found out about this trip . . . ," Sheng adds.

"That just means she cares a lot about you," Mistral tells him, stretching out like a flamingo.

"Tired, huh?" Harvey asks her, sitting down cross-legged on the floor.

"I sure am. I didn't sleep a wink."

"Why not?"

"I was afraid," answers Mistral, rubbing her hands together nervously. "Just like you guys."

The leather briefcase is lying on the floor, hidden under an old white sheet.

"We can always change our minds," Elettra states. "After all, nobody's forcing us to open it."

Their eyes dart around in the dim light.

"I say we do it," Sheng proposes.

"Me too," says Harvey.

"It might be dangerous," Mistral adds meekly. "After all . . . that man was murdered."

"And maybe because of this briefcase," says Elettra. "He was being followed. He was scared. He said that it had all begun."

"He doesn't seem to have been very lucky to me. . . ."

"He was even saying 'twenty-nine.' Like our birthdays."

"And don't forget: yesterday was December twenty-ninth," Sheng says, biting his fingernails.

The light from the bulbs hanging from the ceiling suddenly dims.

"You want to make those blow up, too, Sheng?" Harvey teases.

"Hey! I didn't do it!"

"Oh, no? You mean I just imagined the whole thing?"

"Sheng's right," Elettra says as the basement lights go back to normal. "It wasn't him. There's a street right above us and the lights dim whenever a truck passes by."

"Hear that?" Sheng retorts.

"Besides, yesterday . . . ," Elettra goes on, "I think it was me." She drags her finger over the sheet hiding the briefcase and forces a smile. "I might as well tell you. It wouldn't be the first time it happened to me. . . . But it's never been as strong as it was last night."

Mistral gives her a look of understanding.

Harvey leans back to rest on his elbows. "Sorry, what happens to you?"

"I make lightbulbs explode . . . without even touching them."

"Hao!" cries Sheng. "How do you do that?"

"I don't know. Sometimes I feel strange . . . charged and . . . Well, laugh if you want, but when I feel that way I even make computers go haywire."

"Like some sort of virus?"

"No. I interfere with their electrical current. At least I think that's what it is. Sometimes all I have to do is walk by and the paper in the printer gets jammed or some of the computer screen's pixels burn out. And . . . I make mirrors go dull," Elettra continues. "After I've used them for a while, mirrors lose their shine. They get all blurry and . . . and they fade. They reflect less. I can't explain it any better than this, but that's basically what happens."

"So what happened to you yesterday?"

"I started feeling this surge of energy when we were talking about our birthdays. I felt hot and I couldn't breathe. In the end, when the heat was getting to be more than I could stand, I wound up touching Sheng on the shoulder and—"

"I had my hands on the lamp—"

"You funneled all your energy into him and—"

"And the lamp exploded."

In the basement, there's a long moment of silence.

"Something like that, I guess," Elettra admits, embarrassed.

"Never heard anything like it," Harvey breaks in. "But anyway, that's got nothing to do with this briefcase."

"Actually, the same thing happened to me later on," explains Elettra. "On the bridge, when we ran into that man. I felt hot. The same surge of energy."

"And now?"

The girl shakes her head. "No. Everything seems okay right now."

"So what do we do? Do we open it up?" Sheng asks impatiently.

"And after we've opened it?" asks Harvey.

Sheng brushes his finger against the briefcase, fascinated and scared at the same time. "We see what's inside."

"And then?"

"Then we keep it a secret. We swore we wouldn't tell anyone anything, didn't we?"

"Actually, maybe what we should do is take it to the police and forget this whole thing ever happened," suggests Harvey.

Elettra thinks back to what the man shouted out in the snow. She repeats it aloud. "It's begun."

"No one's going to come here to claim the briefcase," says Sheng. "So we might as well see what's inside."

"It'll be our secret."

"Whatever you guys want."

"So who's going to open it?"

Harvey, Sheng and Mistral look at Elettra. "He gave it to you," Harvey says. "You open it."

She nods, rests her hands on the briefcase and clicks open its gold hasps.

Clack.

The pale sun peeks out from behind a thick layer of clouds. The snow that fell during the night is piled up along the curbs. Beatrice walks along nervously, her green boots getting splattered.

It's eleven o'clock.

She didn't sleep a wink. She kept her bedside light on all night long, looking through the few photos she has of her happy past, when she still lived with her little sister. But she never managed to fall asleep. Every time she tried shutting her eyes, she saw Jacob Mahler with his violin. She could still sense the darkness of the Tiber all around her. And the darkness of that incredibly enigmatic man.

She kept hearing the last words he said.

Before killing him, Mahler had called him the Guardian.

The guardian of what?

Beatrice is stunned, scared and rather disgusted by what happened. Joe Vinile never told her she'd be an accomplice to murder. And he didn't tell her anything about Guardians. Or razor-sharp violin bows.

He told her there was an important job to do and that she'd be paid handsomely, more than she'd ever earned before. He told her that in the world of crime, Jacob Mahler was considered a legend. And that working with a legend, even once, meant joining the big league. It meant smooth sailing for the rest of her life. He told her that Jacob Mahler was looking for a man. And that they'd find the man, follow him and set him up to be captured. But he hadn't told her that once Mahler had captured him, he'd kill the man by slitting his throat with a violin bow.

She's still lost in her thoughts when she reaches Piazza Sant'Eustachio and the café by the same name.

Joe Vinile and Little Linch are already sitting at a table. Beatrice sits down beside them without so much as a hello. Joe's sporting a pair of wraparound sunglasses and a black leather jacket. Beneath this is his Vasco Rossi T-shirt, from which he is inseparable. Joe's convinced he looks so much like the famous Italian rock star that they could pass as twins. Joe Vinile's real name is Giovanni. He's fifty years old, and he is what he is today thanks to a flourishing pirated music racket.

Beside him, Little Linch looks like a walrus squeezed in between the arms of the chair. He has an enormous face, a pudgy, misshapen body and buck teeth. Beatrice doesn't know what his real name is. In Rome's underground crime rings they all call him Little Linch, jokingly distorting *lince*, the Italian word for "lynx," because when he was young he worked doing bit parts at the Cinecittà movie studios, reaching the height of his career by playing a half-blind character called La Lince.

He's the first one to speak to her. "We were expecting you to show up with your friend Jacob . . . ," he begins, trying to rest a sweaty hand on her arm.

"The meeting's for eleven past eleven," she replies, checking her watch. "And there are still two minutes left."

"You sure he'll show?"

Joe Vinile pulls a little square box out of his pocket. He rests it against his throat so he can speak. A hoarse, buzzing voice comes out of the box. "Well, this is . . . *rrr* . . . the right place . . . *rrr*. . . . Want some coffee . . . *rrr* . . . ?"

Beatrice nods and Joe orders with a simple wave of his hand. The waiters prepare the espressos shielded by little screens so their clients won't discover the secret behind their famous blend. That's why many consider Sant'Eustachio to be the finest café in Rome.

The espressos arrive boiling hot in tiny cups that are even hotter. The moment they're placed on the little table, the air fills with the persistent aroma of violets.

"Hello," says Jacob Mahler just then as he sits down in the only free chair left.

Little Linch gives a start.

It's eleven past eleven.

And none of the three even saw him walk up.

"I'm very angry," he begins, not looking at anyone in particular.

Joe Vinile rests the little box against his throat and croaks out, "Mind telling us . . . *rrr* . . . about what, exactly . . . *rrr* . . . ?"

"About how things went last night. Very badly, I'd say."

"The boys . . . *rrr* . . . told me just the opposite . . . *rrr* . . . ," Joe retorts. "Isn't that right . . . *rrr* . . . Linch?"

Little Linch stirs his spoon needlessly in his espresso cup. "I did what I was asked to do. I found our guy in Via del Babuino and started to follow him, pushing him toward the Tiber."

"And you never lost sight of him?"

"No," Little Linch lies, resting his spoon on the saucer, his hand trembling slightly. "Except for a couple minutes, maybe . . . when we reached the river," he admits a moment later. "But that was because of the blackout."

Joe Vinile nods. "Something very . . . *rrr* . . . unusual," he admits. "But that didn't stop us . . . *rrr* . . . from leading him . . . *rrr* . . . into the trap . . . *rrr* . . . if I'm not mistaken . . . *rrr*. . . ."

Jacob Mahler leans down on the table with all his weight. "The Guardian had a briefcase with him."

Little Linch nods his head. "He did, yeah."

"But he wasn't carrying a briefcase," Beatrice breaks in. "Not when we saw him."

Joe Vinile raises his hands in a sign of helplessness. "He must've given it to somebody . . . *rrr* . . . or thrown it into the river. Who . . . *rrr* . . . can say?"

A sharp sneer darkens the killer's face. "Either we find that briefcase or it's all over."

"But that would be impossible!" protests Little Linch.

"You're the one who lost track of him," the killer hisses. "And believe me, finding that briefcase at the bottom of the river will be a lot easier than explaining to my boss that we lost it."

Beatrice looks worriedly at Joe Vinile and then at Little Linch.

Jacob Mahler adds viciously, "And most importantly, it'll be far less painful."

Joe Vinile shifts uncomfortably in his chair and asks, "So what was in . . . *rrr* . . . that . . . *rrr* . . . briefcase?"

9
THE BRIEFCASE

THE FIRST THING ELETTRA PULLS OUT OF THE BRIEFCASE IS A LITTLE black-and-white checkered umbrella. She rests it on the ground and announces, a little disappointed, "Your typical umbrella, I'd say."

A metal tag stitched into the edge of its cloth reads:

ANTICO CAFFÉ GRECO

VIA CONDOTTI

ROMA

"Fortunately there's more," murmurs Elettra. This time she takes out something about the size of an apple, wrapped in dark cloth. The strong smell of camphor fills the air.

"What is it?" asks Harvey.

"Just a sec . . ." Slowly, Elettra unwraps it. Inside the cloth is an old toy. A round object made of black wooden rings of different sizes and a metal tip at one end.

"*Hao!*" whispers Sheng. "Is it my imagination or is that a top?"

"It's covered with writing," Elettra points out, turning it around in her fingers.

She hands it to Harvey, who studies it carefully. "These aren't words. They're drawings."

"Really?" Sheng breaks in, looking over his shoulder. "Drawings of what?"

"I'd say this is . . . some sort of wolf, maybe?"

Sheng takes the top from him, frowning. "Wolf," he confirms.

"Or a dog," Harvey continues.

"Dog," Sheng confirms once again. The Chinese boy rests the top on the basement floor and makes it spin around.

"There are more of them," Elettra announces. She pulls three identical bundles out of the briefcase, each one containing a top. The kids' expressions show how baffled they are.

"This one's covered with spiral designs," says Harvey, looking at the first one. "And this other one . . . hmm . . . It could be some sort of tower, a truncated pyramid, a temple. . . ."

Depicted on the last top are stylized eyes. Mistral examines it closely.

Harvey huffs. "Yeah, but . . . sorry. Why would somebody chase a guy down for an umbrella and a couple of toy tops?"

"How should I know?" says Sheng, making all four toys spin around on the floor.

"And then there's this," Elettra says in a low voice, pulling one last thing out of the briefcase, this also wrapped in cloth.

It's about the same size as a shirt box. As Elettra slowly unwinds the cloth, it reveals a very dark, very worn wooden box. Its entire outer surface is engraved with writing and overlapping drawings, like signatures left behind on the desks at school by generations of students.

81

"What the heck is that?" asks Sheng.

"I haven't got the foggiest idea." The strange object looks like a cross between a jewelry box and a hinged wooden frame, fastened shut by gold clasps. Elettra rests it on the cloth and flicks open the clasps. The inner surface is a rectangle covered with a thick network of grooves, which look a bit like the lines in the palms of people's hands.

"So what are these?"

"It all looks scratched . . . or engraved, maybe. . . ."

"Spiderwebs," says Mistral. "Ripples in water."

"It makes me think of a maze," Harvey remarks.

The grooves inside the object intersect each other intricately, all joined together in a single highly stylized design.

"It's a woman with stars all around her," says Harvey, running his fingers over them.

"He's right," says Elettra. "It's a woman surrounded by stars."

"One, two . . . ," counts Sheng. "Seven stars. *Hao!*" he shouts. "And . . . ?"

"And . . . I don't know. But this thing looks really old."

"And really used."

"This is what the guy wanted to protect, if you ask me."

"Do you think it's valuable?"

"I'd imagine so," says Mistral, studying it with a critical eye. "It looks really old."

Sheng notices something written along its outer frame and asks the others if they can make out what it says. Harvey shakes his head. "They aren't letters from our alphabet. It looks like it's written in Chinese."

"But it isn't Chinese," Sheng snaps. "It's definitely another language."

"Greek," concludes Mistral. "But I can't read Greek." Then she asks, "Is there anything else in the briefcase?"

Elettra checks carefully. "I don't think so. Wait . . . hang on!"

There's a sheet of graph notebook paper and one last, tiny object wrapped in black tissue paper. Elettra looks inside it.

It's a human tooth.

"Bleah!" Mistral cries out. "That's not a real tooth, is it?"

Harvey picks it up between his thumb and his index finger, holding it up in the light. "I think so. A cuspid, to be precise. And . . . whoa! There's something engraved on it, too."

"Let me see! Let me see!" says Sheng, smiling excitedly.

"A circle," Harvey announces, holding it firmly in his fingers.

"A circle . . . a zero, a ring, an 'O' . . ."

He shrugs. "I give up. I don't get any of this."

"So what's on the piece of paper?"

"A paragraph," says Elettra. "But if you think it's going to explain all this stuff, you're wrong."

"Read it."

Elettra takes a breath and reads aloud, " 'Every hundred years it is time to contemplate the stars. Every hundred years it is time to understand the world. What difference does it make which road you follow as you seek the truth? Such a great secret is not to be reached by a single path. If you find it, you must guard it with care and keep others from discovering it as well.' "

A baffled silence echoes through the basement.

* * *

Elettra searches the briefcase inch by inch to make sure it's completely empty. The kids summarize everything they've found: a strange folded wooden box, four toy tops, a tooth with a circle engraved on it, a piece of paper with an enigmatic note, and a black-and-white checkered umbrella.

"So what do we do now?" asks Mistral, a bit worried. Her long, curved eyelashes look like a series of question marks.

"I say we put all this weird stuff back in the briefcase," Harvey suggests, running his fingers through his hair, "and throw it into the Tiber."

"The person who gave it to us—"

"Was a nut."

"But he was trying to escape," remarks Elettra. "He was afraid he'd be caught by . . . someone."

"Exactly. A paranoid nut."

"You think he was crazy, huh? Remember: somebody killed him."

"And they didn't just shoot him . . . I mean . . . you know." Sheng slides a hand across his throat.

"A secret . . . that you can't let others discover."

"Do you think he knew the secret?"

"Sorry, but what secret are we talking about, anyway?"

"'Every hundred years' . . . ," Elettra quotes, rereading the note.

"It's time to contemplate the stars . . . ," adds Mistral, passing her finger over the ones engraved in the wood.

"It says that whoever discovers the secret needs to keep others from doing the same."

"Them!" cries out Sheng. "I get it!"

"Give me a break!" Harvey moans. "What could you possibly

84

get? We barely know anything. We don't even know the crazy guy's name or who . . . who the 'others,' or whatever you want to call them, are."

"All we know is that they're really dangerous."

"And that the man on the bridge wanted to protect these things," adds Elettra. "As though they were really important."

"A mystery," pronounces Mistral, standing up to stretch her legs. "A big, giant mystery."

"Well, I think it's cool," says Sheng. "I mean, this is all really strange stuff."

"'Such a great secret is not to be reached by a single path,'" Elettra says, rereading the note. "Maybe there really is a great secret to discover. And maybe the man was scared because he'd discovered it."

"And let's not forget the 'twenty-nine,'" Mistral reminds them.

"What do you mean?"

"I mean it isn't exactly normal for a guy who's running for his life to keep on repeating 'twenty-nine, twenty-nine' unless he thinks it's important."

"That is, if you're assuming the guy was really thinking. Instead of just being completely off his rocker," remarks Harvey.

"Yesterday was December twenty-ninth," Sheng reminds them for the hundredth time. "And he was convinced something had begun."

"But what?"

"Who knows? But whatever it was, it began on the twenty-ninth of December. That's why he kept repeating 'twenty-nine.'"

"So you guys are convinced that his saying 'twenty-nine' had nothing to do with our birthday?" Elettra asks.

"What do you think?" Harvey blurts out.

"Of course!" answers Sheng. "Yesterday was our night. The Night of the Super Twenty-nine . . ."

"And the blackout . . ."

"You think it's all connected?" Mistral asks in a hushed voice.

"But what if what happened to us last night," Elettra says, cutting them all off, "just happened so we'd go out and end up on Ponte Quattro Capi . . . ?"

Harvey shakes his head. "Oh, come on! We aren't puppets. We did what we did because we decided to do it. And we wouldn't be here talking about this stuff if one of the four of us, who was a little too . . . curious . . . hadn't agreed to take a briefcase full of junk from an old crazy guy who can't come get it back anymore."

"Four of us. Ponte Quattro Capi. Four toy tops," Sheng remarks. "Maybe the number four has something to do with this, too."

Elettra runs her hands through her hair. "None of this makes any sense! I . . . I don't know why I took the briefcase. I felt like I had to. And now that I know what's inside it, I'm even more curious to figure all of this out." She grabs the black-and-white checkered umbrella. "I'm going to try," she says, showing the others the brass tag, "by going to the Antico Caffè Greco."

"Which would be . . . ?" Harvey asks inquisitively.

"An old café in the center of Rome."

"Good idea," agrees Mistral. "The umbrella might be a lead that could point us in the right direction."

Sheng grins. "Why not? After all, what does the note say? 'Such a great secret . . . is not to be reached by a single path,' right?"

Harvey's the only one who doesn't seem at all enthusiastic about the idea. "I say it'd just be a big waste of time."

"Like you've got anything better to do?"

"Well, I could go visit a museum . . . ," he jokes.

Beatrice and Little Linch walk along the right bank of the Tiber. After their meeting with Jacob Mahler at the Sant'Eustachio Café, they're both in a lousy mood. Little Linch is frowning. Beatrice is brooding.

"Here. This is right about where I lost him," the man says. "That's when all the lights went out and he started running. It was only for a second . . . but then I couldn't see him anymore. I figured he'd gone back to cross over the Tiber, so I headed that way to look for him."

"You didn't go down to the island?" Beatrice asks him, staring out at Ponte Cestio, a bridge leading to Tiber Island.

"No," Little Linch admits.

Beatrice tries to reconstruct the scene in her mind. If the man had started running south, he might have reached Ponte Cestio, and from there he could've crossed the square and gone over Ponte Quattro Capi to get to the other side of the river.

"Let's take a look around the island," she proposes.

The two walk along the riverbank, making their way along the parapet. A few pigeons coo, perched among the cold stone bricks.

"What we're doing is totally pointless," Little Linch reminds her, leaning against the parapet. Despite the chilly December air, he's panting and sweating, which makes him look particularly revolting. "What could we possibly find? That briefcase could be

anywhere. If he threw it in the river, it's gone. So then what do we do? Slap on diving masks and flippers and swim out to dig through the mud for it? Bah! That guy doesn't know what he's talking about."

Beatrice doesn't reply. She just keeps walking. Then she asks, point-blank, "What do you know about Mahler, exactly?"

Little Linch splashes through the slush in his boots. "I know he's a snake. A mean one. A devil. They say he's the best there is."

"The best there is at killing . . . ," mumbles Beatrice, not very convinced.

"Joe claims this is the job that could change our lives forever. That we should consider it an honor to work for him."

"For him *who*, exactly?"

Little Linch drags his feet through the snow without answering.

"Mahler was sent here to Italy for this job by someone else, you know."

"The hermit," Beatrice says in a low voice.

"Heremit," Little Linch corrects her. "It's not a nickname. That's his name."

"Heremit? What kind of a name is that? Is he British?"

"Half-Chinese, half-Dutch, from what I've heard. But his full name is even worse: Heremit Devil."

"Heremit Devil?" Beatrice forces a smile. "Quite a reassuring name. Where does he live?"

"In Shanghai, in an incredible skyscraper . . ." Little Linch spits on the ground. "They say he's so crazy he's never even left it."

"What do you mean?"

"I mean he's never left it. He runs his whole life from inside of it. Like a giant glass-and-concrete kingdom. I think he's one of those freaks who are scared of catching something, of touching people, of poisoned air. . . . How should I know? He's bonkers. A total nutcase."

"But still, an intelligent hit man like Jacob Mahler—"

"Shhh!" Little Linch hushes her, gesturing for her to lower her voice. "Are you out of your mind? Don't go around saying stuff like that out loud! Somebody could hear you!"

"But still, the legendary Jacob Mahler," Beatrice says, correcting herself, "the snake, the devil, the very best there is . . . he works for a madman like Heremit Devil. So basically we're working for two insane men who want to find a briefcase, even if it means making us comb through the Tiber inch by inch. What's wrong with this picture?"

The two quickly cross over Tiber Island, looking around distractedly in search of any clue that might tell them if their man passed by there. And since they naturally find nothing, they walk over to the opposite side, down Ponte Quattro Capi.

"Joe warned us not to ask too many questions," Little Linch mutters, "and I'm happy not asking any. Because we're playing with fire, sweets. A whole lot of fire. And I have no intention of getting burned."

"He told me not even to say his name."

"Huh?"

"Mahler. Yesterday, in the car. He didn't even want me to say the name 'Heremit.'"

Little Linch shrugs. "So don't."

"Is he so scary?"

"He's the one who makes the rules. And rule number one is: not one word too many."

Beatrice stops in her tracks. She leans over to pick up something that's half-buried in the snow.

"What is it?" the man asks.

Beatrice turns it over in her fingers. It's a shower cap, on which is written: HOTEL DOMUS QUINTILIA.

10
THE CAFÉ

Via Condotti is packed with people. Piles of snow line the curbs and colorful Christmas decorations hang overhead, forming lines of blinking lights. The gleaming white Spanish Steps of the Trinità dei Monti are animated by the scurrying hustle and bustle of people wearing colorful coats, furs and extravagant outfits.

Just a few steps away from the square is Caffè Greco, which is surrounded by shops with elegant picture-window displays. Outside, a dark marble sign points out the otherwise anonymous entrance. Inside is a series of elegant rooms and little round tables. Hanging on the walls are paintings in gold frames, prints from the 1800s, portraits, articles from old newspapers, sheathed swords and sparkling mirrors.

Waiters dressed in black dart around the tables, carrying trays of hot drinks and steaming cups of punch, while the patrons chat cheerfully in ten different languages, sitting in the shade of statues and gigantic vases that peek out from behind the columns.

"This place is incredible . . . ," whispers Mistral, clutching to her chest a purse in which she's put her sketchbook and some soft-tipped pencils.

"So what are we looking for, exactly?" asks Harvey.

"Anything," replies Elettra, unbuttoning her quilted jacket.

"At last, someplace warm," remarks Sheng, adjusting the backpack on his shoulder and brushing up dangerously close to a statue.

"Be careful with that thing," Elettra warns him. Before leaving the hotel, they put the entire contents of the briefcase into his backpack.

The kids make their way along, dodging waiters and bundled-up customers. They look around curiously until they reach the back of the café. It's a silent, peaceful room shut off by a red cord that keeps people from entering a little room farther on, one filled with antique furniture.

"They say that was a salon where all sorts of important people used to meet," explains Elettra, resting her hands on the cord. "Politicians, writers, artists, poets . . . They say lots of great ideas came about in this café."

"Why can't we go in?" asks Sheng.

"So we don't ruin it," replies Elettra. "It's practically a museum now."

Harvey distractedly glances at the paintings on the walls. A hunting scene, the portrait of a pope, a romantic landscape, a newspaper article from two centuries ago . . . All very interesting, of course . . . but light-years from anything that might interest him. "Okay, why did we come here, again?" he asks.

"I don't know," Elettra admits. "We've just got this umbrella. And this umbrella told us to come here."

"Hot chocolate, anybody?" proposes Sheng, sniffing the air.

* * *

They sit down at the nearest free table, fighting over the most comfortable armchairs, and order four hot chocolates. Mistral pulls out her sketchbook and starts drawing furiously.

"You're good at that," Elettra comments, watching the tip of her pencil gradually transform the blank sheet of paper into a perfect reproduction of the room around them.

Concentrating on her sketch, Mistral doesn't reply.

Sheng rests the backpack under the table, keeping it firmly between his knees.

"I say we ask someone," Elettra suggests after a while. "Otherwise, we'll never find out anything."

"Sorry, but what is it you're hoping to find out?" Harvey asks dryly. "This is a dead end."

"Excuse me . . . ," Elettra says to the waiter who brings them their hot chocolates.

"Elettra, don't . . . ," Harvey whispers, trying to stop her. But it's too late.

The girl holds the checkered umbrella out to him and asks, "A man gave this to us. Does it belong to you guys?"

When he sees the umbrella, the waiter looks far from surprised. "Actually, it does," he answers. "We call those our 'emergency umbrellas.' Did the man tell you his name?"

"Actually, no," Elettra admits. "I was hoping you'd know what it was."

"He was a strange guy," Sheng breaks in, "with a white beard and wild eyes."

Mistral turns to a fresh page in her sketchbook and quickly starts on another drawing.

The waiter tucks the umbrella under his arm. "When did you run into him?"

"Yesterday."

"He was a tall man with a white beard, all dressed in gray, wearing a long raincoat," Sheng goes on, outlining his shape in the air with his hands.

"More or less . . . like this," concludes Mistral, showing him her sketch.

"Ah!" the waiter exclaims. "You mean the professor!"

"The professor?"

The waiter nods his head vigorously. "He's one of our regular clients. Yesterday he got caught in the snowstorm and he didn't know how he was going to get back home. He's a really nice man, but really scatterbrained. I'm not surprised he asked you to bring the umbrella back for him. It's already a miracle he didn't lose it someplace. Is he your teacher or something?"

"Not exactly . . . ," Sheng says softly.

"So he came here yesterday?" asks Elettra.

"Naturally. He comes here every day. In fact . . ." The waiter checks his watch. "No, it's still too early. Let's just hope nobody sits down at his table before four o'clock."

"Which table?"

"The one over there, on the left, just before the cord."

The kids turn around to look at the table he's pointing to while the waiter continues. "The professor comes in every afternoon and goes to sit down at his usual spot. If someone happens to be there . . . he's capable of standing right there beside them without saying a word until the people who've stolen his spot can't put up with it anymore and leave."

"What does he teach?"

"I have no idea. In fact, I'm not even really sure he's a professor. We just call him that because he always shows up with at least two books, one dustier than the next."

"And . . . ?"

"He sits there, all quiet, reading at his table for a couple of hours. If it's too crowded, he gets huffy and makes a scene, trying to drive people away . . . unless there are kids here."

"Why? What does he do when there are kids?"

"He tells them stories. Stories about ancient Rome and emperors. He tells them about Caesar and Nero. . . ."

"Who's Nero?" asks Sheng.

"If you wait until four o'clock, you can ask the professor yourself," the waiter tells him.

"That's unlikely," Harvey sneers.

"Nero was the cursed emperor of Rome," Elettra explains. "He went down in history for setting fire to the city. . . . Although that might just be a legend."

"Sounds like a likeable guy," Sheng remarks.

"No, nobody liked him," says Elettra. "In fact, after he died, his villa was destroyed, the statues of him were smashed up and his face was chiseled off all the monuments."

"That's right. *La damnatio memoriae*, as the professor would say," adds the waiter, who seems to be rather knowledgeable on the subject.

"That's Latin," Elettra explains to her friends. "It means canceling all trace of him from memory . . . like he never existed."

"A bit like the professor," Sheng says beneath his breath.

* * *

95

The waiter goes back to serving his other clients. The moment they see him disappear into another room, the kids rush over to the professor's customary spot. It's a little round table for two, a light-colored marble top resting on three wooden legs. Beside it are two red velvet armchairs.

"You think there's a reason he always sat here?" Harvey wonders, looking around.

"Well, it gives you a full view of the café and the entrance . . . ," Elettra says.

"Nobody can come up from behind you."

"And this is one of the quietest rooms. . . ."

"But besides that, I can't see anything in particular."

"There's nothing useful on the walls . . . ," Elettra points out. "At least . . . it doesn't seem like it."

Mistral looks around for clues.

"Let me sit down in your place," Sheng asks her, getting up awkwardly from his armchair. In doing so, he bumps the girl's arm, knocking her sketchbook and pencil to the ground.

"Oops, sorry!" Sheng bends over to pick them up but freezes halfway down. "Hao!" he cries. And then again, "Hao!"

He hands Mistral her sketchbook and pencil, kneels down under the table and says, "Look! There's writing down here and . . . What the heck is . . . is this?"

"What?" asks Harvey, crouching down beside him. "Wow . . ."

The wooden support on which the marble is resting is covered with rows of indecipherable numbers and letters, written so close together that there's barely any free space left. In the middle of this delirium of signs, stuck on with two pieces of cellophane tape, is a strange, long object.

96

Sheng detaches one piece of tape and then the other.

"Here it is," he declares with satisfaction. On the marble table-top he places a magnetized plastic badge, written on which is:

BIBLIOTECA HERTZIANA
VIA GREGORIANA 30
INGRESSO RICERCATORI — SALA 4
ALFRED VAN DER BERGER
ROMA

"It's a badge for a research hall in a library," explains Elettra.

"Bingo . . . ," murmurs Harvey, amazed.

Elettra runs her fingers over the plastic badge, as if to make sure it's really there. "The professor's name was Alfred Van Der Berger?" she muses.

"Nice to meet you," says Sheng.

"Maybe we should tell this to the police."

"Or maybe . . . he left us another clue," Elettra says, considering. "And we should follow it before someone else does."

"Before one of 'them,' you mean?" says Harvey with a hint of skepticism.

Elettra looks at him. "Exactly."

"Do you know where this library is?"

Elettra twirls a lock of hair in her fingers. "No. But I know where Via Gregoriana is."

"Is it far from here?" Sheng asks curiously.

"Ten minutes away, if we run."

11

THE LIBRARY

At Via Gregoriana 30, they're greeted by a frightening-looking main door shaped like a monster's face with open jaws. Beneath two enormous window eyes is a travertine nose, which acts as the keystone to the mouth-shaped archway.

"Uh-oh," murmurs Sheng the moment he sees it. "We're supposed to go in through that?"

"No way I'm doing it," says Mistral. "If you guys really want to go in, I'll wait for you out here."

Elettra, on the other hand, thinks the building and the monster are totally amusing. "It's just a front door!" she cries out cheerfully.

"It's a hellish front door, you mean," Harvey adds, running his fingers through his hair.

"Just what we needed to boost our spirits: a nice, monstrous old building," Elettra says, flashing the professor's badge to the others and walking through the doorway. "After all, there's a library in here."

Sheng peeks around the entranceway. "All I can see is a bunch of scaffolding."

Harvey slaps him on the back and walks in beside him.

Mistral stays outside, staring at the building's demoniacal sneer and the empty street beside it. It seems like people actually avoid passing by.

"I don't like you . . . ," she says, talking to the monster. "Wait up! I'm coming, too!" she calls out, following her friends inside.

On the other side of the door, the building has been gutted. Walkways and scaffolding cover practically everything, and a tall, metal crane looms overhead. A shiny brass plaque marks the entrance to the library, but the door is locked and a sign hanging on it reads:

CHIUSO

CLOSED

"And here's where our search comes to an end," Harvey remarks with sarcastic disappointment. "Whatever it is we were supposed to discover, we're not going to discover it."

Inside of her, Elettra feels a sharp pang of disappointment. She tries knocking, but no one answers.

"The place looks abandoned . . . ," Mistral comments, looking around at the scaffolding.

"Let's go home!" Harvey urges.

Sheng tries pushing on the door and then notices a magnetic lock beside it. He takes the professor's badge and swipes it through the slot. The door lets out a rather reassuring clack. Sheng pushes it open just enough to peek inside.

A long, deserted corridor.

"It's open now, guys," he whispers, handing the badge back to Elettra.

When they reach the first turn in the corridor, they hear the noise of a coffee vending machine. A little plastic cup, a humming noise, water trickling into the cup and the beep signaling that the process has been completed.

Seconds later, a middle-aged woman holding a cup of espresso appears. She takes a sip, spots the four kids and stops halfway through her second sip. "How did you get in here?" she asks.

Elettra steps out in front of the others and walks up to her without missing a beat. "With . . . with our uncle's badge," she replies.

The woman glances distractedly at the professor's card. She's a thin, bony woman. "We're closed. Didn't you see the sign?"

"Yeah, but . . . we thought we'd try to get in anyway."

"And . . . if you don't mind my asking . . ." She takes another sip of coffee. "Why? In all my twenty years working here, not once have I ever seen kids your age so eager to get *into* a library."

Elettra begins, "We need to—"

"And save me the typical excuse about having to write a school paper."

Elettra cuts herself off. The librarian has practically read her mind.

In the moment of silence that follows, Mistral steps forward and points at her sketchbook. "We're here to pick up our uncle's notes," she explains, tilting her head above her long, slender neck. "He's going absolutely crazy without his notes and . . . he thought he might have left them on his desk. So we made a deal: we come get his notes and he buys us four hot chocolates."

The librarian looks the girl up and down as if she were choosing a fresh peach at an open market stand.

"Well, four hot chocolates are four hot chocolates . . . ," she declares when she's finished her analysis.

"That's right," Mistral confirms.

"It sounds like a fair deal to me," the woman concludes, finishing off the last of her espresso. "Do you know where to go?"

"Uncle Alfred tried to explain the way there to us . . . ," replies Mistral, whose cheeks are painted a rosy color. "But if you could tell us again, it would definitely save us a lot of time."

"I'll take you there," the woman offers.

"Oh, that won't be necessary . . . ," Mistral begins, until an alarmed Elettra nudges her as if to say, "We don't even know what we're looking for!"

"After all, we're closed today and there's not much to do around here," the librarian says, insisting. "Come along. I'll take you to the research room."

As they cross through the large rooms with frescoed ceilings, which house labyrinthine rows of architectural books and codices, the librarian tells them about the endless restoration work that for years has shut off access to a good half of the collection stored in the building. Elettra feels her tension rise with every step. Frowning, Harvey walks to her left, lost in his own little world of troubled thoughts. It's as though walking into the library has stirred up unpleasant memories in his mind. Sheng often trails behind, drawn by one unusual, ancient book after the other, the views from the windows, doors left ajar. The backpack with the tops, the tooth and the strange wooden object bounces against his back. Mistral walks beside their guide, taking in the woman's explanations about the library's dismal appearance.

The large, frescoed halls now behind them, they reach a smaller room with a steep staircase. An elevator takes the little group upstairs to a sunny loft.

The area beneath the wooden beams is divided into several small offices with plasterboard walls. The dormer windows offer a breathtaking view overlooking the rooftops and terraces of Rome, all sparkling in the snow. The wooden flooring creaks beneath their feet.

"These are the offices we've just restructured," the librarian explains. "And here we are. Room number four. Your uncle's private reading room."

She gently pushes on the door and immediately stiffens, stunned by what she sees.

It looks like a tornado has torn through it.

"Uh-oh . . . ," Mistral whispers worriedly.

Inside the room, a large wooden table is stacked high with books lying precariously one atop the other amid mountains of papers. Sticking out from between the yellowed pages are bookmarks, newspaper clippings and sticky notes full of scribbles. The floor is carpeted with papers. It looks as if someone has ripped them up and thrown them randomly down under the chairs. Many of them are covered with bizarre drawings in ink: spirals, circles, stylized flames.

"Whoa . . ." Sheng whistles.

The window is wide open, revealing a gloomy, tea-colored sky.

"I've never seen such a mess in here . . . ," the librarian murmurs, shaking her head.

"Let's go . . . ," Harvey whispers in Elettra's ear. "Right now."

The girl nods and takes a step backward, refusing to set foot in the room.

Mistral, on the other hand, walks into the study, trying not to tread on the papers scattered around on the floor. Without saying a word, she walks over to the window and shuts it.

"It was left open," she remarks. "Maybe the wind made all this mess. . . ."

The librarian nods but clearly isn't very convinced. "Something about this doesn't make sense," she says. "Would you wait here for a moment, please? I need to find a phone."

Mistral bends down to pick up a few sheets of paper from the floor.

Harvey and Sheng walk up to her. "What are you doing?" the American boy says in a low voice. "Let's get out of here. . . ."

"Let's just take a peek," she suggests.

On the professor's table are stacks of all kinds of books. Old writings by Greek and Latin authors. Seneca, Plutarch, Apuleius, Pliny, Lucretius. And books about science, astronomy, all covered with sticky notes.

Harvey walks around the table and picks up a book that's been left open in front of the chair. "Okay, but let's do it quick! What do you think? Could this be of any interest? It might be the last book the professor was reading."

It's a book bound in dark leather, on which the professor had attached a sticky note with the words KORE KOSMOU — THE MAIDEN OF THE COSMOS. The book smells old. The paper is thin and yellowed. It's written in Greek, with lettering in very dark ink. Harvey turns the pages until he reaches one marked with a piece of graph paper identical to the note they found in the briefcase. "And here's another note," he says.

"So what's it about?" Sheng asks with a sigh.

"I don't know," he answers. "It looks like a sort of translation."

He looks up to meet Elettra's eyes. She's still standing stock-still on the other side of the door. "Could you come here and read what it says?"

The girl shakes her head slowly. "No . . . I don't feel up to it."

"You were the one who insisted we come all the way here," Harvey pleads. "And this is a sheet of the professor's graph paper. Just take a look! We'll try to figure out if we need it, and then we'll get out of here."

"It might be another clue," adds Sheng.

"I feel like I did yesterday," Elettra explains, holding up her hands. "I feel . . . hot."

"That must mean we're on the right track!" exclaims Mistral, kneeling down to pick up a few handfuls of the ripped papers from the floor.

Drawn on each of them are hundreds of circles.

Elettra takes a deep breath and walks into the room. Sheng steps aside with a theatrical flourish, making way for her to get to the table. "If you feel like you did yesterday, don't touch me, okay?" he says with a friendly smirk.

Elettra forces a smile, then takes the sheet of graph paper Harvey's holding out to her. The professor's handwriting is sharper than usual, but it looks like he was the person who wrote it, although quickly and hastily.

Slowly, Elettra reads: " 'Once they have discovered fire, men will rip the plants up by their roots and examine the quality of their fluids. They will observe the nature of stones and dissect the bodies of their fellow men, yearning to see how they are made. They will reach the very limits of the Earth. They will rise up to the stars. They will be consumed by the desire to realize their designs, and when they fail they will be overcome by pain and sadness.'"

"That's it?" Harvey asks when she's finished.

"Yeah. That's all there is."

"Cheerful stuff, huh?" Sheng says in a low voice.

"And down there . . . those words that are crossed out?" Harvey insists, pointing at the last two lines.

Elettra holds the sheet up to the light and slowly reads, "'Prometheus should never have stolen the secret of fire. It was a mistake that unleashed the wrath of the gods. And now the gods cry out for vengeance.'"

"Who is it that stole what?" Sheng asks, baffled.

"It's a story from ancient mythology," explains Harvey. "Prometheus was a Titan who stole fire from the gods and gave it to mankind."

"And then?" the Chinese boy insists.

"From that moment on, men felt free because they could use fire, but the gods were furious. They chained Prometheus to a cliff, where an eagle would devour his liver day after day for the rest of his life."

Sheng makes a disgusted grimace. "Bleah!"

"Hey! I found something!" Mistral cries out just then, making the others start. "At least, I think so," she adds when they turn to look at her.

In her hands is a black notebook held shut by a rubber band. "You think this might be his journal?"

Mistral doesn't even get the chance to open it. Coming from outside the room are footsteps and the voices of two people talking.

"They're in there," the librarian is whispering. "They told me they were his nieces and nephews, but I'm not so sure. . . ."

"Well, we're about to find out," a man's voice replies.

"Oh, no!" cries Harvey, alarmed. "We can't let that happen!" He spins Sheng around and grabs his backpack, tossing in the leather-bound book, the piece of paper with the translation, the journal Mistral found and a few handfuls of papers the girl had picked up from the floor.

"Let's move!" he orders the others, turning to head for the door.

"Harvey!" shouts Elettra.

A threatening figure appears in the doorway. It's a man wearing a black uniform, mirrored sunglasses and a little cap with the word SECURITY written on it.

"Where are you running off to, son?" he says, reaching out his arm, trying to grab Harvey.

"Hey!" Sheng hollers. "Leave my friend alone!"

Standing behind the security guard, the librarian calls out, "Let's all stay calm, please! Everything's all right. Gianni just wants to ask you a few questions."

The security guard stretches his arm out, barring the door. "Would you let me see your backpack, please?" he asks Harvey.

The American boy takes a step back. "Um, why?"

"Because I want to see what you've put in there. May I?"

"Forget it!" replies Harvey. "Besides, it's not even mine."

"It's mine," Sheng points out.

The guard casts a long look around the room. "What did you come here for?"

"Nothing!" Mistral protests. "Why all the questions?"

"Please, kids . . . ," the woman breaks in. "It's nothing serious. We just want to understand what happened in here."

"Are you one of them?" Mistral asks the guard.

The man lets out a dry laugh. "One of who, young lady?"

"We're getting out of here," Elettra says curtly. "My uncle's journal isn't here anyway."

"Let me see that backpack."

"No way," retorts Harvey, adjusting it firmly on his shoulders. "You aren't getting it from me."

"Is that so?" The man presses his fingers against the earpiece he's wearing under his left temple and orders, "Security? Send Mauro up, too. Top floor."

"What are you doing?" the librarian asks him.

The guard motions for her to step back. "I'll take care of these little brats, ma'am." Then he walks toward Harvey, adjusting his mirrored sunglasses on his nose. "So you want to be a wise guy, do you?" The man takes another step forward. Harvey takes one step back.

"Please, let us go . . . ," groans Mistral.

"Let me see what you've stolen."

"I didn't steal anything!" replies Harvey.

It was a mistake to steal fire away from the gods . . . , thinks Elettra.

The guard bolts and Harvey tosses the backpack into the air, shouting, "Sheng, catch!"

The Chinese boy grabs it in midair and would have quickly run out of the room if the security guard didn't grab Harvey by the shirt.

"Now you've really made me angry!" he says.

Prometheus unleashed the wrath of the gods, thinks Elettra.

"Let him go!" shouts Sheng. "The backpack's here. Come and get it!"

Harvey tries uselessly to break free, kicking into the air.

"Now I'll take care of the both of you!" Gianni barks, dragging Harvey across the room.

And now the gods cry out for vengeance.

Elettra shakes her head. There's something not right about what's going on. . . . The security guard has no reason to be so furious. It's not their fault the room is in the condition it is. And even if they used deception to get in there, they didn't mean any harm. Like Prometheus, who used deception to steal fire away from the gods. Deception isn't always used to do harm. Sometimes it's the only possible path to follow.

What difference does it make which road you follow as you seek the truth? the note read. *Such a great secret is not to be reached by a single path.*

Elettra suddenly snaps out of her thoughts. Her hands start burning again.

Harvey bites the guard's wrist, and the man responds by lifting him up as if he were as light as a feather and pinning him against the wall. "Damned kid!"

"Don't hurt him!" squeals the librarian from the doorway.

Sheng backs up toward the window. Mistral is in the shadows in one corner of the room.

Elettra walks up to Gianni, raising her hand.

"Excuse me . . . ," she says.

"What do you want, kid?" the man with the mirrored sunglasses growls.

Elettra's hand moves up to the device he has lodged in his ear.

"I want to show you something . . . ," the girl says in a low voice, touching the earpiece.

The guard's eyes open wide. His mouth does the same. Then he shouts as the unexpected heat released from Elettra's fingertips instantly melts the device into his eardrum. He lets go of Harvey and raises both hands to his head, stunned by the pain.

Sheng walks right around him, grabs Elettra by the hand and pulls her toward the door. Harvey gets to his feet, makes sure his head is still attached to his neck and shouts out to Mistral, "Run!"

The librarian instinctively jumps to the side to let them pass by.

"Sorry about this!" Sheng laughs nervously. "But we're really in a hurry!"

"This way!" decides Harvey, randomly choosing a direction.

Behind them, the security guard is still screaming in pain.

The four run at breakneck speed down the stairs, cross through the frescoed rooms, dive into the atrium of the house of monsters and fly out the front door, which is wide open.

And at last, they're outside.

At the Domus Quintilia, the morning flies by.

Linda's whistling an old song by Renato Zero, inspecting all the rooms in the hotel armed with rags and feather dusters in various sizes. She enjoys the sunlight streaming in through the windows and reflecting off the snow, as well as the invigorating December air.

Having cleaned the dining room and the stairs, she goes to the bedroom she's temporarily sharing with her sister. Irene is reading beside her rosebush, in the light pouring in through the French doors. A blanket is draped over her knees.

"Books, books, books!" Linda exclaims the moment she sees her. "Don't you ever stop reading?"

Irene lowers her book with a smile. "Hello, Linda."

"Enough with all those words! They give me a headache! Can't you find anything better to do? There's a very nice program on television right now."

"I prefer Lucretius."

"Oh, how boring!"

"Have you ever read him?"

Linda gives up, wagging the colorful rags with which she's determined to defeat the very last speck of dust hiding in the room. "Don't you try it! I don't even want to know what it is he talks about! Do you mind if I turn on the radio? You could use a bit of music, sis. A little cheeriness is what you need! Not all that boring old drivel by Lucretius and who knows who else!"

Irene points down at her paralyzed legs and says, "Music? Oh, why not? That way, maybe we could dance together for a while. . . ."

"You're such a kidder, Irene," Linda scolds. She gives her a sideways hug, and for a few long moments, they stay there, clasped in their embrace, without saying a word.

"Have you seen Elettra?" Irene then asks, gently freeing herself from the hug.

"She's out showing the other children the city."

"How did they seem to you?"

"They seemed pleased. Although . . . the Chinese boy . . ."

"Linda . . ."

"If you'd seen how filthy his shoes were! Two big gym shoes completely covered with mud."

"They're kids."

"The French one, on the other hand," continued Linda, "is absolutely adorable. Pretty, perfumed and perfect. So graceful. So feminine. If only she'd teach a thing or two to our Elettra, we'd have a niece who's a little more bearable."

"Elettra's just like her mother," says Irene. "Pure energy."

"And all that hair," adds Linda. "I spend more time picking her hair off the sofas than I do cleaning all the guests' rooms. It's like a tangle of poisonous snakes."

Irene leans back in her wheelchair, pleased and uneasy at the same time. "But they aren't snakes. Besides, even poisonous snakes are important, in their own special way. Have you ever noticed that the symbol for pharmacies is a staff with two snakes entwined around it?"

"And no wonder! With what medication costs these days, it'd be better to die by being poisoned for free!"

Irene cackles. "That's not the reason behind the symbol. It's because in antiquity they would use snake venom as an ingredient in their medicine."

"Fortunately they invented antibiotics," remarks Linda Melodia, throwing open the room's French doors to let in some fresh air.

Later on, the tireless lady of the house goes downstairs to the window to check the courtyard. The hotel is silent and tidy. All the guests have gone out, leaving behind only their horrible footprints in the snow. The tire tracks left by Fernando's minibus are two long, dirty furrows. One detail, however, catches Linda Melodia's probing eye: a number of muddy shoeprints heading toward the basement door, and others, now dry, that from there make their way over to Elettra's room. The direction of the heels leaves no doubt. Whoever made them was coming from the courtyard.

The cheerful woman trots outside to check. When Fernando's minibus passed by, it left behind a web of tire tracks here and there in the courtyard, but Linda manages to understand that four pairs of footprints leave the hotel, head outside . . . and then return.

There's only one possible explanation. Last night, Elettra and the other kids sneaked out of the hotel. To have a snowball fight, probably. "Which would explain why they were so tired this morning . . . ," giggles Linda, passing a rag over the muddy footprints that trail from the hallway up to Elettra's room.

"What a mess . . . ," she grumbles when she opens the door to the bedroom. Suitcases and clothes are scattered everywhere. "It looks like there are thirty of them, not four!" Walking around a couple of undershirts, she tries to reach the window so she can let in some fresh air. Meanwhile, she spots other clues of their little escapade last night: a sopping-wet jacket, the American boy's jeans dampened with snow up to the knee, Elettra's sweater left draped over the radiator to dry.

But then she sees something strange. Scattered on the floor are shards of glass. Others are in the wastepaper basket in the bathroom.

"My lamp!" moans Linda Melodia, looking around in search of the dandelion lamp. "What the devil have they been up to?"

It doesn't take her long to find the pieces. Linda collects the shards of glass from the floor as well as what remains of the lamp's base. Then she carries the trash bag out of the room. "That little devil's going to get an earful from me!" she thunders, walking outside, toward the curb.

There's still a lot of snow on the ground. Linda Melodia stomps up to the garbage cans, keeping the trash bag held high, as if she were worried someone would snatch it out of her hands. "My lamp!" she exclaims again, making the pieces of glass clink together. She walks around a young woman with dark brown hair, who says good morning to her.

"Good, you say? *Good* morning?" huffs Linda. "Look at this mess! My lamp! And that's not all! Last night they went out without even asking for permission!"

The young woman smiles at her. "Can I help you with that?" she asks when she realizes Linda's fumbling with the lid.

"Yes, thank you. Hold this! Or better yet, open that up! A pest! That's what she is . . . a pest!" Linda calms down only when the bag with what remains of her lamp has disappeared into the garbage can. "There! Done . . . ," she says to the young woman, who looks at her with her big, beautiful, dark eyes. "Thanks for your help. I don't know what's more difficult, running a hotel or looking after a twelve-year-old girl!"

"Are you the owner of the Domus Quintilia?"

Linda Melodia heaves a sigh and answers, "In a certain sense, yes."

"What luck! Could I ask you a few questions, then?" The woman holds out her hand. "My name is Beatrice."

12

THE JOURNAL

"Hao! How'd you do that?!" Sheng cries excitedly. "I've never seen anything like it! You were like . . . like a cartoon superhero!" He raises his right index finger and yells, "Now I'm gonna show you something!"

Mistral elbows him to make him cut it out. Elettra looks far from happy. She walks along, her head hanging low, her eyes half-closed. Her long black hair looks like dry, thorny twigs.

"How are you doing?" Harvey asks her.

"I feel tired," she answers. "And really confused."

"You're not the only one. Strange things are happening. And quite frankly . . ." Harvey thumbs through the professor's journal. "I think this is going to make us understand even less than we did before."

"We're all shaken," adds Mistral. "We were really in a tough spot with that guy. . . ."

"What, are you kidding?" Sheng snorts, gesturing. "It was fantastic! We ran off like four daredevil robbers and then the stairs . . . whoosh! And the front door . . . bam! And finally . . . on the street! Incredible!"

"Maybe we should stop somewhere to rest," suggests Mistral.

"Yeah," Elettra agrees.

Harvey shakes his head. "I think the best thing for us to do right now is to put some distance between us and the library."

"I could use something to eat," suggests Sheng, looking around. "What time is it? Can't we grab a burger somewhere?"

"Why don't we go back to the Caffè Greco?"

"Burgers!" Sheng insists. "I want a giant hamburger . . . a What's-Your-Beef-Evil-Security-Dude-Gianni Burger!"

Mistral yanks on his backpack. "Would you cut it out with the stupid jokes?"

"You know what we call a stupid joke like that in Rome?" Elettra interjects, a little smile on her face. "A *pasquinata*."

"A *pasqui*-what?"

"*Pasquinata*."

"Which would be . . . ?"

"Pasquino is the name they gave to a statue the Romans would hang comical messages on, to make fun of the people in power."

Harvey holds up the professor's journal. "Then let's go there! We could hang this on it."

Elettra's head shoots up. "That's not a bad idea . . . ," she thinks aloud.

"Um, what isn't?"

"The Pasquino isn't far from here," explains Elettra, pointing down a cobblestone street.

"So what?"

"Right next to the Pasquino," continues Elettra, "is a quiet little place where they serve what's called the *coppetta incredibile*. It's a dessert made with whipped cream, pistachios, strawberries, meringue and custard. What do you say?"

"Approved!" declares Sheng, instantly giving up his plans for a hamburger.

The afternoon light begins to fade, but not the kids' curiosity. Sitting around a little table outside the Cul de Sac restaurant, four empty dishes of *coppetta incredibile* in front of them, the kids listen carefully to what Elettra is reading from the professor's journal. The first pages aren't particularly interesting. They sound like notes from a university lecture about Nero, who, it seems, was his favorite topic.

"He liked crazy people," remarks Harvey.

Elettra turns page after page. "Sure looks that way. Nero as emperor, Nero in battle, Nero's childhood . . . It seems he was tutored by a very important philosopher called Seneca, one of the great minds of antiquity. The greatest tutors often ended up with crazy pupils. Aristotle taught Alexander the Great, Seneca taught Nero . . . ," she summarizes.

"So who was your great tutor?" Sheng asks Harvey, getting elbowed in reply.

"Seneca taught Nero the secrets of the natural world. He told him about Earth, the planets, the moon and the sun. He described the four elements that every other thing is made of: water, air, earth and fire. Nero was particularly fascinated by fire, an element of both life and destruction." Elettra struggles to translate the following pages. "Seneca maintained that mankind was allowed to make advances in discovering some of the secrets of the cosmos, but that there was a limit. There were secrets that were never to be revealed."

"That's just like what was written on the note in the brief-case!" Mistral points out.

"Here the professor added a footnote: 'That's what I'm looking for. And one of these secrets is hidden in Rome.'"

Sheng slaps his hand down on the table. "What did I tell you? Keep going! Keep going!"

"There's another footnote . . . ," says Elettra, turning the journal upside down. "'Study the tops and the wooden map. Find out how it's used. Ermete.'"

"What does 'Ermete' mean?" asks Mistral, resting her pencil beside her sketchbook, in which she's been jotting down the things that seem to be the most important.

"It's a name, actually," Elettra explains. "But I don't know who that could be."

"So the professor calls the thing a 'wooden map' . . . ," Harvey points out. "What else?"

Elettra thumbs through a few blank pages and others on which drawings have been sketched. "I'd say he wasn't as good as you, Mistral. What do you think these are supposed to be?"

The girl studies the sketches in the journal and remarks, "It looks like he was trying to copy down the drawings we saw on the tops."

Elettra nods and turns the page. "Here he goes back to talking about Nero again."

"How boring!" grumbles Sheng. "I want to know what the se-cret is!"

"It looks like Nero wanted to know that, too . . . ," Elettra comments. "When Seneca spoke to him for the first time about a secret that mankind was forbidden to seek out, Nero was furious.

He demanded to know what the secret was, and Seneca replied, 'It is the greatest of secrets, but the time has not yet come for it to be revealed.'"

"Typical answer from a teacher," remarks Mistral.

"And Nero?" asks Harvey.

"I bet he was angry," Sheng throws in.

Elettra giggles. "I'd say so, too. He abandoned the teachings of Seneca and started to learn from tutors from the Orient, who convinced him to worship fire and the sun god."

"Zeus?" Sheng guessed.

"No. His name was . . . Mithra," says Elettra, reading aloud.

"Never heard of him."

"I have," Sheng remarks, amazing everyone. "I think they still worship him in India. Or something like that . . ."

"The professor writes that Mithra was the sun god. A god who came back to life after death, just like the sun sets and then rises again in the morning. And . . . this is weird . . . in ancient Rome he was celebrated on December twenty-fifth!"

"On Christmas?" asks Mistral.

"They didn't have Christmas back then, you know," Harvey reminds her.

"So when did they get all their presents?"

"Nero started to believe he was a god himself," Elettra continues, reading. "And that he was the actual personification of the sun. Basically, he went crazy. 'Foolish mortal, you have gone further than was allowed. You have sought to learn secrets that you should not have sought out. You have discovered answers to questions that you should not have asked.' That's Seneca again, I guess."

"What did Nero say to that?" asks Harvey.

CENTURY

IGNIS

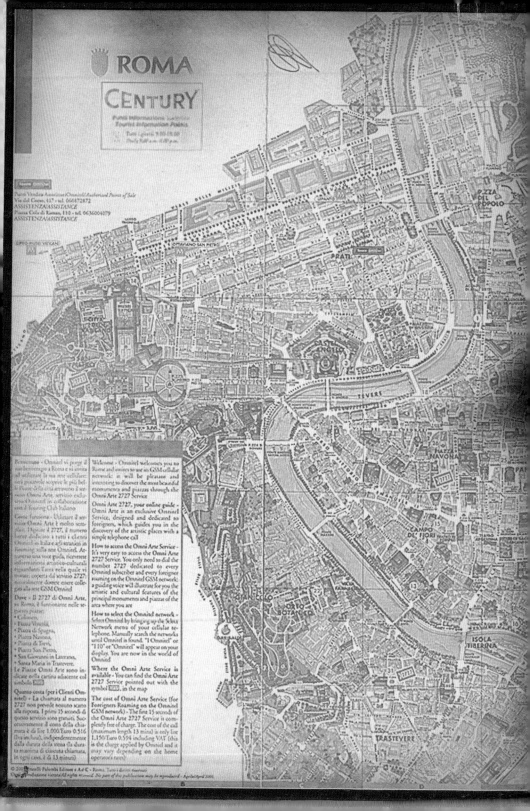

Dearest Vladimir,

I am sending you this material in the hope
that it may be useful to you. I have found
the places in the city where the Pact
began. The places where the four children, <u>our</u> four children, began to follow
the path of Century. What you will find
here is the fruit of a long investigation.
It is a thankless and exhausting task that
we have given ourselves. I beg you, watch
over them. Elettra is my only niece. She
has heeded the call. And this is all that
I know. The rest does not concern us, and
neither you nor I will ever discover how
the Pact decided to speak to them.

After so many years, and after so much
research, the moment has come.

Irene

★★★ HOTEL DOMUS QUINTILIA ★★★

Il Bed & Breakfast nel cuore di Roma

A Trastevere
a due passi da Santa Cecilia
e dall'Isola Tiberina

①

②

...ggero

i ROMA

...asa, abiterà nell'An...

...Agenzia per il Turismo, in via Giulia l'A...

COMITATI DI QUARTIERE

Stop anche a tavolino

...izia che la storica scuola
...Mai di piazza Madonna
...onti non diventerà un cen-
...mmerciale è stata accolta
...oria dalla Rete Sociale
...che da un anno e mezzo
...intrapreso una vera e pro-
...attaglia per preservare un
...di storia del rione. «Questa
...a - commenta Riccardo
...della Rete - dimostra che
...itorio può organizzarsi dal
...divenire in ottimo inter-
...per risolvere dei conflitti.
...u villaggio nella città. E
...va alle manifestazioni,
...0 firme raccolte, alle ini-

...lative in piazza, tutte pacifiche,
...che hanno portato alla vittoria:
...«Siamo le torri d'ascolto del no-
...stro rione - prosegue - e continue-
...remo su questa strada. Ci sono in-
...fatti tanti spazi da riqualificare,
...le Aldobrandini che ha una gran-
...le quantità di spazi e padiglioni
...inutilizzati e che potrebbe diventa-
...re un punto di aggregazione». Ma
...la Rete parla anche di progetti di
...pedonalizzazione e della lotta da
...intraprendere contro i tavolini sel-
...vaggi, perché «Monti ormai è un
...tavolino ambulante». È soddisfat-
...ta anche Marisa di Iorio: «Vende-
...re un immobile a cui tutto il mo-

In delizioso B&B a Trasteve...

Il B&B Hotel Domus Quintilia (Trasteve...

③

Domus Quintilia library

Caffè Greco

'o del Dado

'Argentina

'la Gatta

ofessor's

San Clemente

ANTICO CAFFE' GRECO
SRL VIA CONDOTTI 86
ROMA
PART.IVA 06369221004
TELEFONO 06/6791700

                        EURO
OPER. 4
CAPPUCCINO   5.20
BEVANDE   4.20

TOTALE   9.40

N.PZ 2   CASS. 1
07-01-2004 17:10 SC. 195

/F AE 49401302

ARRIVEDERCI E GRAZIE

④

⑤

⑥

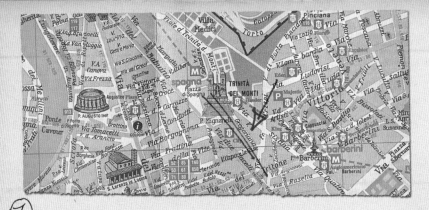

⑦

BIBLIOTHECA HERTZIANA
MAX-PLANCK-INSTITUT FÜR KUNSTGESCHICHTE

Prof. Alfred Van Der Berger
Wissenschaftlicher Assistent/Assistente scientifico

MAX-PLANCK-GESELLSCHAFT

⑧

Via Gregoriana, 28
00187 Roma

⑨

10

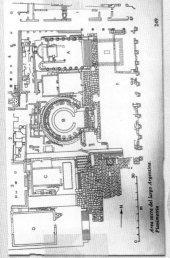

Area sacra del largo Argentino.
Planimetria.

11

VAN DER BERGER

12

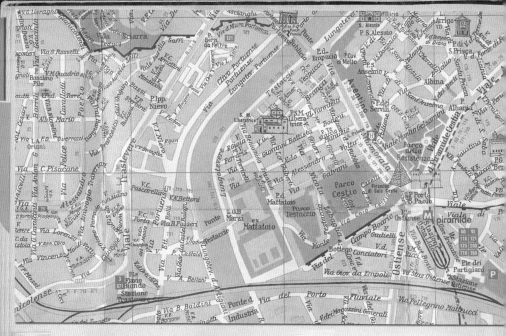

13

14

AL REGNO
DEL DADO

RAYMOND

RIONE DEL TESTACCIO

⑯

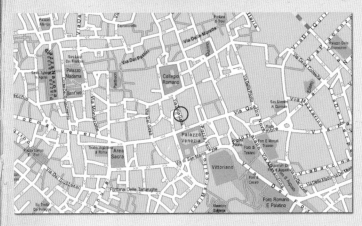

LA RUOTA DELLA FORTUNA

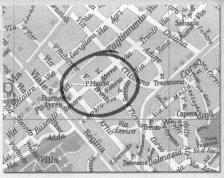

23

22

24

25

26

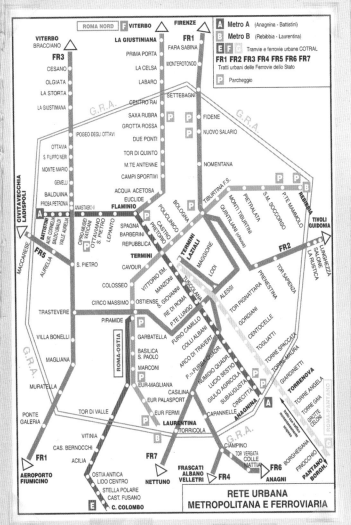

(27)

RETE URBANA
METROPOLITANA E FERROVIARIA

San Clemente
Metro

Sant' Eustachio
il Caffè
dal 1938
SANT' EUSTACCHIO
IL CAFFE' S.R.L.
P.ZA S.EUSTACCHIO 82 RM
P.I. 00936071000
TELEFONO 06/68802048

EURO
CAPPUCCINO (28) 1,30
PASTICCERA 0,90
PASTICCERA 0,90
TOTALE 3,10

05/09/2006   10-00
SCONTR. FISCALE   105
/FMR 42000670
ARRIVEDERCI E GRAZIE

FIRMA
PERCORSO   da   a

Cica Cica Boom
Gelateria artigianale

(29)

Cica Cica Boom
Gelateria artigianale
Via Liguria, 38 - Tel. 06-4884745

TAXI N.
Data   5/9/06
Ore
Importo corsa € 6,50

da
BUCATINO
taverna testaccio
TAVOLO RISERVATO

(30)

Metrebus Roma
P. IVA 06341981006
Euro 4,00
Vale fino alle ore 24.00

2 BIG Biglietto Integrato
Giornaliero

(31)

INDEX

The stars, the lights of the sky,
watch over mankind, for whose
dreaming look they compete as
rivals. But only one is chosen.
There is only one path.
                    — Alfred Van Der Berger

INIZIERA 20 DICEMBRE

32

"He ordered the construction of what's called the Colossus Neronis, the largest bronze statue ever forged. In it, he was depicted as the sun god, surrounded by fiery flames."

"He totally lost it. . . ."

"Yeah. In fact, later on he set fire to the city. As though he were a god, he destroyed the very thing that gave him power. And to do that he used . . ." Elettra struggles to translate the words that follow. ". . . The Ring of Fire."

"What's that?"

The girl shakes her head. She shows them the journal, in which the professor has drawn a ring surrounded by flames. The following pages are brutally torn. Drawn on the remaining scraps are flaming circles and spirals.

When she sees them, Mistral rummages through the backpack and pulls out the sheets of paper she picked up from the library floor. There, too, are circles and spirals copied over and over again, obsessively.

"To be honest, I doodle stuff like that when I need to kill time . . . ," says Sheng. "Maybe the professor talked on the phone a lot."

"I say he was insane," insists Harvey.

"Actually . . . ," Elettra says softly, leafing through the last remaining pages in the journal, "from here on in, nothing else is legible. Except for . . . well, this, maybe. 'The Ring of Fire is Seneca's secret. It's hidden below and hidden above. Search below and you shall find it above. To find the way, use the map.'"

"What does that mean?" asks Sheng.

"Nothing," blurts out Harvey. "Just like everything else we've read so far. It doesn't mean a thing."

"But if it says you need to use a map to find the way there . . . Well, he did leave us a map," Mistral points out.

"But what kind of a map is it, anyway? It's just a hunk of wood," says Harvey.

"Isn't there anything else in the journal?"

Elettra shakes her head. "I don't think so. Except for . . . let's see . . . These look like phone numbers, partially crossed out . . . 'Ilda, news, 06543804. Orsenigo, dentist, 18671903.'" Saying this, she hands the journal to Sheng. "That's all, I guess."

"Can I use one of your pencils?" Sheng asks Mistral. He copies the phone numbers down onto a napkin and looks carefully at the last pages of the journal.

"So what do we do now?" Mistral asks.

Elettra and Harvey exchange glances. "It'll be getting dark soon . . . ," the American boy points out. "And we've been gone since this morning. Maybe we should go back to the hotel."

"Are you tired?" Elettra asks him.

"Aren't you?"

"Yes, but I'm really curious, too. . . ."

Just then, a little melody comes from Mistral's purse. Her cell phone's ringtone is playing the refrain from "You're Beautiful," a song by James Blunt.

"Bleah!" grimaces Sheng, rubbing the pencil across the inside cover of the journal.

Mistral fishes the cell phone out of her purse and answers it. "Hi, Mom!" The conversation soon turns into a monologue of "Yes, of course, I understand, no, no, that's fine, don't worry about it," and quickly comes to an end. The phone plops back into her purse and a look of disappointment clouds the girl's face.

"Bad news?" Elettra asks her.

"Well . . . ," replies Mistral. "My mom needs to leave Rome on business and she won't be back before tomorrow night. She's leaving me her room. Although . . . if you don't mind, I'd rather stay in your room."

"Sure, no problem," says Elettra.

"Do you have to go back to the hotel to say goodbye to her?" Harvey asks.

Mistral drums her ice cream spoon against the saucer. "I'm not sure . . . ," she answers. "But I don't think so."

"Then we can stay out a little while longer," suggests Elettra. "I know a great place to get pizza."

"I'll need to let my parents know," says Harvey.

"What about you, Sheng?"

"What?" The Chinese boy is still busy rubbing the tip of the pencil across the last page of the journal. "That's fine with me. . . . I just need to talk to my dad."

Mistral picks up her cell phone and hands it to Elettra. "You want to make the call?"

The girl punches in the number of the Domus Quintilia, but before hitting the send button, she says, "Actually . . ." She takes a look at Sheng's napkin and punches in a second phone number. After a few rings, a woman's voice answers.

"Is this Ilda? Yes, hello there!" Elettra booms out boldly.

Harvey jumps up from his seat. Sheng's mouth falls open. Mistral smiles.

Elettra goes on, unperturbed. "This is the professor's niece. Yes, Uncle . . . Alfred. Oh, you didn't know? Well, he does. Actually, he's got two nieces and two nephews in all. That's right.

Of course we . . . What? He's . . . he's doing just fine. . . . But . . . well . . . I can imagine. Yes . . . yes, he told us that. We know it's been a long time since he's stopped by. For . . . for news. Sure. So you do have some, right? News, I mean. . . ."

Harvey runs his fingers through his hair nervously and starts walking around the table.

"You set it aside for him," repeats Elettra, "as always? Well . . . great. We could stop by to pick it up. That way . . . that way we can surprise Uncle Alfred. What's that? It's heavy? Oh, it doesn't matter. . . ." Elettra motions to Sheng to jot down an address. "The newsstand in Largo Argentina. Fine. In fifteen minutes. Perfect!" And with this, she hangs up.

"Are you out of your mind?!" Harvey blurts out. "Why did you call that number?"

"Why not?" she responds, handing him the cell phone. "What was your plan of action?"

"I don't know!" Harvey grunts. "But anyway . . . darn it! We should all decide what to do together, shouldn't we?"

"Well?" asks Mistral.

"That was the owner of the newsstand in Largo Argentina. She said she's set a lot of stuff aside for 'Uncle Alfred,'" Elettra answers. "And we're going over there to pick it up."

"Perfect! While we're at it, why don't we call the dentist and schedule an appointment?" Harvey sputters. "In fact, maybe the tooth we found in the briefcase belongs to him!"

"Why are you getting so angry?" snaps Mistral, who's starting to get annoyed by Harvey's attitude.

"*Hao!*" cries Sheng just then.

"What is it?"

The Chinese boy shows them the inside cover of the journal, which he's completely blackened in with the pencil.

"Take a look! I've seen them do this on TV. It shows you the impression of what was written on the page before, so you can read it," he explains. "And it works!" On the blackened page, in a sort of carbon copy, is a large circle inside of which they see the professor's tiny, angular handwriting, which reads:

I have made a discovery
and I have been discovered
the Ring of Fire
they're right behind me
they walk and dig
they watch
they murmur
they creep
they kill
I hear their
words words words words WORDS
it's begun
what was hidden is about to be revealed
no one can
HIDE FOREVER

It's already evening when the phone rings at the hotel. Fernando Melodia folds up his copy of *La Gazzetta dello Sport* with a rustling of paper, grabs the receiver and replies, "Domus Quintilia. Oh . . . hi, Elettra."

"Who is it, Fernando?" a shrill voice immediately asks. Aunt Linda peeks in from the doorway and the man motions for her to be quiet.

"No, that's fine, of course you can . . . ," he says in the meantime. "I think your taking them to the Montecarlo for pizza is a great idea!"

"Is that Elettra?" Linda interrupts, her voice rising in intensity. "If that's Elettra, let me talk to her immediately."

Fernando turns his back on her, letting the telephone cord wrap around him. "Of course, I'll let them all know. . . . Sheng's father hasn't come back yet, and Harvey's parents . . . What's that?"

Aunt Linda angrily sits down on the sofa and demands that he let her speak to her niece.

"Elettra, your aunt wants to—" Fernando manages to say before the phone is ripped out of his hand.

"Elettra!" Linda Melodia shouts out furiously. "Just tell me one thing! What did you kids get up to last night? I saw your footprints!"

Fernando plops down on the couch and grumbles, "Oh, she said they were out buying magazines in Largo Argentina. And that they wouldn't be back for dinner." He smiles sheepishly at a dark-eyed young woman, who's now glaring at him from the sitting room. He escapes into the comfort of his sports paper.

"Tell me what you did last night!" the aunt barks out again.

A long moment of silence follows.

"Elettra!" Linda Melodia thunders out, shocked. "What on earth has gotten into you?!" she exclaims. And with this, she hangs up.

"So what did they do last night?" Fernando asks with amusement, without looking up from his paper.

"Your daughter reads too many books!" Aunt Linda sighs. "Do you know what she just had the nerve to tell me? That last night on Ponte Quattro Capi, they met a man whose throat was slit shortly afterward!"

"Oh, my!" exclaims Fernando, without managing to hide a hint of admiration for his daughter's outlandish excuse.

"She also said that it was on the front page of all the newspapers," Linda continues, returning to speak with their guest. "It's unbelievable! Kids these days come up with the most frightful stories. . . ."

His curiosity piqued, Fernando folds up *La Gazzetta* and takes a look at the front page of *Il Messaggero*. "Actually, they say they really did find a man's body beside the Tiber. . . ."

"Fernando! Don't you get started now, too!"

The man shrugs his shoulders, withdrawing into a dignified silence.

A few minutes later, Beatrice walks out of the Domus Quintilia, overjoyed.

She quickly dials a phone number.

"Little Linch? I think I found something," she says into her cell phone. "Meet me in Largo Argentina. At the newsstand."

13

THE NEWS

Napping among the remains of the temples in Largo Argentina are dozens of stray cats. Not minding the snow or the traffic around them, others stroll around peacefully, like local gods. Not far from them or the crowded bus stops is a little pre-fabricated newsstand, which looks like it's been attacked by an army of advertising posters. The owner's wrinkled face can barely be seen peeking out from behind the stacks and stacks of magazines. When the kids appear before her, the woman can barely keep herself from running out to hug them.

"I was so worried!" she cries. She points at the first page of *Il Messaggero* and says, "When I saw that photo this morning, I almost fainted! That looks just like your uncle's raincoat. . . ."

Elettra, Sheng, Mistral and Harvey try to avoid the subject.

"I'm so relieved! I'm so relieved!" Ilda says, sighing. "I haven't seen him for days now, and if you hadn't called me, I'd have stopped by to take a look in his house tonight."

"It's a good thing we called you, then . . . ," Elettra says softly.

Ilda disappears into the depths of the newsstand and starts to rummage around in the plastic containers full of magazines. She doesn't stop talking for a second. "He's seemed so anxious lately! I've even asked him if he's been eating, because he looks so pale, and he's a lot thinner than normal. I don't think he even weighs sixty kilos! Literally! You read too much, I tell him! And you're always so worried about . . . well, about something!"

The news vendor slips out of a little side door. She's a tiny woman, much shorter than the kids, although she has massive shoulders and arms. With no apparent strain, she holds up four plastic bags stuffed full of newspapers.

"This is all of it," she explains. "In the first one I put all the main daily papers: *Le Figaro*, *Le Monde*, the *New York Times*, the *Bombay Post*. All that's missing is *Pravda*, which they keep delivering late. In this other one I put all the magazines from African missionaries as well as Argentinean and Bolivian weeklies. Polish and Finnish monthlies are here in the third bag. I mean, they're all from up north, aren't they? When I couldn't understand where something came from because I didn't recognize the language, I put it in the fourth bag."

"I'll take that one!" Sheng offers, peeking into the bag, hoping to find a Chinese newspaper.

Ilda stares at him rather curiously, amazed that the professor has a nephew with Asian features. But then, as if she's understood everything, she remarks, "He certainly is a man of the world."

Each of the other kids grabs a bag.

"I'm sorry, but . . . ," Elettra hazards, turning to the woman. "You said that if we hadn't called, you would've stopped by our uncle's place in person. . . . Does that mean you've got a copy of his house keys?"

"Of course! Do you need them?" exclaims Ilda, disappearing

back into the newsstand. She reappears moments later next to the culinary magazines, handing a set of keys to the kids. "This is the copy the professor left with me. He's always forgetting them at home, and he comes here for the spare set whenever he's locked out." On the key ring is a little tag with an address written in ink. Elettra has never heard of the street name before, but she decides not to ask any more questions.

Having said goodbye to Ilda with a world of thanks, they walk down into the nearest subway station, looking for a map of the streets of Rome. "Line B," says Harvey, the first one to find the address. "The last stop."

"Will that leave us enough time to come back for pizza?" Sheng wonders, the bag of newspapers in his hand and the backpack on his back.

The others don't reply.

When they get out of the subway, night has already fallen.

The sun has set behind the hills and the buildings look like ant farms along the street. The cars zoom by, their headlights shining through the night. Many of the streetlights are still off, while others are now blinking on, as if they were exhausted. The asphalt smells of dirt and stray dogs.

Elettra, Harvey, Mistral and Sheng walk along slowly, lugging the four plastic bags stuffed with newspapers. "Do you think the professor actually read all this stuff?" asks Sheng. "And in all these different languages?"

"I don't know," replies Elettra, the keys clutched in her hand. "But I guess we'll find out real soon."

"Nasty little place," remarks Harvey. "Even worse than the Bronx."

The kids walk along tall walls covered with graffiti.

"This is it . . . ," Elettra whispers after a while.

They've stopped in front of the shabby-looking front door to a small gray four-story building, which looks like it's been squeezed in between other cement constructions. The closely set terraces are thick with satellite dishes. Through the windows the intermittent glow of televisions flickers. The street is dark, narrow and covered with potholes. The remains of a motorbike are still chained to the only working streetlight. "Not exactly a great neighborhood . . . ," whispers Mistral, looking around with concern.

Harvey clears his throat, discouraged. "This building looks like it could topple over any second," he says.

"Are you sure this is the right address?" Sheng asks. "Because, if you ask me, it doesn't look like anybody lives here. . . ." All of the building's windows are sealed off with aluminum shutters, making it seem more like a high-security prison than an apartment building.

A car zips down a nearby street, its muffler rattling as if it were in the throes of death.

"In any case, I say we get off the street," Elettra suggests. She climbs up the steps separating her and the main door to the building. On the intercom panel is a single listing, handwritten on a piece of tape. "It's the right address . . . ," says Elettra softly. "Take a look."

Drawn on the piece of tape is a ring.

* * *

They buzz twice but get no answer. Elettra pulls out the set of spare keys and unlocks the main door, which opens up with a creak. Lying in the dusty entranceway are dozens of envelopes that have slid across the old, cracked tiles all the way up to the inner stairway. The railing is made of old black wood. A bicycle has been abandoned on the ground. Everything smells of mold.

Elettra finds the light switch and flicks it on.

Overhead, a crooked ceiling lamp sputters and then turns on with a groan. The harsh light reveals walls eroded by dampness. Metal pipes in various sizes make their way down the stairway to disappear belowground. The electrical meters look like plastic mushrooms growing out of the plaster.

"I'm not going up there . . . ," says Mistral.

"I think it's better to go upstairs than stay here . . . ," Sheng says in a hush.

"You think the stairs will hold our weight?" asks Harvey.

"I've never seen anything more intimidating," Mistral says.

"Come to Shanghai and I'll show you the junks!"

"Anybody home?" Elettra calls out toward the stairway. Not hearing any reply, she leans over the railing and looks up. "What floor do you think he lived on?"

"If you want me to take a wild guess," says Sheng, "given that we've got to drag these bags up with us and there's no sign of an elevator . . . I'd say the top floor."

"I think you're right," the girl replies, starting to climb the stairs.

Harvey shuts the door leading out to the street. "But let's make this quick."

130

"Pizza," Sheng reminds everyone, as though it would be a sort of reward.

They climb the stairs in silence, trying not to look around them.

When they reach the first landing, the lights let out an electrical squeal.

And then they go out.

"There aren't any light switches here," Elettra groans, feeling the wall.

"Or windows, either," says Harvey, bringing up the rear.

"In the dark again!" mutters Sheng. "This is getting to be a habit."

"Did you hear that?" whispers Mistral.

"Hear what?" Harvey asks her.

"The noise the lights made! It . . . it was really creepy."

"They're just lights."

Mistral clenches her fists. "It isn't normal," she insists. "Stairway lights never shut off after only a few seconds."

"It's an old system in an old building," says Harvey. The pessimistic yet logical Harvey seems calmer than the others.

"Wait for me here . . . ," orders Sheng. He rests his bag of newspapers on the ground and slips the backpack off his shoulders. He goes down the stairs and returns to the entrance, where he flicks the first light switch.

"There's nobody living here at all . . . ," says Elettra.

Except for Sheng going down the steps, they can't hear any footsteps or voices or water flowing through the pipes. The stairway is cold, dark, abandoned.

"Oh, man," grumbles Sheng a moment later. He fiddles with

the light switch beside the front door and then gives up. "Looks like it's dead."

"Houston, we have a problem . . . ," recites Harvey.

Elettra turns around in the darkness. She has the impression she's seeing the American boy's eyes glimmer in the dark, as if he is looking back at her. "Light just isn't on our side, it seems . . . ," she whispers.

"Not today, at least," Harvey answers. "Should we keep going? After all, it's just a stairway." With this, they all start to make their way slowly up the stairs in the darkness.

On the fourth floor, a tiny window looking out onto the street lets in a faint glow, barely strong enough for them to read the sign on the only door to be found: PROF. A VANDER BERGER.

"So he really was a professor," says Sheng.

Elettra rings the doorbell. A low-pitched sound echoes through the deserted building. A few seconds later, the girl slides the key into the lock and opens the door. Wafting out of the apartment is the strong smell of tobacco and paper. Flicking the switch, she finds that the lights work. "Thank goodness," she sighs.

But her sigh of relief is cut short the moment she steps inside.

It's frightening.

SECOND STASIMON

"Hello? Vladimir? They've killed Alfred."

"Are you joking? No . . . That's impossible!"

"But it happened, I tell you. It's in the papers, on the front page."

"All he had to do was set things up. That was the easiest part! Of course, he was the . . . the weakest of us all."

"Alfred wasn't the weakest."

"Yes, he was. And you know it. Do you remember the wolves? He was convinced he was being followed. He was obsessed with the idea that he was being followed."

"It seems he was right."

"Did he at least manage to . . . ?"

"He delivered the briefcase. He was killed right after that."

"Do you think that's what they were looking for?"

"I'm certain of it. Someone is after that briefcase. But who?"

"Not me. And not you."

"There are three of us, Vladimir. . . ."

"Then you've just answered your own question."

"Can't we get in touch with her?"

"The last time I heard from her she was in China. Two years ago."

"If what you're saying is true, it means she talked."

"Yes, she talked."

"But who did she tell? And why? Even she knows that once it begins no one is to interfere. . . . Who's behind this, Vladimir?"

"I don't know, believe me. Things have gotten out of control. . . ."

"Are the children in danger?"

"I don't know. I need . . . I need to check. Maybe I could make a phone call."

"Make a hundred of them, then. Otherwise, I'll find a way to stop everything."

14

THE APARTMENT

There isn't any furniture or pictures or carpets. All there is on the other side of the door leading into Alfred Van Der Berger's apartment is a hallway lined by two tall walls of books stacked all the way up to the ceiling. And in the middle of the hallway are other books, arranged one atop the other to form columns, stools, tables, shelves. Magazines, newspapers, pamphlets and notebooks fill every square centimeter of the apartment. Some of the columns are low, others taller than a meter high, while still others reach the ceiling. The piles of books only leave room for a single narrow passageway, barely wide enough to walk through.

"Man . . . ," whispers Sheng.

There isn't even space to put down the bags they picked up from the newsstand. The air is stale and musty. The ceiling light seems totally incapable of illuminating the chaotic mass of papers.

"If you ask me, he could've used a bookcase," Sheng adds.

"If you ask me, he was totally crazy," mutters Harvey.

Mistral shakes her head, flabbergasted.

Elettra takes a few steps into the hallway and feels the floor tremble beneath her feet. "Oh, man . . . ," she murmurs, staring at the masses of books. "There are so many of them!" There's dust everywhere. She runs her fingers over the spines of the books. Old leather-bound volumes, economic textbooks, paperbacks, titles in Italian, English, Russian, Portuguese. Light covers, dark covers, photographic books, lettering in gold and others as black as pitch. "It can't be . . . ," she murmurs, delving into the jungle of books. "The whole apartment's like this."

The hallway leads into two rooms, both completely packed with books. There isn't even any furniture, just narrow passageways between the publications, which all come together to form one massive maze.

Mistral follows behind her friend slowly. All around them is the stagnant odor of dust mixed with paper and tobacco. "Don't touch anything . . . ," she whispers. "Don't touch a single thing." She's afraid that the flimsy construction might collapse on top of her at any moment.

Harvey is about to shut the apartment door behind him when Mistral begs, "No! Leave it open. Otherwise we'll suffocate!"

Harvey nods.

"Let's leave these bags outside," suggests Sheng. "I mean, I don't think anybody is going to steal them from us. . . ."

"What's this?" asks Harvey, stepping into the hallway.

Hanging beside the door is a little board, written on which are two columns of numbers that have progressively been crossed off.

~~1000~~ ~~70~~

~~915~~ ~~68~~

~~560~~ ~~69~~

~~462~~ ~~70~~

$$390 - 69$$
$$345 - 65$$
$$230 - 60$$
$$137 - 58$$

"That looks like the professor's handwriting . . . ," remarks Sheng. "But what does it mean?"

"I have no idea," mumbles Harvey. "Bills to be paid, maybe? Or the number of books in here?"

"It looks like a couple of countdowns."

"But the second column goes up and then down again."

"It might be some sort of diet," Mistral guesses, slowly walking back to them. "My mom keeps a chart like that on the fridge."

"You think the professor was on a diet?" Harvey grumbles dubiously.

"The woman at the newsstand said he was really thin . . . ," Sheng remembers. "All skin and bones. I mean, even when he was alive."

"If I remember correctly, she said he weighed under sixty kilograms, just like this," Mistral notes, pointing to the last number written on the board.

"And before that, he weighed sixty, sixty-five . . ." Harvey checks the entire column. "At most, seventy kilos."

"So what does the first column mean?"

Mistral shakes her head. "I don't know, but . . ." She pulls out her sketchbook and patiently copies down the two series of numbers.

"I think I found the kitchen!" comes Elettra's voice from the depths of the apartment.

"Let's go take a look," Sheng proposes.

Elettra moves around on her tiptoes to avoid the unpleasant feeling of walking on nothingness. She's already gone through what might be the dining room, which is filled with stacks of books and newspapers.

The kitchen is a narrow little room where the air barely circulates. There are dishes piled up in the sink and magazines stacked up on all the shelves, their pages damp. On the refrigerator is a map of Rome, stuck there with four magnets in the shape of spaceships. The professor used a red marker to draw circles around certain areas of the map. He also wrote the words:

It will begin on December 29th
One hundred years later.

Mistral walks in, looking like a ghost as she emerges from the darkness of the dining room. The moment she steps foot in the kitchen, she feels like she can barely breathe. "What did you find?" she asks Elettra.

"Just this map," she answers. "Rome. The professor wrote that it would begin on December twenty-ninth. Which means he knew it right down to the day."

Mistral shakes her head. "Can we get out of here? This place scares me."

But Elettra is still studying the map. "He circled Trastevere . . . ," she says, pointing to the district where her family's hotel is located. "Along with Parioli and Esquilino. Those are three of the neighborhoods that the blackout affected yesterday, on the twenty-ninth. . . . So did the professor know? Had he predicted it? Was that the sign that it had all begun?"

Mistral's stare gives no answer to her questions.

"Elettra? Mistral?" Sheng calls from some other room in the apartment. "Come here. . . ."

"I think I found something!" Elettra cries out, taking the map of Rome off the fridge.

"Us too!" calls Sheng. "Come take a look!"

Mistral doesn't wait for him to repeat himself. She grabs hold of Elettra's hand and pulls her out of the room. "What did you find?"

"Stars," replies Harvey. "Stars, everywhere."

The ceiling of the professor's room is covered by a map of the sky, composed of dozens of sheets of paper carefully positioned one beside the other. Dotted lines join together the brightest stars, creating glowing figures with ancient names: Draco, Orion, Hercules, Canis Major, Auriga, Ursa Minor, Polaris, Ursa Major. Some of the stars are circled in red, like boats in a game of battleship.

"It looks like the professor was studying the stars," Harvey comments, sitting down on the mattress to stare up at the ceiling. There are slightly fewer books around the bed, and the air seems more breathable.

"Together with a million other things," adds Elettra.

"Do any of you understand astronomy?" asks Sheng.

"Not me," sighs Harvey. "But I can ask my dad. That's what he teaches at college."

"So the professor was studying the stars to discover . . . what?"

"The . . . the secret, I guess. The Ring of Fire. To find it you need to use the map, and by looking below you find it above . . .

or something like that," summarizes Mistral, leafing through her sketchbook filled with notes.

"Oh, that explains everything!" Sheng exclaims ironically.

"What could be this important?" wonders Mistral.

"Something other people are looking for, too . . . a secret they mustn't discover . . . but something that people are willing to kill for . . . ," Sheng murmurs.

"'Search below and you shall find it above' . . . ," recites Elettra. "Above us are the stars, right?"

"And below?"

"The floor," Sheng answers.

"So what's on the floor?"

"Us. Plus tons of books."

"And big red circles . . . ," Elettra notes, pointing at a series of marks made on the few areas of the floor that aren't covered with books.

"What could those be for?"

"I don't know," she admits. She walks out of the bedroom to check the rest of the house. "But there are other ones in the hallway."

"They look like circles on a treasure map," Sheng comments. "You know, like 'X' marks the spot!"

"I don't get it," says Harvey, giving up. "I don't get any of this. Maybe . . . maybe we're going too fast. Maybe we should get the book we found in the library translated first. Or reread the professor's journal more carefully."

Sheng pats his backpack. "It's all here, safe and sound."

Mistral points out a book resting beside the bed to Harvey. "Take a look at what he was reading."

The boy reaches over the bed and picks it up. He brushes away the dust and tells them, "I think it's been a while since he last read this. It's entitled *Naturales Quaestiones*. It's about comets. And it's by Seneca."

Sheng snaps his fingers. "Nero's tutor!"

"That's the one," confirms Harvey, thumbing through the pages. "It's all written in Latin, in case any of you know how to translate it. . . ."

"So let's summarize," says Sheng. "We've got a tooth, a thing the professor calls a wooden map, four toy tops, an incomprehensible book in Greek and an incomprehensible book in Latin."

"Very well put," cackles Harvey.

"And finally, there are some mysterious 'thems' out there who've killed the only person who could explain how we can piece all these things together. Am I forgetting anything?" concludes Sheng.

"Apart from aliens, the American Secret Service and an island inhabited by dinosaurs, I don't think so, Professor Sheng," replies Harvey, shaking his head theatrically.

"All right," breaks in Elettra. "What we do know is that we've wound up on the trail of something called the Ring of Fire, which seems to be really ancient . . . and that it's hidden in Rome. We know that the professor had been searching for it for years and that he might just have found it in one of these places." She shows the others the map of Rome with the various neighborhoods circled in red.

At that very moment, the phone rings.

Sheng yelps. Mistral snaps her sketchbook shut.

And an icy shiver runs down the kids' spines.

"This must be it . . . ," says Beatrice, pulling the Mini up to the curb.

Jacob Mahler slips out of the car door in a single nimble movement.

"Hey! Hold on!" protests Little Linch, who's still crammed in the backseat. He grabs hold of the headrest and the roof of the car to hoist himself out. Once on the street, he uselessly tries to smooth out his rumpled suit.

"Couldn't you get yourself a real car?" he complains to Beatrice.

"I'm already lucky I got this one back," the young woman replies.

Jacob Mahler is looking at a gray four-story building. He raises his hand to point at a light coming from the apartment on the top floor.

"Someone's still there . . . ," he says. "Perfect." He takes the bow out of his violin case and brandishes it like a sword.

Beatrice quickly assesses the building. The news vendor in Largo Argentina told them about the professor's nieces and nephews and where they were headed. It must've been a second home, based on what they were told by Little Linch, who'd been following Alfred Van Der Berger for a few weeks and had never seen him in that neighborhood. He was living in a studio apartment in the center of town, not far from the Caffè Greco. A studio apartment that had turned out to be completely empty, with the exception of a few changes of clothes.

"Would you look at this place?" protests Little Linch, squashing something under the heels of his boots. He tries to clean them in a snowbank, but in the end he gives up. "What a dump!"

Beatrice switches on her car's blinkers. "Should we go up and take a look?"

Jacob Mahler shakes his head. "The two of us will go." He nods to Little Linch, who follows behind him, trotting like a wild boar.

Beatrice doesn't breathe. She glares at Mahler's back.

"Keep the engine running," the hit man orders her. Then he slides the tip of his bow into the lock, opening the front door, and walks into the building.

Little Linch follows him. He switches on a flashlight and turns one last time to look at Beatrice. "We'll be right back, sweets. . . ."

After which he disappears inside.

15

THE TELEPHONE

Eʟᴇᴛᴛʀᴀ ʟᴏᴏᴋs ᴀʀᴏᴜɴᴅ ꜰʀᴀɴᴛɪᴄᴀʟʟʏ ᴀs Pʀᴏꜰᴇssᴏʀ Aʟꜰʀᴇᴅ Vᴀɴ Der Berger's telephone rings over and over. It's somewhere nearby, hidden behind the dozens of newspapers that fill the room.

Mistral dives down into a number of yellowed journals, pushes aside a folded-up map of Kilmore Cove, grabs an old telephone in black Bakelite and holds it out to the others. "Here it is!"

"Answer it!" Harvey says encouragingly.

"I can't!" she protests. "It's got to be a man's voice!"

Sheng and Harvey look at each other. Harvey rips the receiver out of Mistral's hands and shoves it up against Sheng's ear.

"Hey!" the Chinese boy exclaims, taken by surprise. And then, immediately: "H-hello?"

"Professor, it's Ermete!" It's the voice of a man. A rather young man. Who's rather worried. "Is that you, professor? I can barely hear you! Can't you finally get a decent phone, for crying out loud?"

Sheng covers the mouthpiece with the palm of his hand in sheer panic, his eyes open wide. Elettra and the others gesture for him to keep going. "H-hello," Sheng says robotically.

"Everything all right? You sound strange. What's going on? I've been trying to reach you all week!"

"Everything's fine," Sheng says, trying to speak in the lowest voice possible. "I . . . was out."

"I see. Anyway, listen . . ." The mysterious caller seems to be in an awful hurry. His voice is partially drowned out by the furious revving of a motorcycle engine. "I think I've figured out how the map works!"

"The . . . map?"

"The map, professor! We've been studying it for months! Yesterday I was reading the comics when it dawned on me. It's just like you said, naturally. It's incredibly easy to use and incredibly old! Do you understand?"

"Incredible . . . ," echoes Sheng, not knowing what else to say.

Elettra sticks her head up near the earpiece, trying to listen in. "Ask him what it is," she mouths.

"I mean, no . . . ," says Sheng. "I don't, really."

An engine is roaring. "Listen," the man continues, "I don't have time to explain this in detail right now, but I'm convinced: it's not Roman and it's not Greek. The writings on the side of it were added later on. And I've deciphered some of the engravings on the back. They're all from a later period. I'm telling you—that map was made far before the times of Christopher Columbus, Seneca or Alexander the Great!"

"Hmm . . . very good . . . ," affirms Sheng sheepishly.

"Excellent, I'd say! Listen! If what I'm saying is right, we've got to try it out as soon as possible! When can we meet?"

"Um . . . well . . ."

Elettra whispers something in his ear.

"Tomorrow, at the latest," replies Sheng.

"At my shop? Is that okay?"

"At your shop," Sheng agrees. Then he looks at Elettra, who opens her eyes wide, imploringly. "*Hao!*" he exclaims. "But at your shop . . . where, exactly?"

"In Testaccio, of course! At the Regno del Dado!"

Elettra looks at Mistral, who's already making a note of it in her sketchbook.

"Excellent," mumbles Sheng.

"I'll see you there. And remember to bring the tops!"

The instant the stranger hangs up, Sheng shuts his eyes, lets go of the phone and falls backward to the ground, which makes the whole room rattle like a drum.

Mistral kneels down beside him. "You were great!"

"It was nuts . . . *Hao!*" cries Sheng, casting a glance at Harvey, who raises both hands to excuse himself for having sneaked the phone over to him.

The boy gives them a recap of what was said during the call and then gets back up, raising a cloud of dust.

"Now what?" concludes Harvey.

"Now we go have that pizza!" answers Sheng, rubbing his belly. "We get a good night's sleep and tomorrow we go see this guy to ask him what he's found out about the map."

"Do you think we can trust him?"

"I guess so."

"But what if he was actually . . . one of them?" insists Harvey. "Maybe the phone call was just a trap."

"You see traps everywhere!" Sheng protests. "What do you two think?"

Mistral agrees with Sheng. Elettra, on the other hand, has her doubts.

"In any case," says Harvey, going to sit back down on the bed, "once we know how the map works, then what do we do with it?"

"We use it to track down the Ring of Fire . . . ," Sheng begins. "The professor wrote that to get to the Ring, first you've got to figure out how the map works. And if this guy's figured it out . . . then our problem's solved."

"Which, just to be precise, isn't even our problem," Harvey underlines. "I mean, it wasn't until *you*, Elettra, had the bright idea of accepting a briefcase from a total stranger."

"That's not exactly how it went," the girl protests. "Or should I remind you about how we all met?"

"Your dad messed up the reservations."

"And our birthdays? And the blackout?"

"And my yellow eyes?" adds Sheng.

Elettra shows the others the map of Rome with its seven circles. "The professor knew all about it. Take a look! He indicated the exact neighborhoods where the lights went out. And listen to what he wrote: 'It will begin on December twenty-ninth.' "

Harvey purses his lips. "So what?"

"So," Mistral breaks in, "all of this ties in together, somehow. . . ."

"But we're here, all four of us. And we didn't get here by chance!" exclaims Elettra.

"Oh, no? How did we, then?"

Sheng looks over at Mistral and frowns. "He's a little slow, isn't he?"

"I'm just trying to be rational," Harvey snaps, "since none of you here seem to want to be. If we keep going on like this, without stopping to think for a single moment, we're going to risk losing touch with reality. That is, we'll risk ending up just like the professor. And Nero." He points his index finger at his temple and twirls it around. "We'll go nuts. And maybe that's what 'they' do. They make you go nuts."

"Want to know what I think?" Mistral says, cutting him off. "I think we should get out of here and go have some pizza. We can always talk it over later on."

And without waiting for the others to follow her, she walks out of the room.

The three kids left in the room look around. Harvey leafs through Mistral's sketchbook, admiring her talent. There are drawings of the four of them at the Caffè Greco, the Hertziana library, the columns in Largo Argentina. "I'm not interested in chasing after a secret like this, guys," he concludes, shutting the book and resting it on his lap. "And I don't feel like being chased by a gang of mysterious . . . 'thems' . . . who are out to get me."

Elettra's face is full of disappointment. "If that's what you want, nobody can force you to stick with us."

Harvey gets up from the bed. "Exactly. I think we should let things slide for tonight. Forget about the map, the weird guy on the phone, the Ring of Fire. . . . It's all crazy. There's nothing solid here to—"

Harvey stops in midsentence.

Someone's coming up the stairs.

* * *

"Do you guys hear that, too?" he asks the others in a low, small voice.

"Where's Mistral?" Sheng asks, looking around.

"Mistral?" whispers Elettra.

No one replies. The three kids freeze beside the professor's bed, listening. Distant cars. The perfectly still air of the apartment. The refrigerator in the kitchen humming and then kicking back into action with a gurgle.

"Mistral?" Elettra whispers again.

A noise. Harvey grabs her wrist.

Elettra nods. She heard it, too. Something clanging against the railing outside.

Footsteps on the stairway.

Someone's coming.

Elettra peers out through the bedroom door and gives a start. Mistral is on the other side of the hall, as still and pale as a ghost. Her round eyes are open wide with fright.

Elettra lies down on the ground and peeks over the threshold, toward the front door to the apartment, which they left open.

Her heart in her throat, she sees the beam of a flashlight dart across the stairway.

Sheng crawls up to her. Harvey stays behind them, crouching down.

"They're coming up here . . . ," whispers Elettra.

"Who?"

"I don't know."

They listen to the footsteps.

There are at least two of them.

Whoever they are, they've reached the last flight of steps. Elettra waves Mistral over, but the girl shakes her head and points down at her feet. Drawn on the floor right beneath her is a red circle.

The flashlight has reached the top floor.

The first person to appear in the doorway looks like a vampire. He's all dressed in black, is tall and thin, has totally gray hair and is holding a violin. Hobbling behind him is a sort of two-legged whale holding the flashlight and dragging his feet as he clings to the railing.

"It's them," whispers Sheng. "They're here."

The tall, thin man stops at the doorway and slowly raises his violin, tucking it between his shoulder and his chin. Gleaming in his right hand is a bow. He rests it gently against the strings and begins to play a gripping, hypnotic melody, which flows through the professor's apartment like honey. They're delicate, perfectly rounded notes. Slow and sweet, they creep their way around the books and gently caress the kids' ears.

Elettra feels her eyelids go heavy. She blinks once, twice, and then closes her eyes. When she opens them again, the music from the violin surges. The man kicks the door, smashing it against the wall.

He's inside.

The music glides along, following him down the hall. The notes speak of sleepiness, of tranquility, of perfect calm. Elettra struggles to keep her eyes open. Beside her, Sheng is already fast asleep. A sudden, terribly deep sleep. Harvey's on the professor's bed, his head hidden beneath a pillow.

"I don't want . . . to sleep . . . ," the girl insists, digging her fingernails into the palms of her hands until they almost start bleeding. Her wrists feel weak, drained, and her eyes are heavy. "You've got to stay open . . . ," she tells her eyes stubbornly. "You've got to stay open. . . ."

Just when her strength is about to abandon her, the music comes to an abrupt halt. Elettra can see Mistral taking a step down the hallway. She's pressing her hands against her ears, crying, "Stop! Stop!"

"Hello, young lady," whispers Jacob Mahler.

Behind him, Little Linch teeters on the landing like a whale hypnotized by the singing of sirens at sea.

Mistral removes her hands from her ears and shakes her head. "No more music . . . no more," she groans.

An evil smile crosses over Jacob Mahler's face. He lowers the violin and the bow to his sides. "So you're the sensible one in the group, are you? I'll stop playing, I promise. But don't start crying, all right? Because I hate people who cry." He takes two steps toward her and adds, "Besides, there's no reason for you to."

At the other end of the hallway, Elettra's lying on the ground. Her eyes are shut, too heavy to open. The music, which is stuck in her head, has made her too groggy to move. Sheng's mouth is wide open and he looks like he's about to start snoring. Harvey is motionless, his head still hidden under the pillows.

The floor trembles threateningly.

Elettra instantly stiffens, as if she were falling into the void. Just like when, sometimes, as she's falling asleep, she suddenly feels like she's losing her balance.

151

She opens her eyes.

Mistral is talking.

"Please . . . ," the French girl says, staring at Mahler as he walks toward her. "What do you want? We haven't done anything. . . ."

"You haven't done anything. True. But I want something from you." Jacob Mahler's cynical gaze studies the walls and columns of books without showing the slightest bit of surprise. "So I'm going to ask you this just once: did you take it?"

"What?" asks Mistral.

"My briefcase."

"N-no."

" 'No' because you didn't take it or 'no' because you don't want to tell me?"

Mistral looks around. She sees Elettra and Sheng lying on the floor in the bedroom. "No, because the briefcase wasn't yours to begin with," she replies.

Elettra shuts her eyes.

"Very well, then . . . ," Jacob Mahler says calmly, raising his violin again.

"No!" groans Mistral, instinctively clapping her hands over her ears. "No more music!"

"Where is my briefcase?" the man asks, taking two more steps into the apartment.

Lying on the ground, Elettra feels her body trembling. But immediately afterward she realizes it's not her body that's trembling . . . it's the floor.

Jacob Mahler has noticed something strange. His voice has become slightly tense.

"Listen . . . ," he says. "I know you took it, you and your friends. . . . So go call them and give me back my briefcase."

Mistral stubbornly shakes her head.

"Why on earth," the man continues, "is a sweet, sensible girl like you in a terrible place like this? What did you come here to do, hmm? If your parents found out, I think they'd be very angry. . . ."

"I've only got my mother . . . ," replies Mistral, backing toward the dining room. "And she never gets angry."

Jacob Mahler smiles, but it's as if his smile is trying to hold back a river of rage ready to burst forth. "You're lucky. Why don't we make a deal, hmm? You tell me where you've hidden my briefcase . . . and I'll let you go back to your mother. What do you say?"

"I don't have the briefcase. . . ."

"Well then, who does?"

"Nero," replies the girl, challenging Jacob Mahler with a resolute stare.

16

THE FLOOR

◯

THE APARTMENT FLOOR IS SHAKEN BY A STRONG TREMOR. A FEW books tumble to the ground. Elettra wakes up with a start. Harvey's beside her, his hand resting on her shoulder. "How much do you weigh?" he asks in a hushed voice.

"Why?"

"I figured out what all those numbers by the door are. They're—" A second tremor, this one stronger than the last one, makes him lose his balance and fall down on top of her. The apartment walls let out a long groan. More books slide to the floor.

"Help!" yells Sheng, waking up with a start and noticing that the floor in the room is lurching. Elettra looks out into the hallway. The walls of books are billowing out like sails. A horrible noise echoes beneath them, followed by a metallic creak, like plumbing being ripped apart.

"It's a trap, you see?" says Harvey, trying to get back to his feet. "The second column kept track of the professor's weight. The first column is the weight that the apartment floor can still support!"

A third tremor.

"And how much is that, right now?" asks Elettra, her eyes open wide.

"One hundred thirty-seven kilograms," replies Harvey, helping her up to her feet. "Around three hundred pounds."

With the third tremor, Little Linch looks around for his colleague. "Hey, Mahler!" he shouts, still a little groggy from the music. "What's going on in here?" He spots the gray-haired killer inside the apartment and takes a few steps toward him. "What the heck are all these papers doing flying around?" he grunts.

The moment he crosses over the threshold, Mahler sees him and shouts, "Don't!"

"H-huh?" stammers Little Linch, not understanding. He takes another baby step and a giant pit suddenly opens up beneath his feet. "Hey!" he manages to shout before plunging down, disappearing in a cloud of dust.

The pit widens, making its way down the hallway. Mountains of books tumble down one after the other like dominoes. "Everything's collapsing!" shouts Mistral.

In the bedroom, Elettra holds on tightly to Harvey, who shouts, "The red circles! Look for one of the red circles on the floor! Sheng! Mistral! The red circles!" The hallway floor lurches up with a boom and then disappears in a cloud of dust with a crash. The walls tilt; the plumbing explodes, spraying water everywhere; and the tiles crumble to pieces.

Elettra clings to Harvey, oblivious to everything except the noise.

She isn't even sure where she is, if she's on solid ground or

155

falling. There's dust. Only dust. Then she hears a shout. It might be Mistral. It might not. She tries to free herself from Harvey, but his arm won't let her go. He's holding her tight, protecting her. She can feel his cheek pressed up against hers. And she can hear his voice whispering, "It's okay. It's okay . . . ," as the world comes crashing down all around them.

The two kneel and then sit down on the ground. They wait. Now they can hear water running. They can see flashing lights. Sheng's coughing. The backpack appears for a moment from behind a cloud of dust.

Elettra tries to move her legs. Little by little, she realizes she's on a sort of raft suspended over a seemingly bottomless pit. Sheng is also perched on a little patch of the floor that has remained intact.

And Mistral?

Elettra shuts her eyes.

Her legs are dangling down into empty space, like an acrobat's.

Sitting in her Mini, Beatrice sees the building's front door fly out into the middle of the street like a cork popped out of a bottle of champagne. It's followed by a cloud of dust. She clicks off the radio, opens the car door and rushes out. Only then does she hear the noise. A deafening, echoing roar that bursts out from the old walls of the building. She sees people in neighboring houses looking out their windows. She hears doors slamming and the first repeated screams of "Earthquake!"

But it isn't an earthquake.

Beatrice covers her mouth with both hands. "It's collapsing!" She doesn't have time to say anything else. The building is already lurching backward, swaying, folding over on itself like a milk carton ready for the trash can.

Beatrice runs for cover behind the door of her Mini. Her blinkers shine through the dust. People begin to scramble out of nearby buildings. Some run off, screaming. Others stop to stare. A man walks calmly toward her.

"It can't be . . . ," murmurs Beatrice, recognizing Jacob Mahler.

He's covered with dust from head to toe. His clothes are the same color as his hair, but he's walking along coolly, as if nothing is happening. In one hand he's holding his violin. With the other he's dragging a girl behind him.

Beatrice feels like she's seeing a ghost.

"Let's go," the ghost says, pushing the girl inside and sitting down in the car.

His face is a thick mask of dust.

Beatrice puts the Mini into reverse and slams down on the gas pedal. The car bumps up against the curb. She throws it into first gear, yanks on the steering wheel, honks the horn and swerves around a couple of people standing in the middle of the street.

"Where's Little Linch?" she asks.

"He's dead," says Mahler.

"How did it happen?"

They hear the first sirens approaching in the distance.

"He ate too much," the killer replies with a smirk.

17
THE BED

Eᴌᴇᴛᴛʀᴀ ᴏᴘᴇɴs ʜᴇʀ ᴇʏᴇs. Sʜᴇ's ʟʏɪɴɢ ᴏɴ ᴀ ᴍᴀᴛᴛʀᴇss, ʜᴇʀ ʜᴇᴀᴅ sunk down into a pillow. Another bed is right above her, like a ceiling.

It's her bunk bed.

She blinks her eyes and looks around. She recognizes the furniture bathed in the half light, the second bunk bed, her room. She can hear Sheng and Harvey breathing. They're sleeping nearby.

It's nighttime.

But what day is it?

She tries to move her arms. Then her legs. She sits up, aching. With one hand she touches her face. There's a bandage on her temple.

It wasn't a dream.

"Elettra?" comes her father's whispering voice.

The girl hadn't noticed him sitting at the foot of her bed. He'd only been a shadow among the many shadows. Fernando leans over to give her a kiss. "Elettra, my little angel . . . What did you kids get yourselves into?" He doesn't hug her. He limits himself to looking at her from the end of the bed. "You were really lucky. . . ."

"Dad . . ." Elettra's throat is dry. "What time is it? How . . . how did I get back here?"

The bedroom door opens up slightly and Aunt Linda walks in. "Elettra!" the woman says, almost shouting. Then she lowers her voice to a hush to avoid waking up the boys. "Thank goodness you're okay!"

Aunt Linda dives into the bunk bed, suffocating her niece in an affectionate embrace. "You're all out of your mind, you and your friends!"

"Auntie, what—"

Linda cups her hands around the girl's face and squeezes her cheeks. "That was foolish! Perfectly foolish!"

"Dad . . . Auntie . . . I don't know what to tell you. I don't remember anything—"

Just then, Elettra remembers the floor caving in, the cloud of dust and the lights shining through the darkness.

"Don't worry. Harvey already told us everything . . . ," Fernando Melodia whispers, pointing to the other bunk bed. "He carried you home. You'd fainted."

"Harvey carried me home?"

Aunt Linda clasps her hands together and waves them right in front of her nose. "Of all places, you kids had to go to a construction site to play? And in winter, of all times?"

Elettra slowly shakes her head, trying to understand what Harvey might have told them. "A construction site?"

Fernando stops Aunt Linda with a patient wave of his hand. "We know. Harvey told us you went there to check out the bull-dozers, but—"

"What on earth were you thinking?" interrupts Aunt Linda, appalled. "With all the things to see in Rome . . . Bulldozers!"

"Since it was so dark, you should've watched where you were walking," Fernando goes on.

"Into a manhole, you fell! Into a manhole!" her aunt says, heaving a sigh.

Her father, on the other hand, caresses Elettra's forehead. "You hit your head and passed out." The girl nods, impressed by the excuse Harvey managed to come up with—and by the feel-ing that her father doesn't really believe a single word of the story but is repeating it to her so she can avoid giving herself away to Aunt Linda.

"Sheng was hurt, too," her aunt breaks in. "I put a nice, sturdy bandage on his arm, but tomorrow, just to be sure, I'm taking all three of you down to the emergency room. I don't care if it's New Year's Eve!"

"What time is it right now?" Elettra asks her father.

"Almost two."

"It was a trap . . . ," Elettra thinks aloud.

"It wasn't a trap," Fernando replies, his voice too low for her aunt to hear. "You got yourselves into it, and you got yourselves out of it all right."

Elettra stares at her father, trying to understand how much he actually knows. "Dad, we—"

"Naturally, we haven't said anything to Harvey's parents or Sheng's father," he continues. "But—"

"But tomorrow we're all going to have a nice little chat," Aunt Linda interjects. "Don't think you can get away with this so easily. You were the one responsible for the boys."

Something dawns on Elettra. "What about Mistral?"

Fernando Melodia stiffens.

"Well, she's with her mother, isn't she?" Aunt Linda answers for him.

Fernando nods. "Harvey told us that she caught a cab downtown and went to meet her at the station—"

"And to think they still have all their luggage here!"

Elettra looks over at Harvey's sleeping form in the half light, grateful for how well he managed to protect them all by keeping their secret.

"Get some rest now. We'll think about all this tomorrow, okay?" her father suggests.

At the thought of Mistral, Elettra feels tears welling up in her eyes. "We shouldn't have gone there," she murmurs.

Her aunt rests a hand on her forehead. "Right now just get some rest. . . ."

Elettra nods and slips back into a deep sleep. She hears the bedroom door closing and her father saying, "It all went extremely well."

Harvey opens his eyes. He's covered with sweat. He's panting and the covers are twisted around his body. His watch is cutting off the circulation in his wrist. He checks the time. It's six o'clock. "The bed wasn't falling . . . ," he says, reassuring himself. "It was only a dream."

He slowly frees himself from the sheets and blankets, trying

161

not to wake up the others. His legs are covered with scrapes and bruises. He rests his feet on the cold floor. He needs to feel something solid beneath them.

The moment he shuts his eyes, he can see pages from books flying through the air. Burnt pages fluttering upward. A sea of dust. He sees Elettra unconscious, her legs dangling into nothingness, and Sheng clutching his backpack like a parachute.

He sees what's left of the floor of the building's fourth story and the ladder that he and Sheng climbed down, carrying Elettra over their shoulders. He sees the firemen's flickering lights and their red fire engines, with their tall aluminum ladders.

They slipped out of the building before anyone could notice them. Then Harvey laid Elettra on the ground and turned to go back inside.

"Where are you going?" Sheng asked him.

"To look for Mistral. There's still a girl in the building!" he shouted.

"We'll go look for her!" a fireman answered, turning to dash nimbly up the extending ladder. Other firemen entered through what remained of the front door, armed with axes.

"Have you seen a girl come out of there?" Harvey asked the people crowding the street. But no one paid any attention to him. They were concentrating on the show provided by the rescue team.

"Have you seen a girl come out of there?" Harvey continued to ask everyone he passed by.

Finally, a woman answered him. "A young girl with straight,

light brown hair? I saw her leave with her father. A man with gray hair. He had a violin. . . . Could that have been her?"

Harvey nodded.

It sure could have.

Harvey gets up, grabs something from the nightstand and walks over to the bathroom. He turns on the lights around the mirror and stands there for a long time, staring at himself.

His eyes are like an old man's.

Then he looks down at Mistral's sketchbook, which he'd picked up from the nightstand. He slowly leafs through the pages, pausing on the last drawing: the four of them in the professor's room.

"Harvey?" comes a whisper from behind him. The boy sees Elettra's reflection in the mirror.

"Can't sleep?" he asks her, shutting the book.

"Not anymore. How are you?"

"Just a few scratches."

"Thanks for carrying me back here."

"What, you think I would've left you there?"

"No, but . . . I mean . . ."

Harvey turns to look at her. He lets the sketchbook slide down along his back and then slips it into his boxer shorts. "It wasn't difficult. You don't weigh much at all, fortunately—otherwise the floor would've collapsed a lot earlier."

"I . . . I talked to my father. He told me your version of what happened."

"It's not my version. I'm not good at making up excuses. It was Sheng."

"Is he okay?"

"He hurt his arm."

Elettra hesitates a few seconds before asking the last question. "And Mistral? Have you seen her?"

"No."

"Do you think . . . she . . . ?"

"No. A woman saw her leave with the man with the violin."

Elettra bites her lip. "Alive?"

"Of course."

The two leave the bedroom and make their way down the hallway, barefoot. They get to the dining room, coming from which is the soft glow of a television. Elettra's father has fallen asleep on the couch. The morning news is on.

"There," whispers Harvey when shots of a collapsed building appear on the screen. "That's us." A helicopter films the scene from above. The professor's house is a box of cement folded over on itself, around which are lights, cranes and fire hoses. The reporter aboard the helicopter excitedly relates the little information he's received. "A dilapidated old building . . . gas leak . . . structural failure . . . thousands of books . . ."

Elettra and Harvey draw closer, trying to hear better. "It's unclear how many families resided in the building . . . other than Professor Alfred Van Der Berger, who lived on the top floor. . . . At this point, rescuers have found no—"

"No sign of a French girl," Elettra sighs with new hope.

"I told you. That guy took her away."

"She's alive, Harvey," whispers Elettra. "And she's in Rome with him."

Harvey shows her the notes in Mistral's sketchbook. "The fact is, nobody will believe any of this. We can't tell anyone anything."

"No," Elettra admits. "But maybe we could try to find her ourselves."

"But how?"

"By asking for help."

"From who?"

"I think there's someone who might believe what happened to us. . . ." Elettra searches through the sketchbook for Mistral's last notes. Then she lets Harvey read them.

Lying on his bed, Sheng knows perfectly well that he's dreaming, but he can't snap himself out of it. The dream scares him, but he just can't wake himself up. He can only go along with it, an involuntary spectator.

He's walking through the jungle with Harvey and Elettra. It's boiling hot and perfectly silent. He can't hear any insects, any birds. It's as if the jungle were empty. From time to time, a Roman monument peeks out from behind the plants—a building, a column, an obelisk—as if the forest has grown right over the city. Then the tropical vegetation makes way for an expanse of fine, pure white sand, which crunches beneath his feet.

On the other side of a narrow inlet of clear blue water is a tiny island covered with seaweed. Elettra, Harvey and Sheng dive into the waves and, once again, Sheng notices there isn't a noise to be heard.

Waiting for them on the island is a woman. Her face is covered by a cloak and she's wearing a close-fitting gown, drawn on which are all the animals of the world.

The first one to get out of the water, Harvey kneels down before the woman.

Elettra follows him but remains standing.

Sheng, instead, stays in the water, hiding. He's scared.

The woman stares at them, standing motionless on the beach covered with seaweed. Then she raises her right hand, slips it into her gown and pulls out an old wooden top, which she holds out to the Chinese boy.

And with this, Sheng's eyes open wide.

"Calm down, Sheng," Harvey tells him, his hand resting on his shoulder. "It was just a bad dream."

The images from the dream whirl through Sheng's mind: the jungle, the beach, the island, the woman, the top . . . "I dreamed about the top!" he cries. "We've got to . . . to use the map!"

"That's what we were thinking, too."

"What time is it?"

"It's early morning. How do you feel?"

Sheng's right arm is throbbing. "My arm hurts a little . . . but it's no big deal. I dreamed about you. There was . . . some kind of jungle covering the city."

Elettra motions that he should stop talking. "You can tell us later on, if you want. We don't have much time."

"To do what?"

"We've got to get out of here before seven o'clock."

"And go where?"

"To get Mistral back."

"But how?"

"Are you coming with us?" asks Elettra.

Like she does every morning, Linda Melodia opens her eyes at seven o'clock on the dot. She rather regretfully slides out from beneath the sheets, her toes seeking out her ever-present Tyrolean wool slippers.

"What time is it?" her sister asks from the bed when she comes out of the bathroom a moment later. Linda mumbles something as she puts on an undershirt, a flowered sweater and a pair of cream-colored slacks.

Irene's head is sunk down into a pillow. "Everything all right?"

Her sister stands before the mirror to do a few breathing exercises. "I wouldn't say so. After what happened to the kids, I barely shut my eyes. If only you'd seen them when they got back . . . They were covered head to toe in dust and grime!"

Irene giggles. "Always exaggerating. I'm sure they were just a little dirty, that's all—"

"Believe me! For a moment I thought Elettra . . . Well, we'd better just forget about it."

"They're only kids, Linda."

"I was a girl once, too! But I didn't feel the need to sneak into construction sites and risk my neck just to see a crane. Or am I wrong? What were you doing when you were their age?"

Irene rubs her eyes. "Me? I was trying to save the world."

Linda rolls her eyes. "Oh, of course! How could I forget?" She plants a kiss on her forehead and says, "If you don't need anything, I'll go down and set the tables for breakfast."

"Would you hand me the phone, please?"

"Who are you going to call at seven in the morning?"

"My secret lover?"

Linda walks out of the bedroom smiling. She goes down the stairs of the Domus Quintilia, which is still silent, and walks into the dining room. She slips a dozen cream-filled croissants and a hazelnut and chocolate tart into a large toaster oven.

Meanwhile, she thinks back to her sister's secret lovers. And her own. Faded images return to her mind. Lying on the beach doing summer school homework, which Irene would check over meticulously before letting her go off to play. She remembers running beside the sea, her little beach sandals, the colored ribbons in her hair, the boat rides . . . and that boy who would dive into the water from the rocks, staring at her passionately.

Oh dear, thinks Linda, warming up a dish of fig cookies. *I can't remember his name.* On the other hand, she remembers everything about Irene. She was identical to how she is now. She could still walk then, and steadily, and her face had fewer wrinkles, her eyes sparkled more. . . . But even back then she would spend all her time huddled over books, her hair billowing out under the sun.

The espresso machine shoots hot steam into the milk, frothing it up for a cappuccino. Linda sprinkles some cocoa on top, makes a little heart shape in the foam and enjoys her customary breakfast before the others wake up. Not far away, Fernando is still snoring on the couch in front of the television, which is still on. He'll soon wake up with a start, check his watch and ask her to make him a *caffè ristretto doppio,* which he'll guzzle down in a single gulp.

A dab of milk foam on the tip of her nose, Linda leaves the dining room and walks down the hall leading to Elettra's bedroom.

She stops to listen.

Perfect silence.

Good, she thinks, wiping off her nose. *They're sleeping. I'd better not wake them.*

18

THE MESSENGER

"Coming! Coming!" barks Ermete De Panfilis, shuffling up to the door of his shop in Testaccio. He casts a glance at the clock along the way. It's not even eight o'clock. Who could it be at this hour?

Whoever it is, it's my fault, he thinks, walking through the room, which is a cross between a living room and a garage. His mother has told him time and time again that you should never work and live in the same place, otherwise you'll end up working day and night.

The bell rings for the millionth time. It's the straw that breaks the camel's back. "Oh, come on!" he hollers, walking past his sidecar, which he's just put back together. "I hear you, you hear? I'm coming, dammit!"

Then he stops.

Where's the door?

He looks around, lost. He has the feeling someone's moved his front door. It's that horrible feeling of disorientation so typical of early morning. As horrible as everything that has to do with mornings: boiling hot coffee, the latest news, milk trucks, kids going to school, urgent phone calls. They're all part of a world that Ermete would gladly do away with forever: the world of "before eleven a.m."

A world his mother, on the other hand, never stops reminding him about when she calls him every Sunday morning at half past seven.

It might be her at the door. Wherever the door is, obviously . . . It would be perfectly natural to see her pop in, her clothes and makeup already perfect, her mood just bubbly enough to irritate him to no end, with her endless list of concerns to nag him about.

Here's the door.

Before he opens it, Ermete De Panfilis scratches his backside for a long moment.

Does he really need to answer the door?

Nothing can be seen through the peephole. But then again, maybe he hasn't even looked through the peephole yet. With a sigh, he slides the bolt to the side and tries to slick back the last few remaining strands of hair on his head, which are sticking up like porcupine quills.

"Here I am . . . ," he says, opening the door wide with a sigh.

An icy gust of wind instantly reminds him that he's still in his robe.

Nobody's there.

Ermete is an electrical engineer, just like his mother wanted. His degree gave her a trump card to play with her girlfriends. And it helped him, too, in a way, by letting him afford an apartment far from home and giving him the chance to follow his real interests as a radio ham, an expert in antique motorcycles, a dabbler in archaeology with a passion for mystery, a collector of pig statuettes, an avid reader of comic books and, naturally, the world's foremost expert on board games from all eras.

"Is this some kind of joke?" the engineer/radio ham/archaeologist/comics reader/gaming master Ermete De Panfilis sputters, standing at the threshold of his front door. "Who's there?"

Not a soul is on the street. Or in his front yard. The sign for his shop, Il Regno del Dado, or "Kingdom of Dice," is naturally switched off.

"Are you the owner?" asks a voice a foot below him.

Ermete looks down with a peeved scowl.

Only then does he notice the three brats: a girl with black hair that looks like an octopus; a tall, lanky boy who looks like the singer from Oasis, only shorter; and a Chinese boy with a bandaged arm.

"Who are you?"

"We'd like to come in, if you don't mind."

"Why?"

"We're here about the map," the girl explains.

"Map? What map?" Ermete quickly tries to recall the events of the last few days.

"Professor Van Der Berger's map."

The man's heart skips a beat. "What have you kids got to do with Professor Van Der Berger?"

"He gave us the map and asked us to keep it until he came back for it," the boy with the bandaged arm replies, holding up a torn, dirty backpack.

"So why hasn't he come back for it?" asks Ermete.

"Because he's dead," the black-haired girl explains. "They killed him two days ago by the Tiber."

"And last night they tried to kill us, too," adds the miniature version of the singer from Oasis, "by making a building collapse."

"And we think they've kidnapped our friend Mistral."

"Can we come in now?"

Ermete staggers back from the door, stunned by the information overload. "L-let me get this straight . . . ," he stammers, inviting the three inside the Regno del Dado. "Yesterday, on the phone—"

"I was the one who answered," explains Sheng.

"But . . . why . . . ?" The man scratches his head noisily. He shuts the door behind him and tightens the belt on his robe. "I mean . . ." A baffled expression is painted all over his face.

Ermete's a rather bright man, although his appearance might make people think the opposite. He's lean but not skinny, with sunken shoulders and a little bit of a belly. He has pronounced cheekbones and blue, often drowsy-looking eyes. He has more hairs on his chin than hairs on his head, and these grow crooked, making him look as disheveled as the furniture in his house.

The Regno del Dado is a cross between a basement, a bar and a garage. On one side are disassembled motorcycles lined up beside their various repainted body parts, mechanic's tools, tires, screws, bolts and nuts. On the other side of the shop is a row of plastic tables with board games, dice and playing pieces. Behind a glass door are the tangled cords of his ham radio, with long antennas set up on the terrace.

"Before coming here we talked it over," explains the girl.

"And we decided to explain everything to you. But I'm warning you: this is going to take a while."

Ermete's stomach growls noisily.

"Is it okay if we go sit in the kitchen?" he suggests. "I must have half a ton of cornflakes to finish."

The kitchen is full of plastic plates piled up one atop the other. A giant King Kong poster towers over the sink, while four black Darth Vader heads decorate the tablecloth. The kids eat cornflakes and, taking turns cutting each other off, begin to describe everything that's happened to them so far.

Meanwhile, Sheng lays the contents of his backpack out on the table: the wooden map, the tooth, the tops, the pages they found in the library, the professor's journal and Mistral's sketchbook, the copy of *Kore Kosmou* in Greek and Seneca's writings about comets.

"They showed up right when we found this book," Harvey says in a low voice. "There were two of them. One was short and pudgy. The other was tall, dressed in black and playing a violin."

Ermete gapes. "What do you mean, playing a violin?"

"He uses it to hypnotize people," explains Elettra. "It was almost impossible to stay awake."

The man scratches his chin, thinking. "Fascinating . . ."

"The pudgy one's dead," says Sheng.

"Yeah, and I suppose they were about to kill you with, I don't know . . . a flame-throwing trombone?" Ermete cackles.

"He died when the professor's apartment building collapsed."

"What do you mean, collapsed?"

"Harvey says it was a trap. He thinks the professor calculated

174

exactly how much he weighed and how much the books piled up in his apartment weighed, and he'd arranged them so that if anybody uninvited came in, the whole thing would cave in."

In the half hour that follows, Ermete has them explain what happened in detail. Little by little, as the kids tell him everything, his face grows more and more concerned.

"So we're all in danger now," he says once they've finished.

"We probably are," Sheng agrees.

"And to think I didn't believe him . . . ," the man murmurs. "He was suspicious of everybody, and the more research we did, the more he was convinced he was being followed. Being spied on. By people who wanted to get their hands on this map, basically . . ." Ermete points to the strange wooden object on which Sheng is resting a protective hand.

"That's exactly what the man with the violin wanted. The professor's briefcase. And he knew we had it."

"Do you know what all these things are for?"

"And why they're out to get it at all costs?"

"I think I do," Ermete replies.

"We're not as interested in the briefcase," Harvey points out, "as we are in finding Mistral. We thought we could make a trade: we give them the briefcase and they give us our friend back."

"But before we do that, we wanted to know what it is we're trading," adds Elettra.

The engineer drums his fingers on the table nervously. "If Alfred knew about this . . . ," he sighs. "You have no idea how long he'd been protecting that map."

"But why is it so important?"

"Because you need it to find the Ring of Fire," replies Ermete.

"Meaning?"

The engineer shrugs. "I don't know. That wasn't my part of the research."

"We think it's something that belonged to Nero," Elettra hazards.

"Oh, no," Ermete corrects her. "The Ring of Fire is far more ancient than that. It might've passed through Nero's hands, but it's far, far older. Older than the Romans, the Pythagoreans and the Greek philosophers. And far more ancient than the pyramids. The professor thought it was a secret that had been guarded for thousands of years, handed down through oral tradition by masters to their disciples." Elettra shows him the map of Rome on which the professor had drawn circles. "He was convinced it was here, in the city."

For a few brief moments Ermete studies the map and then asks Sheng to open the wooden box. He shows the kids how the areas of town that have been circled are arranged exactly like the stars engraved in the center of the wooden map, around the figure of the woman.

"This is Ursa Major."

The kids stare with bewilderment at the rectangular object, with its unintelligible maze of engraved lines. "Can you tell us what this says?" Elettra asks, showing Ermete the Greek lettering that runs all the way around the wooden map.

Ermete gets up from his chair. "'Such a great secret is not to be reached by a single path,'" he replies, disappearing into another room. He returns a moment later with a big book full of photos. "But don't let the sentence fool you, because I think it was engraved there long after the map had been made." He sets the book down in the middle of the kitchen table, opens it up and shows the kids a pyramid-shaped tower topped by a raging fire.

"And now I guess I should tell you everything I know. When the professor showed me the map for the first time, he told me it might be an ancient game. A sort of scoreboard, like the ones the Egyptians used when they played senet. But he wasn't sure, and I wasn't, either. This map is full of clearly contrasting features, all belonging to different eras. The engravings that have accumulated over time testify to the fact that it's passed from hand to hand a great number of times and that some of its owners made additions to it . . . or simply signed it. The sentence engraved on its side is one example. It dates back to the period when the map was in Greece. The days of Socrates and Plato. Ever heard of them?"

The kids nod. "A little . . ."

"They were great philosophers."

"Like Seneca?"

"Exactly. But even before him. If you look at the outside of the map," Ermete continues, "you'll notice that wooden pieces have been inserted here and there, like patches. And these little writings, letters, engravings . . . they've become so worn that they're practically invisible. But with a good camera, I managed to discover something absolutely incredible."

"Which is . . . ?"

"Which is . . . that this is a stellar map made by the Chaldeans!"

The kids' faces make no reaction to this amazing revelation.

"Ah. Cool . . . ," mumbles Sheng, as if he's worried about looking foolish.

Ermete rests his hands on the book full of pictures. "I suppose you guys don't know anything about the Chaldeans. . . ."

"Actually . . . no," Elettra admits.

"Zero," confirms Harvey.

"Never heard of them before!" exclaims Sheng, encouraged by the general confession of ignorance.

"Well . . . the Chaldeans were inhabitants of the most ancient city in the world, a city called Ur. Notice this coincidence: Rome, in Latin, was called Ur-be."

"Wow," exclaims Harvey ironically. "It gives me the shivers!"

"The Chaldeans . . . ," continues Ermete, showing them a photo of ancient ruins half-buried in the sand, "were the first men to look up at the sky and to invent astrology, the science that connects people's destinies with the positioning of the stars. You know, like the signs of the zodiac. What sign are you guys?"

"Pisces."

"Pisces."

"I'm a Pisces, too," says Sheng. "But I was born in the Year of the Monkey."

Ermete sits there for a moment, gaping, and then goes on. "Well, anyway, that was all invented by the Chaldeans. They were great astronomers, great scientists and great priests. Their astronomical knowledge gave rise, in a way, to the ancient Iranian cult of Mithra, which spread through Rome, particularly among the legions and the military. Mithra was the god of fire, the sun god, who died every night and was reborn every morning."

"We read something about Mithra in the professor's journal!" Elettra exclaimed. "We know that Nero ended up thinking he'd become just like him, the sun on Earth—"

"But that was just plain arrogance," Ermete grumbles.

"And we know that they celebrated him in Rome on December twenty-fifth," adds Harvey.

"True. Today, for us Westerners, December twenty-fifth is Christmas. But back in ancient times, the birth of Jesus was celebrated on January sixth."

"On Epiphany?" asks Elettra.

"Exactly. January sixth is Epiphany. And *epiphaneia* is a Greek word meaning 'revelation.' That is . . . the day of the summit, of light. Because it's also the day that the kings from the East appeared. . . ."

"The Wise Men. The Magi . . . ," murmurs Harvey.

"Exactly." Ermete smiles. "And what do we know about them? That there might have been three of them, that they brought gifts and that they got there by following—"

"A comet," concludes Elettra.

"That's right, a comet," Ermete goes on. "And that's why it's believed that the Magi, or Wise Men, were high priests, guardians of an ancient tradition and experts in astronomy."

Harvey shifts uncomfortably in his chair.

"What is it?" Ermete asks encouragingly.

"On the professor's nightstand," replies Harvey, handing him the work by Seneca, "there was this book. . . ."

"*Naturales Quaestiones—On Comets,*" reads Ermete.

"What a mess. Everything seems to be connected somehow . . . ," mutters Elettra.

"And it is. Some people who study the stars believe our existence is connected to the movements of the constellations. And that there are favorable and unfavorable moments to deal with certain aspects of life. The professor thought we were close to a particularly auspicious moment in time. Which, according to his calculations, occurs once every hundred years."

"Man . . . that's a long time."

"Yes. 'The time is ripe,' Alfred kept repeating all the time over the last few weeks."

"When he gave me the briefcase," Elettra recalls, "he said, 'It's begun.'"

Ermete nods. "He was obsessed with time and was rushing me to figure out how to use the map. He said we risked missing our only chance for the auspicious moment. . . . And he was obsessed with signs. He believed the beginning would be marked by a simple coincidence, nothing more."

Ermete's words slide through the air like oil.

A simple coincidence, nothing more.

Like four kids, all born on February 29, meeting each other in Rome in the very same room.

It's midmorning when Linda Melodia decides to make a move. Having walked down the hallway leading to Elettra's room with long strides, she's already raised her hand to knock on the door. "Kids? It's ten-thirty!" she calls through the door. "What do you say you get up now?"

No one answers her.

"Kids?" the woman insists, knocking louder. She opens the door a crack. "Wake up, sleepyhea—"

The room is deserted.

Slightly concerned, Linda Melodia walks into the room.

There's a note on Elettra's bed. Linda snatches it up like it's a parking ticket and reads:

We've gone for a walk.
Don't worry about us.
We're fine.
See you tonight.
And happy New Year's Eve!

In a fit of rage, Linda has the urge to crumple up the note, but she stops herself. She stomps out of the room, looking for Fernando. The moment she finds him, she shoves it right under his nose. "Just look at what your daughter's done!" she yells. "What she got herself into last night, wasn't that bad enough?"

"Linda . . . ," mutters Fernando, trying to read the message and calm her down at the same time.

"A note!" sputters Linda. "After everything that happened to them yesterday!"

Harvey's mother walks up to them and asks, "Why? What happened yesterday?"

Aunt Linda is about to reply, but for once Fernando manages to beat her to it. With a reassuring tone, he says, "Oh, nothing in particular . . . They went a little bit crazy on the streets of Rome." Elettra's message quickly disappears into his pocket.

"Are they still in their room?" Mrs. Miller demands.

"Not exactly . . . ," replies Linda Melodia, thumping her foot on the floor nervously.

"Then where are they?"

"To tell you the truth . . . we don't know," admits Fernando, shrinking beneath the American woman's icy glare. He looks at Linda, hoping she'll back him up, but she promptly refuses. "They went out early this morning without saying anything to us."

Mrs. Miller's face blazes up. "What do you mean, they went out?"

"They went for a walk. But they'll be back soon—"

"A walk where?"

"Um . . . well . . . we don't know."

"This is outrageous!" the woman thunders. "George!"

Her husband walks up to them, powdered sugar on his nose.

"Harvey's gone!" his wife says, summing things up for him.

"What do you mean he's gone?"

"He went out early this morning with the owner's daughter and their new Chinese friend! Without telling us anything! Without even saying goodbye!"

"Where did they go?"

His hand in his pocket, Fernando crumples up the note.

"They went out to . . . well . . . to play some sort of game, I think . . . ," he improvises.

"That's impossible," the professor states categorically. "My son never plays. He's a very mature young man."

"Well, then . . . maybe he decided to go to a museum and wanted to get there before the lines got too long?" Fernando suggests, his face as red as a bell pepper.

"I don't like you, sir," the university professor declares. "If I decided to stay here in this hotel, it was only to make my wife happy . . . but now I think you've gone too far. So I'll ask you one more time: where is my son?"

"He's downtown with Elettra and Sheng," replies Fernando.

Mrs. Miller turns to Linda, hoping to find some female solidarity, and confides, "Harvey doesn't like to waste time with kids his own age. Much less with girls . . . especially the impulsive, flighty kind!"

"What Harvey does is his own business," blurts out Linda, unexpectedly taking Fernando's side. "After all, he seems old enough to decide for himself, if you ask me!"

"How dare you?!" the professor growls, taken aback.

"If poor Harvey's decided to waste time with kids his own age, which includes my impulsive, flighty niece, it's probably because he's been bored out of his skull up until now!"

"Oh, heavens!" gasps Harvey's mother. "George, say something!"

The man raises his finger.

"What does that mean, George?" Linda Melodia asks, cutting him off, her hands on her hips. "That you're going to speak to the dean about this?"

19

THE MAP

Kneeling on the chairs in Ermete De Panfilis's kitchen, Harvey, Elettra and Sheng study the stellar map spread out on the table.

"Look . . . ," the man explains. "You need to start in the center, at the woman surrounded by the stars of Ursa Major."

"*Hao!*" says Sheng, just to avoid losing the habit.

"Ursa Major, or the Great Bear, is the constellation that contains Polaris, the North Star."

"The North Star . . . ," Elettra says, making a mental note of it. But she wishes Mistral were there to take down notes in her sketchbook.

Harvey sputters, "Listen, if you've discovered how it works, can't you just tell us, without all these explanations?"

"Sure, if you like. But that way you'd miss all the good stuff. The fact is, this isn't a normal map . . . and it doesn't simply show you where to go. It's the map of all possible maps. It's the map Alexander the Great used to conquer the Orient. The map the Three Kings followed to journey to the West. The one Plato used to describe Atlantis, the one Marco Polo showed to the Great

Khan, the one that allowed Christopher Columbus to discover the route for the New World."

"*Hao!*" repeats Sheng, leaning forward on his elbows.

"You just listed off a bunch of random names, didn't you?" asks Harvey.

"Not at all." Ermete leaves the kitchen and comes back in with a large envelope. "These are the photos and negatives of all the inscriptions carved into the map. Take a look at this!" he says, starting to sort through them. "This mark might be the only signature Alexander the Great ever made in his whole life. The Assyrian-Babylonian letters 'B,' 'G' and 'M' correspond to Balthazar, Gaspar and Melchior, that is, the Magi. This symbol is the signature of Christopher Columbus, while this squiggle in the wood is the seal of the Polo family, Venetian merchants who traveled all the way to China."

"My home!" exclaims Sheng, pleased.

"I could go on and on for weeks," continues Ermete, setting aside his documents. "But you don't seem to be interested in hearing about the other possible owners of this map, who include Plato, Pythagoras, Emperor Hadrian, Ibn Battuta, Schliemann . . . and all the others, up to Alfred Van Der Berger. And you kids."

"It still just looks like a piece of scratched-up wood to me . . . ," grumbles Harvey, not at all impressed with his explanation.

"Was Schliemann the guy who discovered the treasures of the city of Troy?" asks Sheng, who, unlike his friend, is excited about the idea of being in possession of such an important map.

"That's the one," Ermete confirms, turning the map upside down. "And this is his signature, still perfectly legible."

"It's just plain impossible," mutters Harvey.

"So all these people," Elettra says, cutting in, "they all knew how to use it?"

"Yes."

"Did they use it to find the Ring of Fire?"

"No," replies Ermete. "It isn't a map to the Ring of Fire."

"Hold it! Hold it!" Sheng says, jumping up, his hands held out in front of him like a goalie blocking a soccer ball. "The only thing I've understood up till now was that we needed the map to find the Ring of Fire."

"Yes, but—"

"But if you're telling us it isn't a map to the Ring of Fire, what is it, then?"

"Right now, in Rome, the map can be used for finding the Ring of Fire," Ermete says.

Sheng looks at him warily. "But you just said the opposite."

Elettra grabs Sheng by the wrist. "He said, 'Right now, in Rome,' and 'can be used.'"

Sheng nods, although he still doesn't get it. "Right. Meaning . . . ?"

"Meaning that . . . at *other* times . . . in *other* places in the world . . . this map allows you to find *other* things."

"*Hao!* Now I get it." Sheng grins. "So how does it work?"

"It's quite simple, actually."

Ermete asks Elettra to hand him the map of Rome she found on the professor's refrigerator and spreads it open over the wooden box so that the grooves on the inner section are right beneath the paper.

"You do this, I think," he says.

"What do you mean . . . you *think*?" blurts out Harvey.

"This is the first time I'm actually trying it out . . . ," he explains. "Help me keep the map down flat. . . ."

Elettra rests a cereal bowl on each corner of the map of Rome.

"I bet this is how Marco Polo did it, too . . . ," quips Harvey.

Ermete ignores him. "Good. By overlaying this map, we've established the 'where.' Now all we need is the 'what.'" The engineer picks up the wooden tops resting on the table. "Take a look at the drawings. First top: the tower of silence—that is, a sanctuary, a hideaway, a safe place where people can stop to rest. Second top: the guard dog."

"See? I told you it was a dog!" Sheng says, bouncing in his chair, while Harvey glares at him.

"He guards over something important, something precious," continues Ermete. "But in order to reach what you're looking for, you need to get past him first. Third top: the eye. Only a keen observer can see what other people fail to notice. And finally, the last top: the vortex, the whirlpool. The place that pulls in ships and sinks them. Danger."

Ermete arranges the four tops beside the map.

"So what do we have to do?" asks Elettra.

"Spin them across the map," he replies, with a hint of tension in his voice, "and let the map decide."

The silence that follows is shattered by Harvey, who bursts out laughing. "Give me a break!" the American boy sneers. "You actually think we're supposed to do something so stupid?"

"It isn't stupid."

"It's even worse! It's crazy!" Harvey says, getting up from his chair. "Nine times out of ten the top's going to fall to the ground!"

"And nine times out of ten your horoscope is wrong," retorts Ermete. "But one time out of ten it's right. And one out of ten is better odds than you can expect from life."

"This is nuts!" sputters Harvey. "I don't think you understand a single thing about this map. That's not how it works. Guys, they want this map because it's really old and it's worth tons of money. There might be some art collector out there who can't wait to see it on his mantelpiece. But I really don't think they want to spin a few toy tops on it!"

Ermete is about to say something when he's interrupted by Sheng, who lets out a booming *"Enough!"* and grabs the top of the tower. Then he adds, "I dreamed about it—about this thing with the tops."

Harvey throws up his hands. "Oh, great! Just what we need! Dreams!"

But Sheng looks perfectly serious. "So you think all we have to do is pick up a top . . . and spin it across the wooden board, right?"

"Yes," Ermete says softly, pushing aside the bowls holding the map down to the very edges. "At least, I think so."

"Then let's give it a try." Elettra motions to Harvey to be quiet, while Sheng lifts up the top and rests it in the center of the map. "After all, it can't hurt."

"Of all the stupid . . . ," Harvey starts to grumble.

"Tell me, top of the tower of silence," Sheng pleads, remembering the veiled face of the woman in his dream, "where is our safe place?"

He spins it between his fingers and lets it go. The top begins to whirl around, moving across the map. Its tip follows the grooves sculpted into the underlying wood, dancing along the streets of Rome like a graceful ballerina. Via Condotti, Villa Borghese, Testaccio, Parioli . . . The top moves around in all directions, as if it were trying to choose the very best one.

Not to be reached by a single path, thinks Sheng as the top makes its way up the Tiber, spinning around furiously. It reaches Tiber Island and veers slightly southward. And there it stops, starting to spin around in larger and larger concentric circles.

"Trastevere. Piazza in Piscinula," Ermete reads.

"*Hao!*" cries Sheng. "Then it does work!"

"How can you tell?" the man asks.

Elettra smiles. "Because that's my house."

The top slowly stops spinning and rests on its side, right over the street where the Domus Quintilia is located. "Well, what do you say to that?" Ermete asks the others, his hands in the pockets of his robe.

"I wouldn't believe it if I hadn't seen it with my own two eyes . . . ," Sheng whispers.

"It's just a coincidence," Harvey retorts stubbornly.

"Let me try it this time," Elettra suggests.

She grabs the top of the tower and spins it a second time. The top wanders across the entire map and stops once again in Trastevere, leaving everyone gaping. A moment later, Harvey shakes his head skeptically. But he doesn't say a word.

Elettra grabs the top of the eye. "I'll try this one, too. The one showing . . ."

"Something only a keen observer can see . . . ," suggests Ermete.

"All right, then . . . Come on, top!" The girl spins it around with a skilled flick of her hand. The top begins to whirl around the streets and stops on a little lane in the center of the city.

"Via della Gatta . . . ," reads Ermete. "Does that mean anything to you guys?"

"'She-Cat Lane'?" Elettra replies. "No, I've never even been there before."

"What does that mean?" Sheng asks, clearly disappointed. "That it won't help us?"

"Exactly," says Harvey, once again on the offensive.

"Maybe the top wants to tell us we need to go there and take a look . . . ," Elettra guesses.

Sheng's eyes open wide. "Could Mistral be hidden there?"

Elettra picks up the top of the guard dog. "If Mistral's been kidnapped, like we think she has . . . Couldn't we find out from this one? The dog you need to get past to find something important . . ."

"Sure, why not?" grumbles Harvey.

Elettra throws the top, which starts to spin and then takes tiny little hops across the map. In the end, it stops on a house in the Coppedè district.

"Once again, a total mystery," remarks Elettra, confused.

Harvey cackles. "Two good tries and two useless ones."

The look on Sheng's face is indecipherable. "What does 'Coppedè' mean?"

Ermete shrugs. "It's the name of the half-crazy architect who designed that part of town."

"What kind of a place is it?"

"A residential area, but really bizarre. There are lots of strange houses. I've heard they've even filmed a few horror movies there."

Elettra and Sheng exchange nervous glances. "Cheerful little place," Sheng says. "Is it dangerous, do you think?"

"Why don't we ask the last top?" Harvey suggests provokingly. "This is the one that shows us where the danger is, right?" And, without waiting for an answer, he picks up the top of the whirlpool and throws it onto the map.

The top spins around like crazy for a few short moments.

Then it stops on the very same house in the Coppedè district, right beside the top of the guard dog.

20

THE DISTRICT

MISTRAL OPENS HER EYES AND FINDS HERSELF STARING AT A LIGHT blue ceiling.

Where am I? she wonders, sitting up in the bed.

She's in a little bedroom. A wardrobe, a rug, a beige leather armchair. Streaks of light stream in through the slats of the closed shutters of the room's only window.

It's daytime, then . . . But what happened?

The last thing she remembers seeing is the floor of the professor's apartment bucking like a wild horse, then turning into a massive pit. She remembers Elettra, a few steps away from her, shouting out something about the red circles on the floor and then . . . then nothing.

With great effort, Mistral gets up off the bed. Her whole body aches, her head feels heavy and her legs are stiff. She looks around. Whoever put her to bed also changed her into pajamas. Her clothes are folded and lying at the foot of the bed.

Mistral takes a few moments to peek through the shutters, trying to figure out where she is. Outside the window is a sort of medieval castle with crenellated rooftops. And a garden with dark trees, the corner of a fountain, a yellow house whose walls are decorated with bold floral patterns . . .

If she's in Rome, it sure doesn't look like Rome. Mistral grabs her sweater and slacks and begins to slip them on directly over the pajamas. Then she spins around.

Someone's opening the door.

It's a man. A man Mistral recognizes instantly.

She lets her sweater drop to the floor.

And she screams.

Jacob Mahler utters a single word. "Stop."

Mistral's scream dies in her throat and she backs up toward the empty space between the bed and the nightstand, shaking her head. *This is a bad dream*, she thinks. *It's just a bad dream.*

Mahler stands there in the doorway, stock-still, an icy stare on his face and a large bandage just below his hairline.

"I'm not going to hurt you," he says.

Mistral feels the wall pressed up against her back. "Who are you?"

"I'm the person who saved your life."

The girl shakes her head in disbelief.

"I pulled you out of the building just as it was collapsing," continues Mahler. "And I brought you here so you could rest."

"You're one of them . . . ," hisses Mistral. Her hands grope the wall nervously, searching for something, anything.

"I'm well aware that you don't like me. And I don't care. But I suggest you trust me. What's your name?"

"Mistral."

Jacob Mahler takes a few steps into the room, just reaching the bed.

"Very well, then, Mistral. I'm Jacob."

The killer reaches out his hand. It's long, slender and covered with tiny scratches. It remains there, suspended in the air, but the girl never reaches out to shake it. After a few seconds, the man lets his arm fall back down to his side.

"As you wish. But I'm warning you: you're making a mistake."

"You're one of them," the girl insists.

Mahler laughs. "And you? Who are you? Or who do you think you are?"

Mistral feels a lump in her throat, but she forces herself to overcome her fear.

"If you keep this up, I won't be able to help you," Jacob continues.

The girl nervously runs her hand through her hair. "Help me . . . how?"

"To get back home, for example. Where do you live?"

"Paris."

"Hmm . . . That's awfully far from here, isn't that right?"

"That depends. Where are we?"

Mahler raises an eyebrow. "Nice try. You're bright."

"And I'm sure you don't really want to help me."

"Well, just realize that I don't want to hurt you. All I want is one thing. And you know what that is."

"No, I don't," the girl replies stubbornly.

"Mistral . . . ," Mahler says insistently, pointing to the open door behind him. "Do you want to tell me what you did with that briefcase . . . or do I have to go get my instrument?"

The memory of the violin's hypnotic notes hits Mistral like a punch. At the very thought of hearing that music once again, her eyes open wide with fear.

"Well?"

"You said you dragged me out of the building when it was collapsing. . . ."

"That's right."

"What happened to the others?"

"What? There were others?" asks Mahler, pretending to be shocked.

"You know perfectly well there were."

"I have no idea how many of them there were. Won't you tell me?"

Mistral shakes her head.

Mahler leans against the bed. "In any case, I don't think anyone could've saved themselves. The whole floor collapsed. Boom! And it swallowed up Little Linch along with your friends."

Mistral feels tears well up in her eyes.

"That's the law of nature. Some die. Some live. You're alive, Mistral, thanks to me. Don't you think you owe me at least a little favor?"

Mistral shakes her head slowly. "I don't help people like you."

Mahler walks over to the window and peeks outside. "Ah, kids today . . . ," he murmurs to himself. "They want to play the heroes, but instead they've simply watched too much TV. Do you watch TV shows, Mistral?" He opens the window, letting in the cold air and the noise of traffic. "You don't? That's too bad. I love them, because they last twenty minutes at the most. Twenty minutes. And when they're over you can forget about them, at least until the following week. Isn't that wonderful? Wouldn't it be perfect if life were broken down into twenty-minute episodes that you could forget about afterward?" His face whirls around to look at Mistral. "Wouldn't that be wonderful?" he repeats.

Although she doesn't understand what he's getting at, she nods her head.

"There now, you've started to think clearly. Well, I'd like for this little show of ours to be over soon. I'd like for you to go back home to your mother and forget all about this, just like you would do with a bad TV show."

"Until next week," replies Mistral.

"Exactly. Don't you want to give your mother the chance to see the next episode of the show about Mistral?"

"What do you mean by that?"

"I mean," replies Mahler, slamming the window shut, "that either you tell me what you've done with that briefcase . . . or I'll have your little show end right here, right now. Forever."

Mistral doesn't doubt it for a second. The man's serious. She tries to keep her knees straight, although she feels her head reeling from fear.

"That briefcase, Mistral," Jacob Mahler continues, "is mine. And I'm very angry that you stole it from me."

"We didn't steal it. . . ."

"Very angry."

"We didn't even want to take it. . . . He gave it to us."

"Keep going."

"When we met Professor Van Der Berger on the bridge, he was running away from them . . . from you. He said that something had begun and that we had to take care of the briefcase for him. But we—"

"What did you do with it?"

"We . . . we threw it into the river." Mistral struggles to keep her head held high, but her eyes are no match for the intensity of Jacob Mahler's stare.

The killer raises his right hand and slowly starts to count down the seconds until her show comes to an end. "Five . . . four . . . three . . . two . . . one . . ."

"It's in the basement!" Mistral cries out just before he gets to zero. "We . . . we left it in the basement."

"The basement of the Domus Quintilia?"

Mistral bites her lip, not answering.

"There's a good girl." Jacob Mahler smiles. "I'm going over to get it. And then I'll take you back to your mother. Agreed?" Without waiting for an answer, the gray-haired man walks brusquely out of the room and shuts the door behind him. The key turns in the lock.

Beatrice is outside.

"Keep her quiet," Mahler orders, handing her the keys. "And don't let her out for any reason. Any reason at all. I'm going over to get the briefcase."

"What are you going to do with her?"

"She's seen me. She could identify me."

"So what? She's only a girl. You don't mean to—"

"I don't kill children," Mahler cuts her off. He thrusts a hand into his pocket and pulls out a slender, shiny gun. "I have others take care of that, when need be."

Beatrice stares at the killer's hand, horrified. "You're joking, right?"

"No. If she tries to escape and you can't stop her any other way . . . shoot her."

He hands the gun to Beatrice.

Mahler walks briskly down the stairs of the house. "I know you're a bright young woman. Don't disappoint me."

Lingering in the air is the faint smell of violets.

The front door opens and shuts. From the window, Beatrice watches the oval shape of her yellow Mini cross the square. Then she looks down at the gun she's holding, torn apart by conflicting thoughts. Jacob Mahler asked her not to disappoint him, but she's not willing to go to such extremes.

It's one thing to go pick him up from the airport, naively thinking she's taking part in a classy operation, like the ones in spy movies where they exchange briefcases. It's another thing to witness a man being murdered on the banks of the Tiber and then discover that the briefcase is in the hands of a group of kids, who are going to be killed for no better reason than that.

She's not sure she's doing the right thing. She's not at all sure.

She heads toward the room where Mistral is locked up.

She presses her ear up against the door and hears her crying, "Mom, where are you?"

Beatrice's female heart shrinks down to the size of a little speck. *I'm not your mother,* she thinks. *But I could be your sister.*

"I'm not going to hurt you," Beatrice whispers to the closed door. "And he isn't going to hurt you, either."

She has the gun in her pocket.

"Trust me, sweetheart. Trust Beatrice."

THIRD STASIMON

"Well?"

"Well, I can't tell you much. She's not answering the phone. She might've gone off on an excavation somewhere. . . . The people at the university can't tell me anything more than that."

"We've got to find her. And we've got to find out if she's the one who talked."

"Any news on your end?"

"Nothing good. Only three of the kids are left now. They lost Mistral."

"What do you mean they lost her?"

"She didn't come back. They're saying she went out of town with her mother."

"But didn't you set everything up so they'd all have enough time to look for the Ring of Fire?"

"Something seems to have gone wrong."

"Like last time, you mean."

"Last time it was different."

"Why, because it was a hundred years ago?"

"No, it was just different."

"I wouldn't say so. The kids have hit a dead end and now they risk making the same mistakes."

"I didn't say they'd hit a dead end. I just said they'd lost Mistral. The others were already back working on it this morning. Maybe . . . maybe there's still hope."

"But it's never been done with only three of them. It's unlikely, don't you think?"

"Unlikely, but not impossible."

"If the kids fail this time, too, it'll be . . . the end of the world, in a sense."

"Then look for her, Vladimir. Keep looking for her."

21

THE STREETS

AT ELEVEN PAST ELEVEN ON THE LAST DAY OF THE YEAR, ELETTRA arrives in Via della Gatta. Walking around a Gypsy woman, the kind who asks for money to read your palm, she crosses through a sunny little square used as a parking lot. In her pocket is the top with the eye, along with the tooth they found in the briefcase. Before leaving Ermete's house, they divided up the tasks . . . and the treasure.

Via della Gatta is a total disappointment. It's a dark, narrow, dirty little street tiled with porphyry and flanked by tall buildings in dark travertine. Tall black bars protect the windows on the ground floor.

What is it you were trying to show me here? Elettra asks the top she's carrying in her pocket. *Don't tell me Harvey's right and you don't work at all, okay?*

She turns into the lane with the best intentions, but no matter how hard she tries, she can't find anything that seems important. After a few meters, the street broadens into a square and continues on, becoming a sunnier, paved area.

Elettra sees a bookshop, a library, a few stores, the customary cars parked sideways over the sidewalks, a beat-up van bearing the name of a moving company and . . . basically, that's it.

She's reached the end of Via della Gatta.

It might just have been a coincidence, she tells herself, turning back.

She searches high and low, remembering what was written in the professor's journal: *Search below and you shall find it above.*

And of us three crazy kids, I just might be the craziest.

Four crazy kids, she corrects herself instantly. *Four, not three.*

She searches the lane a second time, checking the names on the intercoms in search of a sign.

"We'll find you, Mistral . . . ," she whispers. "Don't worry. We'll find you."

This conviction is stronger than any other thought in her mind, stronger than her concern about calling home to let them know everything's okay. Elettra's totally committed to her task, to her friends. She's never felt so close to other people before. It's like she's known them her whole life.

Sure, Harvey's grouchy, but deep down he believes in their adventure, too. Elettra can still feel his cheek pressed up against hers as he protected her in the professor's apartment. . . . Then there's Sheng, who's so enthusiastic he might even seem a little naive. But he's got undying faith in the others.

"Can't find it, can you?" asks a portly man with a big mustache who's standing outside a café.

Elettra stops in her tracks.

"You're a tourist, right?" the portly man asks bluntly. "I'm good at spotting tourists. Never get it wrong. You're here in Rome to celebrate New Year's Eve! Got it right, didn't I? Where are you from, Paris? I bet you've never had a real dish of spaghetti!" The portly man bursts out in a hearty laugh, and Elettra doesn't know whether to answer him directly in Roman dialect or to ignore him completely.

She decides to ignore him and continues walking down the street.

The man looks at her, amused, and shouts after her, "In any case, you need to keep your head up. The cat you're looking for is up there, on the cornice of the corner building! Second floor. You can't miss it! It's a statue!" He lets out another hearty laugh.

Elettra looks up. Resting on the cornice of one of the buildings is a statue of a cat. *So that explains the name of this street!* she thinks.

But the man standing outside the café isn't done. "Everybody comes here for the same reason. . . . Legend has it that a treasure's hidden in the very spot where the cat's looking. But I say the cat's turned its head over the years. If you ask me, it used to be looking down here at the café! What other treasures could there be around here, do you think?" And, with a final burst of laughter, he turns around and walks back into the café.

Sheng elbows his way out of yet another crowded bus and, once on the sidewalk, makes his way briskly down the blocks separating him from the Coppedè district. He's armed with a giant map of the city that, at least in theory, can be refolded, along with a pen and pencil to take down any notes he might need, a half-used stack of bus tickets and a professional camera that makes him look just like Peter Parker, the only reporter able to unmask Spider-Man himself.

In his pocket he's carrying two of the tops they spun around on the map: the one with the dog and the one with the whirlpool. He's hoping that what he's trying to do will actually help them somehow.

At the first intersection, Sheng spreads the map out in his hands, examines it carefully and, without thinking twice, goes the wrong way. When he realizes this, it's almost too late to fix things. The sun's high in the sky, the trees in the park in Villa Borghese are a beautiful sight with their centuries-old trunks . . . but Rome is clearly far too big a city for anyone to be wandering around lost.

He sits down, taking stock of his situation.

He's never been good at getting his bearings, especially in a city that's so different from the one where he grew up. If he were in Shanghai, he'd call one of his cousins to come get him or flag down a palanquin. But he isn't in Shanghai. He's in Rome. And just trying to understand how the buses work is already enough to drive him crazy, staring at all those signs in Italian. . . .

He checks the time, tries not to think about how late he's made himself by getting on and off all the wrong buses and heads back to the Coppedè district.

The camera bangs against his chest and sharp pangs shoot through his bandaged arm, but Sheng's happy to be there. He has no idea what he'll find at the spot he's circled in red, nor what he'll learn from the photos he'll manage to take, but he'd rather try doing everything possible than sit there feeling sorry for himself or being mad at the world, like Harvey.

"It's not my fault!" Sheng shouts after a while, when he realizes that the street he's turned down goes uphill instead of downhill. "These streets are all crooked!"

* * *

Meanwhile, at the Regno del Dado, Harvey paces back and forth nervously.

It's noon.

Ermete's still in the shower. He's been in there for at least half an hour.

Harvey can hear him singing away as steam swirls out from the door, which is slightly ajar. When the man's voice cracks for the millionth time, Harvey paces around and checks the time yet again.

"How much longer is this going to take, anyway?" he asks. It's a question aimed at just about everything: Ermete's endless shower, Elettra and her mission in Via della Gatta and Sheng, who by now must've gotten lost in the streets of Rome.

Harvey's convinced that their splitting up was a terrible idea. Just like his decision to stay there, spending the morning listening to Ermete's phone calls with a series of friends, each one shadier than the last.

On paper, at least, their task seems to be the most critical one. They're supposed to go see one of Ermete's unscrupulous connections to find out if he knows anything about the man with the violin. Or Mistral's kidnapping. But after a million useless attempts, just when he seemed to be on the verge of talking to this unknown friend, the engineer said he was tired and that he needed to take a shower so he could concentrate better.

"An hour-long shower?" yells Harvey, exasperated by the wait.

Inside of him, he feels a growing rage, which he's perfectly unable to vent. He wishes he knew whether Elettra and Sheng have discovered anything by following the directions given to them by the tops. And he's not sure what answer he'd rather hear, because if those pieces of wood actually work, it means he's losing his mind.

"It's all crazy . . . ," he mutters, staring down at one of Ermete's board games. "This is what I feel like. A pawn in someone's hands."

He walks through the apartment for the millionth time, and, hearing the engineer crooning blissfully, he clenches his fists in anger. "You're such a big help!" he snarls impatiently.

When he goes back to the kitchen, he passes by the phone and decides to make a call. He picks up the receiver. He puts it down. He picks it up again. Then he quickly dials his father's cell phone number.

"Dad?"

"*Harvey? Where on earth are you?*" his father shouts immediately. There's a muffled noise as the phone is handed over to Mrs. Miller, who, in a single breath, gives him a seemingly endless third degree.

"Everything's fine . . . just fine . . . ," Harvey tries to tell her. But his mother is like a raging river. "No, really, we're perfectly fine! Yes, we'll be back soon. . . . We're just . . . No! No! Mom! Listen to me! Would you listen? *No!* I can't come back right now! And don't come looking for me! At a friend's house. Yeah, a friend! I don't know his name! *I'm fine!* Mom! I just wanted to . . . I just . . ." He brusquely hangs up before his ear catches on fire.

"Yeah, happy New Year's Eve to you, too!" he mutters, staring at the phone.

The bathroom door opens. Ermete's finished his shower.

"Everything okay?" he asks, drying off the few strands of hair left on his head.

"Nothing's okay!" yells Harvey. "Let's get going!"

What treasure is the cat pointing out? wonders Elettra, staring up at the graceful statue in black marble perched on the cornice. The girl moves closer to the building and then draws back, looking for the best vantage point to find out where the statue's gaze is directed. *Well . . . ,* she decides, after countless attempts. *The cat's not looking at this street. She's looking toward Piazza Grazioli, where the parking lot is.*

Elettra twirls a lock of hair in her fingers, deep in thought.

I'm not looking for a treasure . . . , she tells herself. *I'm looking for Mistral or, at most . . . the Ring of Fire.*

If the cat is what the top was indicating, then what the cat's indicating is . . . an elegant building in Piazza Grazioli. But its stony stare might be focused on any one of the windows. Or the front door. Or the cellar.

Elettra steps over a snowbank and checks the names on the intercom.

But as she's drawing near, she notices for the second time the Gypsy she avoided before. The woman's sitting cross-legged in the doorway of a building on a makeshift mat of cardboard.

Could it be? she wonders. Elettra looks back to check the position of the cat again. *Could it be?*

She walks up to the Gypsy, not even knowing what to say to her.

The woman turns her wrinkled face up from the thick pile of

old coats she's bundled up in, trying to protect herself from the cold. She holds out a plastic dish with a few copper coins resting in it.

"Good luck to you, young miss. I wish you much good luck, to you and your family," she mumbles, like a sad refrain.

A little good luck couldn't hurt, thinks Elettra. "Oh, why not?" she blurts out.

Slipping her hand into her pocket to grab a few coins, she pulls out first the top and then the tooth. She finally finds a fifty-cent coin and holds it out over the Gypsy's dish. "Here," she says.

The Gypsy gives a start. Her expression suddenly changes and the moment the coin clinks against the others, she gets up from her cardboard mat and turns to leave.

Elettra looks over her shoulder to see if a policeman is coming toward them. But, with the exception of a few people crossing through the square and the cat perched on the cornice, she doesn't see anyone.

"Where are you going?" she asks the woman.

The Gypsy waves her hands over her head and, turning her back on the girl, exclaims, "No, no! Go away! Go away!"

"Are you talking to me?"

The Gypsy nods. She walks off in her bundle of coats, repeating, "Don't! Don't!"

"Don't *what?*" Elettra insists, baffled.

The woman doesn't reply. Instead, she starts running.

Sheng stops to check the not-exactly-foldable map in front of a large, dark archway crowning the main road. After a brief struggle against the wind, he heaves a sigh of relief. Unless he's making another massive mistake, the bizarre-looking archway divides Coppedè from the rest of Rome.

The archway is menacing, light and heavy at the same time, supporting a structure that looks a lot like a prison.

"It's up to us, guard dog . . . ," murmurs Sheng with a heroic attitude as he rolls up his sleeves while trying not to crumple the map any further. "It's up to us, whirlpool. . . ."

As he walks through the arch, he has the strong sensation that the city has changed. In the middle of the square he sees a fountain with four frogs, surrounded by patches of gray snow. All around him are buildings that look like they've been quilted with dark travertine.

Sheng checks the position of the house he's there to see, raises his camera and starts snapping off shots.

Yellow-and-red checkered house. Click.

Windows held up by leering masks. Click. Click. Click.

Balconies resting on the shoulders of Titans. Click. Click.

Knights in suits of armor holding up copper drainpipes. Click.

Slanting rooftops. Click.

He photographs these subjects with the speed of a sharp-shooting gunslinger. He continues on, never slowing his pace, with the professional expression of someone who's being forced to do dirty work and wants to get it over with as soon as possible. None of the passersby even bothers to look at him, assuming he's just an average tourist.

And so, totally undisturbed, finally Sheng reaches his intended destination. It's a little house with a somber-looking turret surrounded by an iron gate topped with twisted spikes that look so strange they deserve four shots of their own. Click. Click. Click. Click.

On the other side of the gate is a dismal-looking yard (two clicks) and a series of tiny prints made by a raven (one click).

The boy looks up to study the rest of the house. Its facade is completely asymmetrical. Columns and canopies hide side entrances and rooms. Sheng aims his camera and starts snapping shots.

And then, just as he's focusing on a window with closed shutters, he has the odd feeling someone's standing behind it. He zooms in and out without being able to see anyone, and, his voice so low he can barely hear it himself, he asks, "Mistral? Are you in there?"

He stands there, waiting for an answer, which naturally doesn't come. He lowers the camera and looks around. He can see stoplights and road signs. Heroes and monsters, swords and fleurs-de-lis. Coats of arms and blazons. The iron gate and the garden.

"Man . . . ," he murmurs. "This place gives me the creeps."

He walks along the gate, reaching a narrow path that's been cleared of snow and leads up to the entrance of the house. A few red spots dotting the ground like tiny wounds catch his eye.

"Bingo . . . ," murmurs Sheng, snapping pictures of them. Zooming in, he confirms that they're tiny patches of blood.

Click. Click.

Then he lowers his camera and turns around to look behind him. No one's there. A street. Cars. Stoplights. Road signs. Coats of arms and blazons.

"More than the creeps . . . ," he says. He tries to concentrate on the house again, but he finds it's no use. He lowers the camera and admits to himself that he's scared out of his wits.

He walks away without looking any further, clumsily bumps into some passersby, apologizes and keeps walking.

That's enough pictures, he thinks.

Dogs, dragons, sculptured animals, eyes, hands of stone.

That's really enough. He's had all he can take of Coppedè.

He starts running.

He reaches the frog fountain and flies through the archway, stopping only when he's on the other side. He's in Rome again.

"Stop!" Elettra shouts out to the Gypsy woman.

The woman runs, hobbling awkwardly in her thick layers of coats. "Go away!" she answers without slowing down.

Elettra follows her, first walking with long strides and then running. "Why are you running away?"

The Gypsy woman simply shoos her away with her hands, still running. Elettra runs faster and soon catches up with her. The woman finally gives up, leaning against the wall.

"Would you mind telling me why you were running away from me?" Elettra hounds her.

"In your pocket . . . ," the old woman pants, her face red with exhaustion.

"What? This? The top? Do you recognize this top?"

The Gypsy woman shakes her head, a foul odor wafting up all around her, one of dirty hair, sweat, grime.

"This, then? Do you recognize this?" insists Elettra, showing her the tooth.

The woman covers her eyes with her hands and tries once again to run off. "No! Go away! It's not me!"

"You're not what?" yells Elettra, holding her back. The Gypsy manages to pull herself free and starts running again.

Elettra, panting, chases after her. "Won't you explain, please?" Then something dawns on her. "Do you know Alfred Van Der Berger?" she shouts. "The professor?"

When she hears the name, the old woman slows down slightly. She turns to look at the girl, shakes her head, and starts running again.

"You do! You know the professor!" Elettra shouts, doubling her speed. "I know him, too! He's a friend of mine!"

This time, the Gypsy woman stops in her tracks. Elettra catches up with her, walks around the misshapen bell form of her coats and repeats, "Alfred Van Der Berger. The professor. He's the one who gave me the tooth."

"He's dead," says the Gypsy.

"I know."

"They killed him the other night. . . ." Tears run from the Gypsy woman's eyes, leaving two glistening trails down her dirt-covered cheeks. It's snowing. And the river is howling.

"Yes, yes, yes . . . ," Elettra says, overjoyed to have found another person who knows what happened. "It was them. . . ."

The woman looks around, frightened, and her hands gesture as if to cancel out everything around her. "Shhh!" she hisses between her black teeth. "Speak softly. There are . . . shadows . . . listening. Shadows that make the river howl."

"I was there that night, too. I was on the bridge!" continues Elettra.

"No," replies the Gypsy. "You weren't there. There was only

snow. The river crying. And the violin. The violin was there, the other night, when he died."

In her mind's eye, Elettra can see the man with the gray hair crossing over the threshold of the professor's apartment. She can still hear with crystal clarity the sweet melody that was making her fall asleep. And, even after so many hours, for a moment she's forced to close her eyes.

"Did you see the man with the violin, too?" she asks with a low voice.

The Gypsy woman shakes her head. "I only heard him. I didn't see him."

"Was he the one who killed the professor?"

Instead of an answer, she's given another question. "When did he give you the tooth?"

"The other night, on the bridge."

"And did he tell you why?"

"No. But I think it's for the same reason he gave me other things . . . so the man with the violin wouldn't find them."

"He told me that, too," says the Gypsy. Her hand disappears beneath the layers of her clothes. A moment later, it reappears with a black leather cord, hanging from which is a second tooth.

She holds it up beside the one in Elettra's hand.

On it is engraved the letter "M."

22

THE BASEMENT

"I'M SORRY, MR. HEINZ," FERNANDO MELODIA TELLS THE MAN WHO'S walked into the Domus Quintilia looking for a room. "We're booked solid." The man is dressed entirely in black. With him he has a violin case and a broad-brimmed hat that hides the upper part of his face.

"Are you certain?" he insists. "Your hotel was recommended to me by a friend. . . ."

"I'm sure," replies Fernando. "Besides, in any event, we aren't exactly in the right mood to receive guests, believe me."

"Has something happened?"

"Yes, you could say that," says Fernando Melodia, without offering any explanation. "And now, if you'll excuse me . . ."

But the man seems to have no intention of leaving. "Couldn't you at least show me the rooms," he continues, "or let me have a look around?"

"No, I'm sorry. We're really very busy. My daughter's caused a little bit of a crisis, so . . ." Fernando is reluctant to add anything else.

"How old is your daughter?"

"Twelve."

"I understand, then. That's the age when they begin to rebel against their parents."

Fernando shakes his head. "No, I don't think you understand. The fact is, she convinced our guests' children to . . . I'm not sure what . . ." He gestures, as if to say, "What can you do?" Then he makes his way around the reception desk to walk the man to the door. "In any case, I hope you'll come back here next time."

"Where's the basement?" the man asks him, point-blank.

"Um, sorry?"

"I asked you where the basement is."

"B-back there . . . ," stammers Fernando, pointing out a door hidden behind some plants. "But why . . . ?"

The man's hands shoot out only twice, striking him in the chest. With the first blow, Fernando doubles over, the wind knocked out of him. With the second blow, he falls to the ground like a sack of potatoes.

"Thanks for the information," hisses Jacob Mahler, stepping over him.

He bends down to grab him under the arms and drags him behind the reception desk, hiding him from view. Then, with a quick glance left and right, he opens up the reservation book and hastily leafs through it, looking for the names recorded that week.

But there aren't any names in the book. It's as if the hotel doesn't have a single guest. *How could that be?* wonders Mahler. He opens up the drawers in search of registration documents or receipts, but again finds nothing. No passports. No identity cards. "Dammit!" he hisses, turning toward Fernando's motionless body. "How do you run this hotel, huh? You haven't copied down a single name!"

Giving up all hope of discovering the identities of the other kids in the group, Mahler shuts all the drawers. He'll have to make do with the names he already knows: Elettra and Mistral.

"Meanwhile, the briefcase," he murmurs, moving the plants aside. That is the thing he was paid for. The thing Heremit Devil ordered him to track down.

He flings the basement door open. A stone stairway makes its way down into the darkness. Mahler looks for the light switch and flicks it. A series of bulbs light up an underground room with a red brick ceiling.

"Basement." Jacob Mahler looks around and smiles.

At the bottom of the stairs is a mouse. A little mouse that stares at him, surprised by all the light. Jacob loves mice. They're just like him. Silent creatures who for years have been battling against mankind. Creatures whom mankind will never succeed in defeating.

The moment it senses danger, the little mouse scurries off to hide in its underground home.

Mahler walks down the steps two at a time, being careful not to let his coat drag on the ground. He breathes in the dusty air, walks up to the first piece of furniture and lifts up the sheet covering it: a trunk. He lifts up a second sheet: an art nouveau wardrobe. And then a third: a pair of nightstands.

He grits his teeth with frustration. The basement is immense. Where could his briefcase be hidden? Mahler scans the room with his eyes. It doesn't take him long to spot signs of a recent gathering held on the floor.

He follows the footprints up to a lopsided dresser.

First drawer.

Second drawer.

Third drawer.

His lips twist into a smile.

"Briefcase," he says.

But the moment he grabs it, he realizes something's wrong.

The briefcase is light. Too light.

"You shouldn't have done this, kids," growls Jacob Mahler. He rests the briefcase on top of the dresser and opens it. It's empty. Completely empty.

He hits it with his hand, making it fall to the ground; then he clenches his fists, trying to hold back a howl of rage. He starts to slowly hum the scale of C in an attempt to calm down. By the time he's finished his third scale, he's succeeded. But he also realizes he's made too much noise.

He raises an eyebrow. The basement ceiling trembles. Approaching footsteps.

Mahler picks the empty briefcase up from the floor. He takes one last look around and mutters to himself, "Clever, Mistral . . . very clever."

The footsteps come to a sudden halt. Mahler listens and starts to count the seconds. He understands immediately when it's time to leave. He doesn't even have the chance to rest his foot on the first step when a woman's cry comes from upstairs. "Fernando! What are you doing down there?"

Mahler climbs the stairs. He reaches the basement door and, through the branches of the plants, sees a woman leaning over the reception desk.

Without making a single leaf rustle, he tries to slip out.

But the woman snaps upright. "Who are you?" she exclaims.

Jacob ignores her, heading toward the front door.

"Excuse me!" insists Linda Melodia. "Might I know who you are?"

A second voice cries out with alarm from behind Mahler's back, "Linda, look out!" It's a woman in a wheelchair. Her features are withered with age and her hands are clutching the armrests of the chair.

"Stop!" warns Linda Melodia.

Jacob Mahler tries to push her away, but instead of stepping aside, she raises a broom and hits him over the head with it, snapping it in two. "I'll show you, you filthy thief! Get out of here at once!"

The man grabs her arm with a steely grip. "That's exactly what I was trying to do . . . ," he hisses.

"Leave me alone!" screams Linda, trying to break free.

Mahler could break her wrist. Or kill her.

But he doesn't. Deep down, he admires the way the woman defends her territory. He limits himself to pushing her away and walking over to the door. The old woman in the wheelchair shouts something that he doesn't bother to listen to.

He walks away from the hotel, carrying the useless, empty briefcase.

Something warm slides down his face.

He touches his forehead. The woman's blow seems to have reopened his wound.

23
THE RIVER

"Follow me," the Gypsy had said, and Elettra had obeyed her.

She left the known city to delve into the invisible world of the Gypsies, thinking of all the things she knew about them, none of which were flattering. *Don't trust them. Don't look at them. Don't let them read your palm. Don't let them touch you. Stay away from them.*

But instead, a few hours away from the night of San Silvestro, Elettra agreed to follow one of them through the hovels built beneath a bridge spanning the Tiber.

She follows her past a broken parapet, along a path of muddy snow that makes its way past shrubs, rocks by the riverside and dry branches, caught on which are strips of plastic that flutter in the wind like little flags. She follows her into the ice-cold shade of a bridge. Below the noise of cars. She leaves the city behind her.

Her guide is a mass of dirt and patched-up coats. But once in a while, a golden glimmer can be seen through her hair. It's a single gold earring dangling from her right earlobe.

The Tiber's current rages along, driven by the snowfall of the previous days. It's like a song that drowns out the noise of the traffic. "We're there . . . ," the Gypsy announces after a long while.

She shows Elettra a makeshift hovel built with sheets of metal, plastic, old boards and broken window shutters. It has no lock. It's entered by simply pushing open a door made of streetside posters that have been pasted together.

It's cold inside. Seeping through the walls is the icy chill from outdoors and the cold from the stones of the bridge looming overhead.

The Gypsy tries to light a small gas heater. At first the flame won't catch, but a few well-planted kicks to a tank lying on the ground make the last wheezes of gas hiss through the pipe.

Elettra stands warily by the door. The floor's covered with plastic. Patches of insulating material cover the walls. It smells pungent, foul.

"Come . . . ," says the Gypsy. "I'm not going to hurt you." She heads toward the back of the shanty, where trunks and boxes of old clothes are piled up. She starts searching for something.

Elettra gulps and walks inside.

"Help me . . . ," says the woman. "It's heavy."

Moving the boxes aside, the two lift out into the light a wooden trunk that was hidden against the back wall of the hovel. It's very heavy, as if it were full of stones.

"Why did you bring me all the way here?" asks Elettra.

The Gypsy rummages through various baskets full of golden trinkets, looking for the key to the trunk. When she finds it, she kneels down on the ground to unlock it. "The professor brought this to me . . . ," explains the Gypsy. "After I'd read his palm."

Elettra stares at the chest, amazed. "He gave you that trunk? What's inside it?"

"Wait and see."

"When did you read his palm?"

"When I met him, he was searching. And I was waiting. We met in Piazza della Gatta."

"What was he looking for?"

"A treasure, he told me. But he was sad, regretting something for which he wasn't to blame. I could tell. I saw it in his eyes. I walked up to him and asked if I could read his palm."

"What did he say?"

"He agreed, but . . ."

"What did you see in his palm?"

"The end of the world . . . ," whispers the Gypsy, closing her eyes and turning the key in the old lock.

She opens the lid.

"I don't know why he wanted to give me these . . . ," she explains with a faint voice, having cast a glance at the contents of the trunk. "I think it was because I'd seen the end of the world in his palm. He already knew about it, you see? He asked me how I understood that."

Elettra remains silent. It's too dark for her to see what's inside the trunk. All she can make out is some writing engraved in the lid: ORSENIGO 1867–1903.

The name rings a bell, but she doesn't know what it means. Maybe she's seen it in the professor's notes . . . one of the many things he'd scribbled in his journal that Mistral copied down. But the strange familiarity of the name makes her heart beat faster.

The Gypsy raises her hands. "I don't know how I understood

it, but I really did see the end of the world in his palm." She points to her left hand. "All of his lines were broken, and they came together to form a big spiral."

"Like a whirlpool," says Elettra.

"Like a whirlpool, yes . . . ," the Gypsy says, nodding. "The whirlpool of peril."

Elettra clutches the wooden top in her pocket, thinking of Sheng and the top of the whirlpool.

The woman's voice grows more intense. "Every one of his lines was wrong. I saw other lines within them. I saw men shouting. I saw tears. I saw flames. Terrible winds that shook everything to the core. The earth opening up beneath people's feet. A salty, black sea wiping away everything. This is what I saw in the professor's palm."

Elettra has the sudden urge to get out of there. The Tiber gurgles outside of the hovel.

"But I don't know why he brought me these . . . ," the Gypsy continues with a hushed voice. Her hands dive down into the trunk. "He paid me to keep these for him. He paid me well and he said, 'No one will come here to look for them. But hide them anyway. And if anyone ever comes here asking questions . . . go . . . go at once. If you're frightened, destroy them. But let no one see them. No one at all.'" Her earring sparkles. "Then he added, pointing at the lines showing the end of the world, that they were also looking for the treasure. That they mustn't know where to look for it."

Her hands in her pockets, Elettra takes a small step forward, trying to see what's inside the trunk.

"I hid them here, as he wished," the Gypsy continues. "And no one came to look for them. Until today. When you appeared."

"And you ran away."

"Yes."

"You wanted to come here to destroy them."

"Yes. I considered it."

"So why did you change your mind?"

"The professor told me that what he was looking for had something to do with the end of the world. That's why he was afraid. Because he thought there were other men who had the end of the world in their palms," the Gypsy replies. "But, you . . ."

"I what?" Elettra asks, taking a step back.

The woman removes her hands from the trunk. "You're not afraid."

Elettra lets out a laugh. "Oh, you're wrong. I'm really afraid. A lot more than you can imagine."

"Let me see your hand," says the Gypsy.

"No!" cries Elettra, alarmed. A shiver runs down her spine like a drop of ice-cold water.

"Let me see your hand," the Gypsy insists.

"Why?"

"I want to study your lines."

Elettra shakes her head. "I . . . I don't want you to . . ."

"At times what you want or don't want isn't important."

"I'm not interested in knowing what's written in my palm."

"You can see your reflection in the mirror even with your eyes closed."

"How did you know that? How do you know about the mirrors?"

The Gypsy tilts her head slightly over her right shoulder, a pose that makes her look incredibly sweet. She's reaching out for her hand as though she were inviting Elettra to dance at a ball.

"Well, just don't tell me anything . . . ," Elettra says in a hushed voice. "If you see something, don't tell me."

The Gypsy nods her head.

It's agreed.

Elettra holds out her left hand, palm up, to the Gypsy.

"Please . . . ," she whispers, as if praying.

The woman's fingers grasp Elettra's firmly and she begins to slide the tip of her index finger over the girl's palm. She moves it up and down, in long circles, pressing down here and there. She does this for a few minutes and then releases her grip in a single swift movement.

"Well?" asks Elettra.

"You asked me not to tell you anything. So I won't tell you."

Elettra's heart beats faster and faster.

"Now take a look. . . . Look at what the professor left us," the Gypsy says, waving her over to the trunk. Holding her breath, Elettra rests her eyes on a mass of white, irregularly shaped objects. For a moment, she doesn't understand what they are.

"It can't be . . . ," she whispers. She kneels down beside the trunk with a mix of horror and curiosity. She shakes her head. On her palm she can still feel the spots where the Gypsy woman pressed down on it. "Are these what I think they are?"

The woman smiles. "Teeth," she says.

The trunk contains hundreds, perhaps thousands, of human teeth.

"Hello . . . ," Beatrice says in a soft voice as she opens the bed-room door slightly. Sitting on the bed, Mistral doesn't react at all. She just looks straight ahead, a distant, stubborn look on her face.

Beatrice takes a few steps into the room. "How do you feel?"

The girl stares at the closed shutters and doesn't say a word.

"It won't be long now . . . ," Beatrice insists, trying to be as re-assuring as possible. "He'll be back soon."

"But he isn't going to take me home, is he?" Mistral asks point-blank.

Beatrice walks over to the bed and rests her hands on it. "Why do you say that?"

"Because you guys are . . . *them*."

"And who are *they*?"

Mistral's stare is cold. "I'm not stupid," she says. "Let's just say you're *them* because I don't know your names."

"But—"

"So who are you, anyway? Why have you kidnapped me?"

Beatrice bites her lip. "It'll all be over soon, you'll see. It's just that . . ." Mistral's eyes are deep, intense, begging the woman not to lie to her. To tell her the truth. Beatrice sighs. "I work for him, that's true . . . ," she admits. "But I don't know anything about all this. All I can tell you is I won't let him hurt you. Believe me."

"He's really dangerous, isn't he?" asks Mistral, glancing at the door behind the young woman, which is ajar.

Beatrice stares down at the blanket. She thinks about how hard it is to lie to a girl like this. And how hard it is to tell her the whole truth.

"Yes," she says in a low voice. "Very."

Mistral goes back to staring at the shutters. "I knew it," she mumbles. "And I bet he was the one who killed the professor."

Beatrice quickly tries to change the subject. "I had a little sister like you. That is . . ." She smiles. "A bit like you. She'd be more or less your age today."

"Where is she?"

"They split us up. That happens sometimes, when parents . . . fight."

"I haven't got both parents. I've only got my mom, so she doesn't have anyone to fight with," Mistral remarks.

"Sometimes it's better that way, you know? I grew up with my dad and—" A series of bad memories flashes before her eyes. "And it wasn't much fun."

Mistral stares at her, not understanding, but she doesn't ask any questions. She wipes her eyes with her hand.

"Do you want a tissue?" asks Beatrice.

"I'm not crying."

A heavy silence fills the bedroom. Through the window come the muffled sounds of traffic.

"What's your name?"

"Beatrice."

"I'm Mistral."

"Hello, Mistral."

"Were you serious? Do you really think it'll all be over soon?"

Beatrice nods nervously. She looks at Mistral and sees herself at age twelve. Locked up in her room, waiting for her father to decide that her punishment is over and let her out. "Of course I was serious. Of course."

Mistral fidgets nervously. Beatrice listens to the noise coming in from the street. She thinks she can make out the engine of her Mini. And then a door slamming at the bottom of the stairs.

"What is it?" asks Mistral.

"Nothing," replies Beatrice, rushing out of the room.

Jacob Mahler is back.

24
THE LETTERS

"OKAY. DON'T MOVE!" ERMETE SHOUTS INTO THE PHONE. "I'LL BE right there!"

"Where are we going?" asks Harvey, watching the engineer rush from one end of the house to the other, his sparse hair still damp. He opens and shuts all the drawers, one by one. As always, the keys to his motorcycle have disappeared.

"How is this possible?" he yells furiously. The phone rings again. "You get it!"

Harvey picks up the receiver and hears a woman's voice shrieking nonstop. Guessing who it is, he covers the receiver with his hand and calls out, "Ermete! It's your mother!"

"Tell her I'm not here," the engineer replies, rummaging around in a pile of dirty T-shirts. "Where the heck did I put them?"

Harvey uncovers the receiver and stammers, "Um, ma'am? Right now Ermete is—"

"*I'm not here!*" the man shouts from the back of the room. He's finally found his keys inside an empty vase. He grabs them, walks up to Harvey, yanks the phone out of his hand and says in Italian,

"Hi, Mom. Listen, whatever it is, I don't care. No no no no. Really. Today I can't!" And with this, he hangs up.

Then he crouches down beside Harvey and explains, "Elettra called. She seems to have found . . . well, something incredible. . . ."

"What?" asks Harvey, his heart thumping.

"Oh, it's an old legend in Rome. . . . Years ago there was this monk over on Tiber Island—"

"I've seen that," Harvey bursts in. "That's the island where all this started."

Ermete ignores the interruption and goes on. "His name was Friar Orsenigo. He was a tooth-puller."

"A what?"

"A kind of dentist. It's just, he didn't take care of teeth. He only took them out. And he did it with his bare hands."

Harvey instinctively raises a hand to his mouth. "Not for me, thanks."

"Well, all of Rome used to go to him because he didn't ask for money. He'd slip his fingers into your mouth and . . . Crack! Goodbye tooth, goodbye pain. They say the pope even went to see him and that this was the only time the monk's fingers were particularly gentle. The only thing Orsenigo asked in return for his services was that he be allowed to keep all the teeth he pulled. They say he collected almost two million of them during his lifetime."

Something suddenly dawns on Harvey. "Does this have anything to do with the tooth we found in the briefcase?"

"It sure looks like it," Ermete confirms. "Elettra found one of Friar Orsenigo's trunks. Which, naturally, is full of teeth . . . and each tooth has something written on it."

Harvey gapes. "You mean there's some sort of message on them?"

"You got it. I'm going over to take a look."

"I'm going with you."

"No," Ermete says, stopping him. "You're going to see my friend. Without me."

"But I'll just get arrested—"

"I don't think he's under surveillance. He's not a big fish. He's more of a movie and music pirate. But he's one of those guys who knows everything about everybody. You know the type."

"No. I don't know the type."

"Try to work with me here. . . ." Ermete walks over to the table and scribbles something on a piece of paper. "He might just know something about the man with the violin. Like if anyone's seen him. Or if there are rumors spreading around . . ." He hands him the piece of paper. "Go and tell him I sent you. Ask him for everything he knows. But don't give him too many details, and most importantly, don't tell him your real name."

"It all sounds pretty shady to me," Harvey remarks.

"And it is. But didn't you want to do something, too?"

"So what's 'Bucatino'?" the boy asks, reading the note.

"It's a restaurant a few blocks from here. Go down three hundred meters and take the first right. You can't miss it." Ermete opens the garage door.

"How do I recognize your friend?"

"That'll be easy," the man mumbles as he slips on his helmet. He climbs onto the motorcycle and revs the engine. "He looks just like Vasco Rossi."

"Who?"

232

"You guys don't get Vasco Rossi in America?"

"Never heard of him."

The motorcycle roars like a military helicopter. "He's a little guy, with a bit of a belly and long hair. His name's Joe. You'll recognize him because they operated on his vocal cords. In order to talk he needs to keep a little amplifier box pressed up against his throat."

"Amplifier box," Harvey says, making a mental note of it.

"And close the garage door!" shouts Ermete, peeling out through the snow.

Elettra and the Gypsy woman are sitting cross-legged on the plastic-covered floor of the shanty. Neither one says a word. They've begun to take the teeth out of the trunk, dividing them into little piles according to the letters engraved into them. So far, they've made five piles.

"Were the lines bad?" asks Elettra suddenly, fishing a handful of incisors and molars out of the trunk.

The Gypsy doesn't reply. She continues to sort through the teeth with methodical precision. "There are no good or bad lines. There are only lines," she explains after a moment.

"The lines about the end of the world are bad lines."

"That depends on the world you live in," the woman rebuts.

Elettra can't think of anything to say to that. She lets more time pass before she says, "If I asked you to tell me what you saw in my palm . . . would you do it?"

"Only if you really wanted me to. Do you?"

"I'm not sure."

"Then I won't tell you." The Gypsy's eyes dart over to look at the door of the shanty. They hear footsteps drawing near.

"That must be my friend . . . ," Elettra guesses. She goes up to the door made of streetside posters and opens it up to let Ermete in.

"What a disaster . . . ," the man complains, brushing off his muddy jacket. "I tripped and almost took an ice-cold bath in the Tiber."

Once inside, he raises his hand to greet the Gypsy woman. "Ermete!" he says, introducing himself. She replies, a hint of gold sparkling through her hair.

"This is incredible!" Ermete cries a moment later, staring at the trunk. "Why didn't Alfred ever tell me about this?"

"There's one letter on each tooth," explains Elettra, showing Ermete the little piles they've made on the floor. "So far, we've found five different letters."

"It would take a whole day to sort through all these . . . ," the engineer begins, looking at the hundreds of teeth still lying in the trunk.

"That's why I called you. I was hoping you'd show up here with Harvey and Sheng."

"They were busy. Besides, they wouldn't both have fit in the sidecar. Let me see the letters . . . ," Ermete says, changing the subject.

The letters are "I," "T," "E," "R" and "M."

The man scratches his head. "What do you think this is all about?"

"I don't have the foggiest idea," the girl replies. "But the professor did, it seems."

"Didn't he explain any of this to you?" Ermete asks the Gypsy.

"He just said they were looking for it. And that they mustn't find out where to look."

"So there's something we need to look for in this trunk. . . ." Ermete's hands dive down into the teeth, all the way up to his elbows. "But what?" he wonders.

The three continue to sort through the teeth until, an hour later, the gas heater sputters off and the bitter cold once again starts to creep in through the walls of the shack. Elettra looks at the piles of teeth. "Still the same letters . . . ," she points out.

"The only thing I can think of is that you can spell my name with them . . . ," Ermete notes, rubbing his hands together to warm them. He picks up a canine, three molars and two incisors and lays them out one beside the other, forming a grinning yellowed ERMETE. Then he uses the teeth as tiles in a macabre mosaic, trying to form other words. " 'Meet' . . . 'Rite' . . ."

The Gypsy tries to get the heater working again, but it's no use. Elettra rubs her fingers, which have grown numb.

" 'Tremiti.' That's the name of a group of islands. . . . Could that be it? Maybe what we're looking for is there. Or . . . 'terrier' . . . ," Ermete says aloud, still trying. " 'Meter' . . . 'Miter' . . . 'Remit' . . ."

Elettra's fingers are tingling. "What did you say?"

" 'Term'?" mumbles Ermete. " 'Termite'?"

"No, wait. Go back. You said a word that made me think of . . . the sun god. Nero. Fire . . ."

"Maybe you're just getting a little too cold," says the engineer with a smile as he rearranges the teeth, one beside the other. "Anyway, I know what you're thinking of: Mithra. But we can't

235

spell it with these. Unless there are teeth with the letters 'H' and 'A' in that trunk."

"Hold on!" cries Elettra, struck by a revelation. "Actually, we do have another letter."

"Which one?"

The girl thrusts her hand into her pocket and fishes out the tooth they were given by the professor. "There's a letter here, too! I thought it was a circle, or a ring. . . . But what if it was actually the letter 'O'?"

Elettra lays the tooth down beside five others.

OMITRE.

"Ah . . . ," Ermete murmurs, reading the letters. "That's it! But the 'O' doesn't go here. . . . It goes on the other end."

MITREO.

"Meaning . . . ?" asks Elettra.

"The *mitreo*!" Ermete explains. "That's the name of the temple where they worshipped Mithra centuries ago."

"Keep going. . . ."

"There was a really famous one in Rome, one underground, beneath two other churches." Ermete grabs Elettra's hand, clutching it tightly. "And it's completely surrounded by water. An underground river that flows all around it. . . ."

"A ring of water?" asks Elettra.

"Precisely!" Ermete cheers. "What better place could there be to hide a Ring of Fire?"

"So where is it?"

"San Clemente," replies Ermete, rising to his feet.

* * *

236

"We've got to go," Jacob Mahler orders Beatrice. He's as calm as a summer storm. He hurls an empty suitcase to the ground, slams the violin case on top of it and adds, "Immediately."

"Go where?"

"You just get the car started."

"And you?"

The man walks by her, leaving a trail of his characteristic cologne behind him. He opens up a wardrobe, yanks out his wheeled carry-on bag and throws it into the hallway. "I've got to talk with the girl."

"To tell her what?"

"She lied to me." Jacob Mahler walks back and kicks the empty suitcase, making the violin case tumble down at Beatrice's feet. "And I don't intend to let her get away with it again."

"What are you going to do?"

"Ask her questions."

"And if she doesn't answer them?"

Jacob raises an eyebrow, as if to warn her that she's pushing his buttons. "Go downstairs and get the car ready," he orders.

But Beatrice insists. "If she doesn't answer them?"

An instant later the wind has been knocked out of her. Mahler has pinned her up against the wall with catlike grace and thrust his face up centimeters from hers.

"Listen up," he says. "Because I'm not going to tell you this a second time. I'm going in there to talk to the little brat. And she's going to tell me what I want to know. Because it just so happens that, who knows how, she and her friends are keeping me from tracking down what my boss wants me to deliver to him."

"Are you afraid, Jacob Mahler?" Beatrice hisses, suffocating in his grasp. "Are you afraid of Heremit Devil?"

Mahler strikes her with his open palm and throws her to the floor. The slap echoes through the room. "I told you never to say that name."

"Heremit . . . Devil . . . ," the young woman coughs, staying on the ground, her face shielded behind her arm. And she repeats it again. "Heremit Devil."

Jacob Mahler clenches his fists.

Beatrice props herself up against the wall. She slowly wipes her mouth with the back of her hand, noticing that her lips are red with blood. And then she says, "Behold! The great Jacob Mahler, the infallible killer . . . who beats women and gets fooled by a group of kids."

The man glares down at her with a sneer. "You're pathetic."

"Maybe. But you need me."

"I don't think so."

"Oh, but I think so," replies Beatrice. "And I'm telling you, don't go near that girl."

"Who's going to stop me? You?"

"If I have to, yes," retorts Beatrice, pulling the gun out of her pocket.

Mahler lets out a laugh and turns his back to her. "You don't know what you're doing. It isn't even loaded."

"Oh, really?" Beatrice says threateningly.

"Go warm up the car . . . ," Jacob Mahler orders, leaning over to get something from his carry-on bag.

"And you go to hell!" shouts Beatrice, pulling the trigger.

FOURTH STASIMON

"I know who he is. His name's Jacob Mahler. He's German. Former child prodigy. Ex–secret service. He went underground ten years ago to pursue a career in crime. They say he's got a passion for music. And that Mahler isn't his real name."

"I just want to know why he was sent to Rome."

"To kill Alfred, I imagine. And to get the briefcase."

"So . . . they're actually willing to commit murder."

"They already have, it seems."

"And there's nothing we can do?"

"The agreement was not to interfere with the kids."

"The agreement was also not to kill Alfred."

"I don't know what to think. I don't know who's behind all this. Or why. I haven't even managed to track her down. Maybe Alfred was the one who let something slip. . . ."

"I don't think so."

"Well, then?"

"Well, a high-profile professional killer like him doesn't decide to come to Rome all on his own. He must've been hired by someone, someone who knows about the Ring of Fire. About everything, basically. So the question is . . . who is it?"

"I don't know, but they're definitely dangerous."

"We've got to warn them."

"What you're actually thinking is: we've got to stop them."
"No, we can't stop them. Not any longer."
"Why not?"
"Because I know my niece."

25

THE SANCTUARY

WHEN SHENG GETS BACK TO ERMETE'S PLACE, NOBODY'S THERE.

He rings the doorbell once, twice, three times, but no one answers.

He walks all the way around the building to make sure it's the right one, he rings the bell again, he shouts, but all he gets for his efforts is an annoyed neighbor who glares at him from the floor above.

Sheng waves, smiling sheepishly.

Then he looks around, frenetically counting the seconds and regretting he doesn't have either a cell phone or a number to call. The only thing that comes to his mind is to go back to the Domus Quintilia, which is . . . somewhere in Trastevere, he thinks.

He spreads the map open in front of him and starts looking. He'll need to cross back over the bridge and then, maybe, take bus number nine. Or twelve.

"Why is it so complicated?" he says hopelessly.

He folds up the map angrily and decides to wait five more minutes. "But only five," he says aloud.

The seconds tick by slowly, and when four of the allotted five minutes have gone by, Sheng sees Harvey appear at the end of the sidewalk.

"*Hao!* Harvey!" he says, greeting him.

"Sheng! When did you get here?"

"An hour ago, maybe two?"

"That's impossible. I've been gone less than thirty minutes."

"Where've you been? Why isn't anyone here?"

Harvey pulls out a set of keys and unlocks the garage.

"I went to a restaurant down the street. It was fantastic! I'd never eaten *bucatini* before!"

"Gee, you seem so worried . . . ," Sheng chides him. "Elettra? Ermete?"

The garage door goes up with a metallic hum. Harvey goes over everything he knows: the trunk full of teeth that Elettra found, Ermete taking off in his sidecar, and his own meeting at the restaurant with the man's really shady friend.

"So what's the guy like?"

Harvey shakes his head, disappointed. "He didn't make a very good impression on me. Actually, we didn't talk much at all. Also the guy wasn't really talking . . . he . . . he was wheezing through a little box. But when I asked him about the man with the violin . . ."

"What did he tell you?"

Harvey snorts. "Barely anything. But when I asked if he knew him, the moment I brought up the subject, it's like he . . . woke up. He had me sit down, he ordered me a dish of *bucatini* and he asked me around three hundred questions."

"And you?"

"I ate my pasta."

"And his questions?"

"I made up a bunch of stuff." Harvey smiles. "I'm getting to be almost as good as you are at inventing stories. But I'm telling you, I don't like that guy one bit."

"Did you tell him about the briefcase?"

"What do you think I am, an idiot?"

"*Hao!* You're great, Harvey. . . . So did you tell him or didn't you?"

"No!" the American boy snaps. "I didn't tell him anything!"

Sheng goes to open the fridge and comes back with an ice-cold Coca-Cola. "I don't know. . . ."

"You don't know what?"

"There are so many things I don't know right now. . . . I wonder if it was a good idea to tell Ermete about all this."

"I've wondered that, too," admits Harvey.

"And . . . ?"

"And I thought he might even be one of them."

Sheng gapes at him. "How come?"

"We know he was working with the professor, but we have no way of knowing if the professor really trusted him. . . ."

"But in his journal he wrote down Ermete's name right after 'Study the tops and the wooden map. Find out how it's used.'"

"The fact is . . . I don't know how to explain it to you, Sheng, but I had the funny feeling . . . that Ermete's friend knew all about the man with the violin."

"What made you think that?"

"He never asked me anything about him. He just asked questions about me and how I knew Ermete. Listen . . ." Harvey starts to count points off on his fingertips. "Ermete knew Professor

243

Alfred Van Der Berger. Ermete's friend knows the man with the violin. The man with the violin kills the professor. What's the only common denominator?"

"Ermete," Sheng admits, but then he adds, "But he helped us. And he showed us how to use the map."

"Of course, but we were the ones who had the map," Harvey reminds him.

Sheng is silent for a moment, thinking things through. "And we basically brought it over to him."

"Exactly. Speaking of which, what did you find out about the house over in Coppedè?"

Sheng shows him the photos and admits how he was suddenly so scared he turned around and ran off.

"Scared of what, exactly?"

"I don't know. Just plain scared. It's like, in that house, there was something . . . something scary, I guess."

Harvey looks at his friend with a faint smile. "Well, that explains it."

Just then, a phone call comes in. The sudden, metallic ring makes them start.

"Should we answer it?" Sheng asks on the second ring.

"It might be Ermete's mother. She's called ten times already."

"How do you know that?"

"Just listen. The answering machine picks up automatically on the fifth ring."

And, in fact, on the fifth ring, they hear the woman's shrill, nagging voice. The boys exchange a grin and then the answering machine cuts off the monologue with a beep.

"We'd better get out of here," suggests Harvey when the room is quiet again. "The more I think about that guy I talked to, the more I feel like putting a few miles between him and me."

"And if he knows Ermete, he must know where he lives, too. . . . So where should we go?" asks Sheng. "We don't know where Elettra and Ermete are, and—"

"Unless . . ." Harvey suddenly remembers Ermete's cell phone number. He tries calling, but hangs up again after a moment. "It's switched off. Or dead. In any case, it's not working."

"That's bad news."

"We've only got two alternatives."

"Try out one of these fantastic board games?" suggests Sheng.

"No. The first is going back to the hotel and calling it a day. At least for today."

"And the second?"

"We could—"

"No!" cries Sheng, guessing what Harvey's going to suggest.

"I haven't said anything yet!"

"But I can already tell. . . ." Sheng continues to nervously pace across the room with long strides.

"Sheng? What can you tell?"

The Chinese boy picks up his backpack and puts all their gear into it. "Let's at least pack up all our stuff first."

"Do you want to hear the second alternative or not?"

"I know . . . ," sighs Sheng. "We go back together to the Coppedè district. And we look for Mistral."

Harvey tosses the journal into his friend's backpack. "Sometimes you amaze me."

"*Hao* . . . ," mumbles Sheng. "But I'm warning you: to get there we'll need to take a bunch of buses. And we're almost out of tickets."

A few minutes later, Harvey and Sheng walk out of the apartment. The overcast sky threatens to snow. They reach the sidewalk and look around suspiciously. But the few people who are walking along, chilled, don't seem to take any interest in them.

"How can you tell if someone's following you?" asks Sheng.

"You just keep your eyes open," Harvey answers.

They head toward the bus stop.

"Harvey?"

"What?"

"This is all really exciting . . . ," Sheng admits. "But . . . now . . . I almost wish it was over."

"So do I," the American boy replies.

Behind them, the telephone in Ermete's empty apartment rings five times. The answering machine automatically clicks on. "Harvey! Sheng!" the engineer's voice is heard shouting as it's recorded on the tape. "I just saw that you called! You've got to come immediately to the Basilica di San Clemente! I repeat: the Basilica di San Clemente! We might just have found . . . well, the you-know-what. . . . Come on! We'll be waiting for you!"

26

THE WATER

THE BASILICA DI SAN CLEMENTE LOOKS LIKE AN ANIMAL CROUCHED beneath the snow. Inside, the golden dome over the altar is filled with the whispers of the few tourists and the echoing of their footsteps.

Elettra and Ermete walk in through a side door.

"I've never been in here before . . . ," says the girl, looking around. "It's a very pretty church."

Ermete points at the nave to their left, where the ticket booth is. "Lucky you," he sighs. "This must be my thirtieth time here. I think I know all the churches in Rome inch by inch."

Elettra glances at him inquisitively.

"My mom made me be an altar boy," the engineer explains. "Back when she was still proud of me."

The ticket booth is closed, but Ermete takes advantage of his old acquaintances and, after a brief chat with the priest, who's as tall and gaunt as a sardine, he's given keys that unlock a very large door. On the other side of the door is a stairway that makes its way steeply underground in a long series of white steps.

"Where's the *mitreo?*" asks Elettra.

"Way, way down," replies Ermete.

Below the church of San Clemente is a second church. A row of floor lamps turns on with a chorus of clicks. Once she's reached the foot of the stairs, Elettra has the impression she's walked into a stone forest lit up by torches. The ancient walls are like canopies of intertwined branches. The tombs carved into the walls, the niches and the writings on the tombstones are like wrinkled bark. There are Latin inscriptions and fragments of mosaics. Frescoes paled over time. Faded images with dull colors.

And a damp silence.

"Is this it?" Elettra asks, making her way through the strange forest of bricks and stone like a nocturnal animal.

"No. This is the old church. The *mitreo* is even farther down," replies Ermete, leading her toward the nave on the left, to a strange sculpted stairway that looks like a well. On the floor are the remains of columns, which jut up like truncated tusks. "We have to go down this way," he says.

Beneath the old underground church is an even older temple.

They can hear the river now.

The temple beneath the church is dark and damp. Water gurgles around it, inside the walls. Elettra has the sensation she's been caught up in the current of an invisible river held back by only stones and darkness.

She fights back a shiver.

"It's this way, if I remember correctly . . . ," says Ermete, turning down a corridor with a tall, narrow ceiling and then down a second one illuminated by a single beam of electric light reflecting off its golden archways.

All around them is the sound of the water. And it's cold. But since the very moment they stepped into the temple, into the damp embrace of the underground river, Elettra's felt hot.

"We're close. . . . I can feel it . . . ," she whispers.

The *mitreo* is a long, narrow room with a vaulted ceiling and a row of seats carved into the stone walls. In the center is an altar, rising up over which are four head-shaped sculptures. Elettra stares at the altar through the bars of the gate, the only way in.

"That's the third altar, the oldest one of them all," Ermete says, pointing. "If I remember well, over it is a sculpture of the god Mithra battling a bull. Funny, don't you think?"

"Yeah," replies Elettra, although she doesn't see anything funny in it at all.

Ermete kneels down by the gate's lock. "An altar to the sun god, located underground and surrounded by water."

Maybe that's what he finds funny. . . .

"An altar over which is the depiction of an ancient god defeating a bull . . . ," murmurs Ermete, examining the lock carefully. "Who knows what the bull ever did to him?" He pulls a Swiss Army knife out of his pocket. "I used to be crazy about locks. And I found that basically none of them are really foolproof."

"You're going to pick the lock?"

"Something like that, yes," the engineer admits. "If I'm lucky, that is." At first, the little knife turns around uselessly, and then, suddenly . . . the lock gives off a clack. "Done."

The gate creaks open.

"After you, *mademoiselle*!" jokes Ermete, spreading his arm out into the empty room.

Elettra takes a deep breath and walks in.

"See anything?" the engineer asks, his hand brushing over the seats carved into the walls.

"No. But it's really small."

"Hey, are you all right?"

"I'm burning up," replies Elettra.

They walk all the way around the room twice. The altar to Mithra is a sculpted parallelepiped with the image of the god in human form. The floor around it is slick and smooth, having been worn down over the centuries. There are eleven openings in the ceiling.

"Is this where Emperor Nero worshiped the sun?" Elettra asks in a hushed voice, afraid she'll disturb the atmosphere of such an ancient place. Her hand brushes over the bas-relief work on the altar and she can feel her skin burning.

Ermete shrugs. "I haven't got the slightest idea. But if you need to search a *mitreo*, this is the right place to start."

"We don't even know what we need to look for."

"Or how to look for it. Ring of Fire?" whispers Ermete. "Ring of Fire, you there?"

Elettra can't help but smile. "I don't think you can just call it like it's your pet cat. . . ."

"Who knows?"

It's not easy to find anything unusual in the ancient simplicity of the room. Stone, shadows and eleven niches in the ceiling. An altar with four heads sculpted over it. And the water flowing by on the other side of the walls.

"Well, unless you have any ideas, I give up," Ermete says after a while. He leans against the damp wall. "It's like playing a game when you don't know the rules."

"Ring of Fire . . . Ring of Fire . . . ," repeats Elettra, standing in the center of the room. "It's hot in here."

"You think so? I'm freezing."

The girl kneels down on the ground and rests her hands against one of the stones.

Cold. Cold. Cold.

She starts to move, crawling along on the floor.

Cold. Cold. Cold.

"What are you doing?"

"Shhh . . . ," responds Elettra. "You can't understand how much energy I've got inside of me." She shuts her eyes and tries to concentrate, keeping her hands resting on the stones. The further she goes, the more her fingers start to move on their own, like antennas. They're sensing the *mitreo*'s ancient signals, which have remained unchanged over time.

Cold. Cold. Cold.

Warm.

"I think I'm getting closer . . . ," she whispers.

She touches the stones around the warm one. Cold. Cold. Cold.

But the one in the center is hot.

"It's here . . . ," the girl tells Ermete, resting the palms of both hands against the stone, which is identical to the others and yet so different at the same time.

The engineer kneels down beside her. He raps on the surface of the stone with the handle of his Swiss Army knife.

"It sounds hollow," he says with a faint voice.

Elettra doesn't reply.

"I could try to pry it out," suggests Ermete. "But I'm not sure I'll be able to."

"Try," the girl whispers.

Just then, they hear the sound of footsteps. Ermete barely has time to say, "I think someone's coming . . . ," when a creak echoes through the underground room. A stocky man in a black leather jacket and a dirty T-shirt walks into the *mitreo*.

"So in the end . . . *rrr* . . . I found you, huh . . . *rrr* . . . ?" he exclaims. His rough, raspy voice is amplified by a little black plastic box pressed up against his throat.

"Joe?" Ermete asks, astonished. "What are you doing here?"

"Let's just say . . . *rrr* . . . that I stopped by to hear . . . *rrr* . . . your . . . *rrr* . . . answering machine . . . *rrr* . . . ," hisses Joe Vinile. "And I said to myself . . . *rrr* . . . It looks like old Ermete . . . *rrr* . . . wants to do this all on his own."

"Ermete," asks Elettra. "Who is that man?"

"Ermete . . . *rrr* . . . ? Who is that girl . . . *rrr* . . . ?" Joe Vinile lets out a burst of bloodcurdling laughter.

Ermete starts to get to his feet, but the man stops him in his tracks by aiming a shiny black gun at him. Then he coughs. "Hold it . . . *rrr* . . ."

Elettra doesn't understand. "Ermete!" she cries in disbelief.

"Be a good girl . . . *rrr* . . . you brat . . . *rrr* . . . . You know, I think Ermete . . . *rrr* . . . tricked . . . *rrr* . . . both of us . . . *rrr* . . . ."

"Why are you following us?" the engineer asks.

Joe Vinile's gun darts around threateningly with his every

move. "No, you tell me something . . . *rrr* . . . Are they all . . . *rrr* . . . little kids?"

Ermete nods.

Joe Vinile cackles. "So who's going to tell . . . *rrr* . . . Mahler . . . *rrr* . . . that he's been fooled . . . *rrr* . . . by a group of little snot-noses . . . *rrr* . . . ?"

Beatrice walks into Mistral's room and orders, "Let's get out of here, now!"

The girl jumps to her feet. "Was that a gunshot I heard?"

"It doesn't matter!" shouts Beatrice. "We've got to get out of here! Right away!" She goes back into the hallway, finishes tying up and gagging Jacob Mahler, grabs him by the arms and starts to drag him toward the bathroom. She kicks the door open and lifts up the killer's body just enough to dump him into the bathtub.

"Be good, now. . . ."

"Beatrice?" Mistral calls out to her.

"Coming!" The young woman looks down at Mahler one last time and runs out of the bathroom.

Mistral is standing in the hallway, staring down at the bloodstains on the floor. "Is he dead?"

"No, I don't think so. But I put him out of action for a while," Beatrice says in a low voice. "Now we've got to do one last thing. Grab that!" she orders, pointing at the violin case. "And I . . . I'm calling a few friends."

She runs into another room, picks up the manila envelope full of computer-printed photographs and returns to Mistral's room. "A little evidence here . . . ," she says, scattering photos around on the floor. "And a little in the other rooms." She leaves only a couple of pictures inside the envelope. "We might need these, just in case." She looks at Mistral. "Ready?"

"Yeah."

"Good."

They rush down the stairs.

Once outside, Beatrice points at the yellow Mini parked at the curb. "Good," she repeats. She grabs her cell phone out of her pocket and hurriedly punches in the number of the carabinieri.

With the shadows of the afternoon stretching out like dark clouds, the archway leading into Coppedè looks like a portal in a fantasy film, the kind that divides the world of the heroes from the world of the villains.

"Everything okay?" Harvey asks Sheng.

"My arm hurts, but it's nothing," he answers, clenching his teeth.

"Should we keep going?"

"Well, since we came all the way back here . . . I guess so."

The two boys walk through the arch. Once on the other side, nothing seems to have changed. The same crisp air, the same people rushing along and the same heaps of snow. But the buildings rising up all around them have different expressions.

"See what I mean?" asks Sheng.

"It's fantastic . . . ," replies Harvey.

Sheng shakes his head, reassured by his friend's calmness. "Glad to hear you say that." After a while, he adds, "I was thinking about Ermete. If he really is one of them . . ."

"Yeah?"

"If he really is, then something doesn't make sense: the phone call last night at the professor's apartment."

"What about it?"

"Well, if Ermete was one of them, he wouldn't have called. He'd already have known that the professor was dead."

Harvey nods, impressed. "You're right," he says. "You're absolutely right."

Sheng looks up and points down one of the tree-lined lanes. "There. That's the house."

The little villa's windows and shutters are still closed. An icy wind whistles through the empty arcades. Seen from the outside, its layout escapes all comprehension. It's as though it changes shape depending on which side it's viewed from.

The boys walk all the way around the garden, protected by the wrought iron gate. Twisted frost-covered trees rise up in the winter snow like skeletons. On the opposite side, a black gate creaks in the wind.

"It's open," says Harvey.

Cleared of snow, a little path and three steps lead up to a patio with two small yellow columns.

"The front door looks open, too . . . ," adds Harvey.

"That's strange," Sheng murmurs. "Why would it be open? It wasn't open before."

Harvey walks through the gate, keeping his eye on the front door. It's definitely ajar. Sheng follows him, his heart thumping wildly in his chest. Harvey stops a few meters from the partially open door.

He sees a doorbell.

He rings it.

27

THE STONE

METERS AND METERS BELOW THE BASILICA DI SAN CLEMENTE, THREE people are struggling with a large stone. With their panting, pulling and pushing, the stone has begun to give, wobbling like an old loose tooth. The time has gone by slowly. No one has come down to disturb them.

After much effort, the stone is finally pushed to the side, revealing a large niche. Full of dust, the space is about as large as a shoe box. Barely big enough to trap a mouse in.

As the niche is revealed at last, Joe Vinile raises his gun. His raspy voice warns Ermete to move aside. Then he points the gun at Elettra. "Take a look . . . *rrr* . . . ," orders Joe. "See what's inside . . . *rrr* . . . !"

Mice in a trap, thinks Elettra, kneeling down beside the gap.

There's dust. Her hands are as hot as lightbulbs. Beneath the dust is more dust. And beneath that are strips of linen.

"Anyone home?" asks Harvey, slowly pushing open the front door to the house.

On the other side of the door is a dark room with a stairway leading up to the second floor. A few paintings on the walls. A little table. A lamp, which is switched off.

A cold wind howls down the staircase.

Harvey repeats his question and then walks in. The foyer leads into other rooms. The doors are all arch-shaped. The ceiling is painted light blue.

Harvey turns around. Sheng joins him, his face pale.

"Scared?"

"You bet."

"What do we do now?"

"I don't know." Sheng looks around. "The top warned us about the guard dog . . . maybe we'd better not bother him."

Harvey stares at the steps leading upstairs. "Should we go up?" he asks.

Crouching down on the floor of the *mitreo*, Elettra brushes away the dust. Her fingers touch an object carefully wrapped in old strips of linen. It's long and slender, sticking out edgewise from the niche.

"Well . . . *rrr* . . . ?" Joe Vinile asks impatiently.

Water gurgles noisily from behind the walls around them.

In the opposite corner of the room, Ermete nervously bites his fingernails.

Elettra grabs hold of the object and begins to pull it out, discovering that it's very light. Her hands are burning up. Trembling, she rests the bundle of linen on the floor of the room.

It's held together by a golden seal.

"Well . . . *rrr* . . . ?" rasps Joe Vinile. His voice is as pleasant as a handful of salt on an open wound. "Take off . . . *rrr* . . . the cloth . . . *rrr* . . . !"

Elettra turns toward Ermete, but the engineer is staring off into space.

"What are you waiting for . . . *rrr* . . . ?" coughs Joe. "Open that thing up . . . *rrr* . . . ! Let me see . . . *rrr* . . . what the heck . . . *rrr* . . . it is!"

Elettra touches the ring-shaped seal. She pulls on it gently, just enough to undo the strips of cloth.

Inside is a circular object. It's made of iron.

Elettra's hands hastily unravel the last strips of linen.

She takes it in her hand. She holds it up.

It's a mirror.

On the second floor of the house is a hallway with four doors. One is open, and it leads into a small bedroom with a light blue ceiling. Closed shutters seal off its only window, and streaming in through the slats are the last traces of daylight.

"Whoever was staying here," observes Harvey, "they didn't leave very long ago."

Sheng picks up a few of the photos and then drops them with a shout. "The professor!" Harvey picks them up again and takes a look. They're all very similar: Alfred Van Der Berger's lifeless body sprawled out on the ground. And, standing beside him, the man with the violin.

A shiver of terror runs down the boys' backs.

"We've got to get out of here . . . ," murmurs Sheng.

Harvey steps out of the room and into the hallway. Trailed across the floor is a long smear of blood. It leads into a bathroom.

"Harvey . . . ," Sheng insists. "It's not a good idea to stay here."

Harvey follows the red smear, his heart in his throat.

The bathroom door is open. Inside is a large mirror, a sink and a bathtub hidden behind a plastic shower curtain.

The trail of blood disappears behind the curtain.

Very slowly, Harvey moves closer.

And, very slowly, he pushes it aside.

"Harvey . . . ," Sheng whispers from the hallway. And then, the instant he hears his friend scream, he shouts, "Harvey! Harvey!"

28
THE RING

Joe Vinile's gun snakes around before Elettra's eyes.

"Let me see . . . *rrr* . . . !" the man growls, making her move back.

His forehead is beaded with sweat and his hair is plastered down against his shiny skull. He kneels on the ground, panting, and rests his sweaty fingers on the mirror.

"That's . . . *rrr* . . . all . . . *rrr* . . . ?" he remarks. He turns it over in his fingers, baffled. "What the hell . . . *rrr* . . . did we find?"

Ermete comes closer. The object casts out gleams of cracked silver and mercury. And it looks just like what it is: an old concave mirror, its reflective side slightly larger than a melon. It has an irregularly shaped edge, as if it was one piece of a much larger mirror, later set in a bronze frame.

"The Ring of Fire . . . ," whispers Ermete.

Elettra refuses to look at it. *It's a mirror*, she thinks.

"A mirror . . . *rrr* . . . a broken mirror . . . *rrr* . . . !" growls Joe Vinile. His large, flabby body shakes in a violent fit of laughter. He sets it down on the ground and struggles back to his feet. "We . . . *rrr* . . . did all that . . . *rrr* . . . just to find . . . *rrr* . . . a

broken . . . *rrr* . . . mirror . . . *rrr* . . . ? Ha! Ha! Ha! If Little
Linch . . . *rrr* . . . knew what he died for . . . *rrr* . . . ! A stupid . . .
rrr . . . mirror . . . *rrr* . . . !"

"A mirror . . . ," Ermete whispers. Then he adds, as if in a
trance, "Light that turns into fire. Life that turns into destruction.
Why didn't I think of it before?"

"What are you . . . *rrr* . . . babbling about?" croaks Joe Vinile.

Ermete looks at Elettra, his eyes sparkling with excitement,
but this time she's the one staring into empty space. Her curly
black hair is an impenetrable barrier around her face.

The engineer continues to think out loud. "That's what
Prometheus used to steal fire from the gods! A simple concave
mirror! Just what you need to concentrate the rays of the sun and
transform light into fire."

"So what : . . *rrr* . . . ?" breaks in Joe Vinile.

But Ermete is a raging river. "Now I understand all those ref-
erences, those incomprehensible steps that Alfred was trying to
piece together. The entire history of the Ring of Fire, which reappears every hundred years . . . and was passed down from hand to
hand. From the ancient Chaldeans, who worshiped fire, to the
Greeks, who invented the myth of Prometheus, from Magna
Graecia, with Archimedes using mirrors to defend Syracuse from
the Romans, to the Romans themselves, who brought the mirror
here. Don't you see, Elettra? Nero didn't burn down Rome at
night, but during the day . . . with this!"

Joe Vinile snorts. "You're saying . . . *rrr* . . . that this . . . *rrr* . . .
piece of glass . . . *rrr* . . . is worth something?"

"It could have tremendous value," replies Ermete. "Or none
at all."

Elettra is silent. She doesn't look up. She's thinking.

She thinks of Ermete and Harvey and Sheng and Mistral.

She thinks of the professor.

She thinks of the mirror.

She thinks of the Ring of Fire. Which is a concave mirror. Perhaps the most ancient one in the world. Perhaps the very first one. It's the mirror of fire, and she's burning up with a single desire: to get out of there.

To get outside. Under the starry sky.

Joe Vinile uses his foot to flip the mirror over. Carved into the bronze frame are a drawing and an inscription. "And this . . . *rrr* . . . ? What is it? A comet . . . *rrr* . . . ? And this . . . *latinorum*? You've studied this stuff . . . *rrr* . . . What the heck does it say . . . *rrr* . . . ?"

Ermete leans over to pick up the mirror, but Joe sticks out his foot to stop him. "Look at it . . . *rrr* . . . but don't touch it . . . *rrr* . . . !"

Ermete squints in the darkness. He reads the inscription on the back of the mirror and lets out a little laugh.

"What's so funny . . . *rrr* . . . ?"

"The professor had it right," the engineer says in a soft voice, once again trying to catch Elettra's eye. "It's a quote from Seneca. It's from his book about comets."

"And what does . . . *rrr* . . . it say?"

" 'There is an invisible purpose behind the visible world.' "

Joe Vinile grunts. "That doesn't mean . . . *rrr* . . . a damn thing."

"That's not true . . . ," Elettra cuts in, whirling around.

Her hair is flowing as though moved by an approaching storm.

And her eyes are completely yellow.

* * *

A man is sprawled out inside the bathtub. His hands and feet are bound, his mouth is gagged and his chest is covered in blood.

"Harvey!" shouts Sheng, bursting into the bathroom and hugging his friend. "Are you okay?"

The boy nods.

"That's him, isn't it?" murmurs Sheng.

"The man with the violin," Harvey confirms in a whisper. "But what's he doing in there?"

"Is he dead?"

The man's eyes are closed and he seems to have lost a lot of blood. The whole tub is stained red.

"I think so." Harvey takes a step closer.

"What are you doing?" cries Sheng.

"I just want to make sure. . . ."

"Harvey, don't do it! Let's get out of here!"

The American boy takes a second step toward the tub. And then a third. He doesn't take his eyes off the man's motionless face.

"Come back here!" pleads Sheng.

Harvey takes another step, leans over and touches the man's arm with his fingertips. Then he takes a small step back, stiff with tension. He turns to look back at Sheng and murmurs, "Yeah . . . he's dead."

Suddenly, a hand tries to grab him around the waist. Harvey doesn't even have time to turn around.

Sheng shouts, "Harvey! Look out!"

The man with the violin has opened his eyes.

Harvey trips over the plastic shower curtain, yanking out its rings. He slips and falls to the floor.

"No!" screams Sheng, running up to him and trying to drag him to his feet. The man with the violin thrashes around in the tub, trying to free himself. The boys don't stay there a moment longer. They race out of the bathroom. They rush all the way up the hall and down the stairs, out the front door and across the path.

They don't even stop when they've crossed through the front gate.

Or even when they're past the arch.

They don't stop. They just keep running.

When he sees Elettra's yellow eyes, Joe Vinile backs up toward the exit of the *mitreo*. "Hey . . . *rrr* . . . kid . . . *rrr* . . . what the heck is . . . *rrr* . . . happening to you . . . *rrr* . . . ?" he croaks. The moment he reaches the door, a shadow appears behind him. A dark shadow revealing a tiny glimmer of gold. Joe lets out a grunt and turns his head just enough to face the person standing behind him. "And who . . . *rrr* . . . the devil . . . *rrr* . . . are you?"

Ermete lunges at Joe Vinile, giving him a punch that the man resists as though it were a caress. Ermete tries a second time, but Joe rushes at him, head down, ramming him up against a wall of the *mitreo*. The two are locked in a desperate struggle, with Joe rushing at Ermete and Ermete trying to hoist Joe up by the belt.

Elettra just stares at the Gypsy woman, stunned.

"I came to tell you, child . . . that your life line is still very long," the woman announces.

"Do something!" grunts Ermete, punching Joe Vinile in the back wildly.

"Stop!" shouts Elettra.

But the two continue to fight.

"The gun! Look out!" the girl screams.

Only then does Joe Vinile seem to remember that he still has a gun in his hand. He easily breaks free from Ermete's awkward hold and takes a step back. He opens his mouth to say something, but without the amplifier box his voice is just a series of throaty grunts.

He raises the gun over his head and takes a second step backward.

Mistake.

His foot lands right inside the niche in the floor and he loses his balance. His head smacks against the altar to Mithra with a deafening thud. The gun falls to the floor with a metallic clatter.

A long silence fills the room.

The Gypsy woman is still standing at the door, bundled up in her thick layers of coats. Ermete pants, counting the ribs he thinks might still be intact. "Elettra?" he asks. "Are you okay?"

"Yes . . . At least I think so. Are you?"

The engineer coughs out a yes and then takes a few unsteady steps toward Joe Vinile. "He's unconscious," he says, kicking the gun away. "We've got to get out of here, right now. . . ."

Ermete looks around for the mirror, but the Gypsy darts out and stands between him and the Ring of Fire.

"Not you," she orders, raising her hand.

The man rubs his aching bones. "Not me . . . what?"

"You aren't the one who should take the Ring," the Gypsy explains. "She is."

Ermete shakes his head violently. "Listen, don't you get in the middle of this, too, okay? What difference does it make who takes it?"

"The Ring belongs to the one who is to wear it. And the mirror belongs to the one who is to look into it," the Gypsy replies adamantly.

"But I don't want to look into it!" Elettra protests.

"You can see your reflection in the mirror even with your eyes closed," the woman reminds her.

Ermete stares at her, not understanding. "Am I crazy, or are you two in on this together?"

Elettra walks up to him. "Are you one of them?" she asks, point-blank.

29

THE BETRAYAL

"WHY ARE WE STOPPING?" MISTRAL ASKS BEATRICE.

The young woman puts on her emergency lights as she pulls the yellow Mini up to the curb.

"We've still got one more thing to do . . . ," she says enigmatically. She motions to Mistral to get out of the car, and together they walk down a narrow lane. The air is cold and they can see their breath.

"Is he following us?" asks Mistral, hunching over slightly.

"No. He can't follow us," replies Beatrice. "At least I don't think so." Her lip has turned purple, and she can feel her temples throb with a dull pain.

Around them, Rome is immersed in the last chilly night of December. The night of San Silvestro. "Do you know why we call it that?" she asks Mistral.

"What?"

"New Year's Eve. We call it the night of San Silvestro, or Saint Sylvester." She even manages to smile. "I mean, if you mention the name Sylvester, the only thing that comes to my mind is the black-and-white cat who's always trying to catch Tweety, but always fails."

This even seems to amuse Mistral. "Well, we've got to try to be just like Tweety. And be good at not getting caught."

Beatrice nods and lifts the lid.

"Come on, Mistral," she orders, nodding her head toward the open Dumpster. "It's time for a little spring cleaning."

Mistral lifts up the violin case and throws it in.

"To hell with you!" exclaims Beatrice, slamming the lid shut.

She can feel the adrenaline in her body drain away, like hot water melting through snow. She realizes she has to move fast, before she collapses. She has to go away, far away, before she thinks back on what she's done.

"Okay," she says.

Mistral looks at her with her big, kind eyes. "Now what?"

"We get back in the car and I take you home."

"What about you?"

"Don't worry about me," she says. "I know what to do."

It's not true. But it's something, at least.

Ermete's eyes are open wide. His lip is trembling. His hands are nervously pressed up against his aching abdomen.

"Are you one of them?" Elettra asks him a second time.

"How could you think such a thing?"

"Isn't that man a friend of yours?"

"He's an acquaintance."

"He's one of them."

"H-how was I supposed to know that?" Ermete stammers. "I have nothing to do with . . . with *them*. How could I know who was following the professor . . . or me?"

"Why should I believe you?"

"Just do it," the engineer insists.

"Let the Gypsy see your hand," Elettra orders.

Ermete De Panfilis gapes. "What are you talking about, Elettra?" he exclaims. "What could showing her my hand possibly accomplish? Be serious! Let's . . . let's just get out of this place before Joe comes to!"

"Are you scared?" asks Elettra.

"Of course not!" he protests, shocked. "Dammit, Elettra!" he cries when he realizes the girl means it. "Do you want to know my star sign, too? And my rising sign, maybe?"

"All she needs to do is read your palm."

"Elettra! We don't have time for this!" Then, with an exasperated sigh, Ermete lets the Gypsy woman take his hand.

"What do you see?" the girl asks her.

"What do you expect her to see? She sees a hand covered with dust!" Ermete grumbles.

At their feet, Joe Vinile lets out a gasping noise.

"What do you see?" Elettra insists.

"Have you gotten to the part where I forged my parents' signature in high school?" Ermete says mockingly. "Or that unforgettable weekend when I had dates with two different girls on the same night?"

The woman shakes her head.

She reads his hand and shakes her head.

Seeing her so focused, Ermete yanks his hand back, trying to get free. "No funny business, okay?"

"What do you see?" Elettra asks for the third time.

The Gypsy woman's face melts into a calm smile. "I see the hand of a man who's never worked a single day in his life."

"And I'm proud of it!" Ermete blurts out.

"And I see a giant string of lies. . . ."

Elettra and Ermete stiffen.

"But they're all amusing lies. Pranks . . . and games. Child's play," the Gypsy concludes.

"Long live the truth!" cries the engineer, taking a deep breath. "Can we go now?"

"So he isn't one of them?"

The Gypsy woman smiles. "No, not unless by 'them' you mean people who just like playing around."

Ermete bends over to pick up the Ring of Fire and brusquely hands it to Elettra. "Here. Take this, before madame gets angry!"

"I'm sorry," the girl tells him, accepting the Ring of Fire.

"That's all right," says Ermete. "It's just . . . I wasn't expecting . . ."

Elettra rises up on her tiptoes to hug him. "I'm really sorry, Ermete! I just don't know who to believe anymore."

"Well, this time, believe me: we've got to get out of here!" he says, returning the hug.

Harvey and Sheng are running at breakneck speed. Harvey's racing out ahead, deciding on the spot when and where to turn, finding his way through the streets of Rome without hesitating.

And without ever looking back.

They're running in order to put as much distance as they can between themselves and the man with the gray hair. And despite the ice, which makes each step dangerous, they run without ever slowing down, even when taking curves, barely dodging the passersby.

When they finally decide to slow down, the city around them

is once again Rome. Nothing around them reminds them of the crenellated walls of Coppedè. They see white cupolas, rows of monumental columns and series of archways. They see the ruins of the ancient empire proudly illuminated by spectacular lights.

Rome is protecting them and hiding them.

But the city is too big and too ancient for them to keep challenging it like this.

They need a safe place where they can rest.

A place where no one can touch them.

The Domus Quintilia.

Jacob Mahler finally pulls himself out of the tub and lies there on the cold bathroom floor. He manages to spit out the gag in his mouth and starts to drag himself toward the sink, his hands and feet still bound. His chest is exploding with pain.

First he gets to his knees, and then he crouches on his feet. He leans against the edge of the sink. He pushes himself up. The mirror reflects his face. It looks like a skull.

"Don't think it ends here . . . ," he growls, staring at his reflection. "Don't think I'm not going to come looking for you."

His head's throbbing. The wound in his chest makes it difficult for him to breathe.

He moves awkwardly up to the medicine cabinet beside the mirror, opens it, clasps the corner of his medicine bag between his fingertips and dumps it into the sink, making its contents spill out. He rummages through it, finds his razor, opens it up and slips the handle in between his teeth. Then he raises his wrists and starts to rub the cords against the blade, up and down, up and down, barely slicing them with each stroke.

A minute later and he's free. He spits out the razor and frees his ankles.

He pants.

His whole chest is covered with blood.

He staggers out of the bathroom. He reaches Mistral's room and looks around. Empty. Or actually, not entirely empty. Photographs are scattered everywhere. He recognizes them. He was the one who ordered them to be taken and sent in to the newspapers. They're pictures of Alfred Van Der Berger.

"AAAARGH!" he howls, ripping the sheets off the bed and dragging them down the hallway.

First he needs to take care of his wound. Then he has to take care of the girl. But when he returns to the bathroom, he hears music, the notes of the song "You're Beautiful" by James Blunt. It's coming from the sheets he's dragging behind him. Jacob Mahler kneels down and untangles them. A cell phone tumbles to the ground.

It's Mistral's phone.

"Hello?" he practically roars, answering it.

"Good morning," comes Beatrice's voice. "Have you looked outside the front door yet?"

Mahler doesn't breathe.

"You're through, Jacob . . . ," the young woman continues. "It looks like they just caught the Tiberside Killer."

"You didn't . . . ," he snarls, rushing furiously down the stairs.

He throws open the front door.

And he backs up, staring into the blue blinking light. Two police cars are parked outside the house.

"Freeze!" a carabiniere warns him. "Put your hands up!"

Jacob Mahler gapes. He sees the gleaming of guns being trained on him. But he doesn't raise his hands.

Instead he goes back inside, locks the door behind him and runs upstairs, wheezing from the pain in his chest. He walks over to his carry-on bag and pulls out his special satellite cell phone to be used in case of emergency.

From the garden he can hear the voices of the carabinieri as they spread out to surround the house. "Come out with your hands up!" The blinking lights are streaming in through the shutters.

Jacob hits the cell phone's On button and punches in the three-digit code. Any other combination of numbers will make the telephone explode.

He punches in the code.

Six-six-six.

He holds the phone up to his ear as the policemen break down the front door. "Come on . . . ," mutters Jacob.

Purrrr. Purrrr.

"Come on. . . ."

Purrrr. The satellite receives the signal, beams it over to Shanghai, directs it at a black crystal skyscraper that no one can enter without authorization.

First ring.

A carabiniere starts to climb the stairs.

Second ring.

Jacob walks down the hallway, heading toward the round window.

Third ring.

He looks outside: a snowy garden.

273

Fourth ring.

No blinking lights. Footsteps pounding up the stairs.

Fifth ring.

"Devil," says a voice on the other end. It's barely more than the hissing of a snake. As sharp as a dragon's claw.

"Jacob," he replies. "They got me."

The carabiniere suddenly appears at the top of the stairway, his gun cocked in front of him. "Freeze!" he shouts. "Nobody move!"

Jacob ends his phone call.

He's not sure the devil will send anyone to help him.

But while he waits, he'd better prepare for hell.

"Hands up!" the carabiniere shouts again. "Drop it!"

Jacob Mahler raises his hands slowly.

His fingers punch three random numbers into his cell phone.

"As you wish," he calls out to the policeman.

He drops the cell phone onto the hallway floor.

He counts to five.

And the entire hallway explodes in a burst of flames.

30

THE FIREWORKS

BEATRICE PULLS HER MINI OVER IN VIA DELL'ARCO ANTICO. THE
engine steams in the crisp night air. "You need to go through that
archway. Turn right," she explains to Mistral, "and you'll be in
Piazza in Piscinula. From there, you should be able to find the
hotel on your own."

The girl nods. She leans over in her seat to kiss her on the
cheek. "Thanks for everything you've done."

Beatrice waves her hand with mock indifference. "Don't mention it. After all, I promised you. . . ."

Mistral opens the door and rests one foot on the snowy ground.

"Be careful," Beatrice warns her.

"Are you sure you don't want to come, too?" the girl asks. "We
could tell everything to the people who run the hotel and—"

Beatrice stops her. "I can't. It's no place for me."

"Why not?"

"Because I'm not a good person. . . ."

"You're wrong."

"Don't say that again." Beatrice feels as though her insides
were turning to jelly. "Or I might just change my mind."

Mistral gets out of the Mini. "Keep in touch, if you want."

"I will. Straight down that way and take a right," Beatrice reminds her.

She waits, watching the girl walk away, waves to her one last time and then puts the car into gear. As she's driving away, she feels her chest pounding, tears welling up in her eyes. Her seat belt is suffocating her.

She doesn't know where to go.

She doesn't know what to do.

All she knows is that she did the right thing.

She reaches the Tiber, drives over Ponte Quattro Capi and takes the road along Piramide. From there, she drives down to the Colosseum, seeking out the lights of Via del Corso and the noise of bars. It's almost midnight, the end of a very trying New Year's Eve.

She clicks on the radio and turns up the volume, hoping it will relax her.

The city lights go whizzing by.

She enjoys the sensation of the road zipping along beneath her tires.

She checks the time. Only a few minutes left until the New Year.

"A new year . . . a new life," she whispers, waiting for the noisy burst of fireworks that will announce that it's midnight at last.

The capital of the ancient world awaits the sound of the bell that will toll the New Year. Thousands of people have turned on their television sets to synchronize their watches. Elettra, Ermete and the Gypsy woman emerge from the depths of San Clemente. An eerie silence awaits them. The very last minutes of the year.

Colorful banners flutter between the buildings. Blinking lights decorate the streets. The windows flicker with the glow of TV screens. Behind the panes of glass are laughter, corks being held back, hands seeking out other hands, lips ready to be kissed.

"This is the strangest New Year's Eve of my life . . . ," says Elettra, walking through the bustling city, the Ring in her hands.

The first windows are now being opened. The voices of television hosts echo from building to building.

"You're telling me!" Ermete smiles. "I've never been out with two girls on New Year's Eve. What about you, Gypsy Queen?"

The woman doesn't answer. She walks ahead of them with the steady pace of someone who's well familiar with the city streets and the tranquil eyes of someone who's accustomed to watching others celebrate from afar.

Through the open windows, they can hear people start their countdown of the last twenty seconds of the year. The three stop to listen to the chorus of people who, as a single voice, testify to the last remaining moments until midnight.

The Gypsy woman turns to face Elettra and says, "It's time."

She's asking her to do something. Something important. Something that needs to be done.

The seconds fly by.

It's a very special night. The night of San Silvestro, the pope who celebrated mass on the last day of the year 999. The day that many had believed would be the very last day before the end of the world. After that midnight, everything changed.

Elettra stares at the Gypsy woman. And the Gypsy woman says, "It's time for the world to change once more."

Elettra. *Kore Kosmou*. The Maiden of the Cosmos.

She's the one who has to decide. She's the one who has to use the Ring of Fire. The time has come for her to do it.

Or to refuse.

The seconds fly by. The countdown grows louder and louder.

Elettra's hands snap open the seal and unwrap the linen.

The Gypsy woman says, "Look."

Ermete smiles.

And Elettra raises the mirror to look into it.

The first ones to go are the blinking strings of holiday lights hanging over the streets. They turn bright white and burst one by one, like popcorn. Then come the streetlights, which flare up in whitish flames. The energy spreads out like a wave, transforming television screens into blinding sheets of whiteness, lightbulbs in the houses into sudden flashes, home appliances going berserk, tubes in neon signs melting. A blaze of whiteness flies over the city, bursting out from San Clemente in a giant explosion of light. Rome blanches in a single, massive electrical surge that hits it like a gargantuan gale of wind.

Then, as suddenly as it appeared, the light vanishes. Choruses of spark plugs and circuit breakers begin to click wildly in every street, in every building, in every neighborhood. Their rhythmic snapping sets the beat, joined by the sound of champagne corks and the first celebrations.

Exhausted and overcharged, Rome is plunged into darkness.

The laughter comes to a sudden halt. Champagne flows out in

suddenly silent rivers. After the pure whiteness that had blinded it like a star mirrored in the snow, the capital suddenly disappears in a vast pool of darkness.

Blackout.

"Elettra?" comes Ermete's voice after an endless moment. "Elettra, are you all right?"

The girl opens her eyes. It's dark. Ermete is leaning over her.

"What happened?" she asks.

"You looked at your reflection in the Ring of Fire and there was a giant burst of light. . . . Then you fainted," the engineer explains.

Elettra feels weak, drained. "I don't remember anything." She gropes around and feels cold metal. She's sitting in Ermete's sidecar.

"Can you hold out until we get to the hotel?"

Elettra stares at the windows of the buildings around them. The glow from the televisions has been replaced by the flickering glow of candles.

Candles.

Thousands and thousands of candles, lit on every windowsill in the city.

"Why?" the girl asks.

"There's been another blackout," replies Ermete. "It seemed like a massive power surge."

Elettra looks over at the street and sees the Gypsy woman dancing. But she's not making a sound. "What's she doing?"

"Oh, who knows?" Ermete says softly. "But she sure looks happy."

"Ask her . . . ," whispers Elettra. "Ask her what she saw on my palm, would you?"

Ermete shrugs. "I could try . . . but I'm not so sure she'll tell me."

He walks away from the sidecar, leaving Elettra to contemplate the captivating sight of the candlelit street. When she looks back toward the Gypsy woman, the girl only sees Ermete.

"The minute I asked her," the engineer says, walking back to the sidecar, "she burst out laughing and whispered the answer in my ear. Then she ran off."

"What did she tell you?" asks Elettra.

"That she saw a star on your palm. And that by looking at your reflection, you summoned it."

31

THE NEW YEAR

FERNANDO MELODIA IS LYING ON A SOFA AT THE DOMUS Quintilia with two broken ribs. But what's really hurting is his pride. Pride that was squashed by the thief the day before. And by Linda, who, unlike him, managed to drive him off with her broom.

She, on the other hand, doesn't miss a single opportunity to remind him about the embarrassing episode. "There, there, Fernando . . . ," she coos. "Does it still hurt where that nasty man hit you?"

It wouldn't hurt so much if she'd cut it out.

He sighs.

It's been a very strange morning. Ever since the lights went back on, the newscasters have done nothing other than talk about the city's second blackout, a total power outage that forced the inhabitants of Rome to celebrate by candlelight. Even at the president's dinner. Even at the most important gala events.

Not everyone was disappointed, though. The city was immersed in an atmosphere of times past. Some people are even suggesting that the New Year always be celebrated that way from now on, without electricity.

Meanwhile, the local politicians are blaming the power company. The power company is blaming international politics. International politicians aren't available for comment.

Meanwhile, the electricity has gone back on.

But the blackout, thinks Fernando, *certainly wasn't the strangest thing. Not as strange as the way the kids came back to the hotel.*

Including Mistral.

Harvey's parents and Sheng's father had been ready to give their children a severe punishment, but the moment they saw the two scared, exhausted boys walk through the door, they ran over to hug them. And when Mistral showed up, Harvey and Sheng almost fainted from relief. They hugged her and asked her a million questions, all whispered, all out of the adults' earshot.

And Elettra? Elettra was the last to come home. She was somber and quiet. Linda claimed she'd been dropped off by a boy on a motorcycle. A motorcycle with a sidecar!

Fernando decided not to say anything to her. Besides, Linda grabbed the spotlight with the story of her having driven off the intruder with her broom, even showing off the pieces of the broken broomstick like they were relics in a museum.

Then they celebrated the New Year together, forgetting all about that afternoon's arguments. And the threats of legal disputes and police reports. And everything else that was best left forgotten.

Irene was the one who insisted they celebrate. Really celebrate. Fernando went down into the basement to get one of his special bottles, one from the Ulysses Moore reserve, which he'd bought with his wife during their honeymoon in Cornwall.

There were four of them left.

Boom! The cork shot up and hit the ceiling, which promptly inspired Linda to complain, "So, who's going up there to get rid of that stain?"

They had a toast.

"Cheers!" Irene said as she clinked glasses with Sheng's father.

Sitting on the basement floor, Harvey, Elettra, Sheng and Mistral hold what just might be their last group meeting. Mistral's still waiting for her mother to return, at which point they'll leave for France. In the afternoon, Mr. and Mrs. Miller will be leaving Rome to head to Naples, where Harvey's father will be attending a conference. They'll come back into town only to catch their flight to the United States.

Rather than a meeting, it feels more like a sort of farewell party. In a few short hours, thousands of kilometers will divide them.

"But I'm staying in Rome for a month!" exclaims Sheng when the general mood has become a bit too glum. "Elettra and I want to cause a few more blackouts."

All four smile.

They've all told each other exactly what happened, minute by minute. They know they need to make some important decisions. And they go over and over the questions they still can't answer. In particular, the second blackout has everyone baffled. Elettra has already explained that it happened right after she looked into the Ring of Fire. When Mistral asks her what she saw in the mirror, Elettra shakes her head, unsure. She'd seen herself, herself transformed into light, but she answers, "Nothing in particular, I guess."

The ancient mirror is lying there in front of them, perfectly harmless. All four have looked into it, contemplating their blurry reflections made grainy by time. They've read Seneca's writing engraved on its back, passing the Ring of Fire around from hand to hand in awe. And they've told each other, in hushed voices, that it was Professor Van Der Berger's search for the mirror that led to his years of studies—and to his murder.

But they still don't understand why. They feel weighed down by a feeling they can't shake, something they aren't able to explain, a place, a time or a face. However, the more they study the object found beneath the Basilica di San Clemente, the more they're convinced that the mirror is only one piece of the puzzle, a starting point.

It's a mystery that in turn hides other mysteries, which may be found somewhere in the professor's journal or in the books he'd been reading. Or maybe in their all having met in Rome. Whatever it is, it's a dangerous mystery.

"They won't stop looking for it . . . ," says Harvey.

"And they know you live here," Mistral warns Elettra. Her part of the story, her kidnapping, was the one that impressed the kids the most. Harvey and Sheng's part, with Jacob Mahler thrashing around in the bathtub, scared them out of their wits.

"Maybe they arrested him . . . ," Sheng guesses, always the optimist. "If that woman, Beatrice, managed to call the police, I say they caught him."

"We'll have to wait and see . . . ," says Elettra.

No one can know what happened yet. On January 1 there aren't any newspapers to read, and on TV they're still focusing on the blackout.

"In any case, he doesn't have that violin anymore—" says Mistral.

"He isn't the problem," Harvey breaks in. "Even if he's dead or they arrested him, they'll send someone else in his place. And whoever it is, they'll come here. To this hotel."

"But this is our sanctuary. Our safe place," Elettra protests.

"It's already been infiltrated," Harvey replies. "Just ask your dad."

"It's too dangerous now," agrees Sheng. "Even if the tops told us that this place was safe, we've got to be careful. You've got to be careful."

Elettra nods.

"Maybe the tops meant to tell us that it's safe for us. But not for the Ring. Or for other people."

"What do we do with the Ring, then?"

Harvey suggests donating it to a museum. "That way, it'll be safe."

But Elettra has another idea. "I think we need to keep studying it ourselves. And investigate everything Ermete and the professor found out."

"But how?"

"Sheng's staying in Rome for a month. He and I could—"

"*Hao!* You bet!" he says, cutting her off. "We could keep going."

"But with Ermete, of course," adds Elettra. "After all, he's the one who's studied the map of the Chaldeans. And the two things are connected, right?"

The kids look at each other doubtfully. Mistral, who's the only one who hasn't met Ermete, lets them decide. "And the Gypsy woman?" she asks.

"She seems to know a lot more than she told me," Elettra admits. "Not only because she followed us to San Clemente . . . but most importantly because of later on, when she convinced me to look at my reflection. She seemed to know that . . . that I had to do it. I'll go find her. I'll ask her why."

The kids sit silently for a long time.

"Plus, there's the question of the teeth. Who engraved all those letters on them? And why?" Mistral wonders.

"Ermete says the teeth are really old. Over a hundred years old," adds Elettra.

"A hundred years, a hundred years," Harvey thinks aloud. "The number one hundred keeps popping up in all this."

"Guys," Sheng says after a bit, "there's no point in our racking our brains about this right now. We've obviously got a lot of work to do. We've been given some sort of gift. A dangerous gift, sure, but we can't just pretend like nothing's happened. We've got to . . . use it. See where it takes us. If we're able to understand it, I mean. I think Ermete's the only one who can help us. The only person we can trust."

"The only *adult* we can trust," Mistral clarifies. "From what you guys have told me, he knows a lot more than we do."

"But he's in danger, too. He shouldn't stay here in Rome," Harvey insists. "It's not only Mahler we have to worry about. Joe Vinile is somewhere out there, too."

"I guess you're right," admits Elettra.

"And Joe knows Ermete, too."

"Why don't you invite him over to your place?" Mistral suggests.

"What, to New York?"

"Nobody would think to look for him there."

"I don't know . . . I'd have to ask my parents," says Harvey. "But that's not such a bad idea."

"Otherwise, I could ask my mom," Mistral suggests. "I could talk to her today, when she gets back. I've got a big, gigantic house in Paris. And it's always empty." What Mistral doesn't mention is that once she's back in France, she'll be scared of staying all by herself in that big, empty house.

"Do you think Ermete would be willing to leave Rome?" asks Sheng.

"I doubt his mother would give him permission . . . ," jokes Harvey. "But my guess is he'd jump at the chance."

"If we ask Ermete to keep the mirror," Mistral breaks in, "what do we do with the map? And the tops?"

"We can split up the tops," Sheng suggests. "We each take one. Then we can decide who has to keep the map."

Elettra shakes her head.

"Not me. I can't."

"Why not?"

"For the same reason I can't keep the Ring of Fire. If there's one name they know . . . it's mine."

"She's right," agrees Mistral. "And I can't, either. They know who I am, too."

"Well, that leaves the two of us . . . ," says Sheng.

"So how do we decide?" asks Harvey.

"Dice?" He holds up a pair of red-and-black dice Ermete had given him. "The one who rolls the highest number keeps the map."

Sheng rolls the dice and gets a three and a two.

Harvey rolls a six and a five.

"No! I knew it!" he moans, shaking his head.

Elettra hands him the wooden map. "Well, take good care of it, but don't tell us where you hide it. It'd be better if we don't know where it is."

"Right," affirms Sheng.

Harvey opens the map one last time. Then he snaps it shut and rests it on his lap. "All right. But we need to make a promise."

An ancient silence fills the basement.

"We'll never use this map unless all four of us are together. I don't know when that might happen. Maybe when you two have discovered more about the professor, or when Ermete tells us what the Ring of Fire is really used for . . . In a year, maybe? Or maybe never. But the agreement is this: only when all four of us are together, or never."

Elettra nods and adds, "And all of this will be our secret."

"All four of us, together again," repeats Sheng, resting his hand on top of Harvey's. "I'm in!"

Mistral smiles. "Yeah!" she says, adding her hand to the stack. "Me too!"

"At this point, we could use a better expression than 'All for one and one for all,'" says Elettra. "But . . . after all, there were actually four Musketeers."

"So you're with us?" Harvey asks her.

Elettra rests her hand on those of her new friends.

"No matter what happens. No matter what the future has in store for us," she says solemnly. "Yes. I'm with you. And you're with me."

32

THE STARS

AUNT IRENE IS WAITING FOR THE MOON TO RISE UP OVER THE rooftops. She clutches the arms of her wheelchair and listens to the silence echoing through the house. The Domus Quintilia is peaceful.

The only sound is her sister, Linda, tossing and turning in the bed. She's always been a restless sleeper, at times even having long conversations in her sleep.

Irene wheels her chair past the rosebush, up to the French doors leading to the terrace, and unlocks them. The chilly night-time air whirls up, dancing.

Dressed in her nightgown, the woman wheels herself out onto the terrace and shuts the door behind her.

It's freezing cold outside.

It's January saying hello to her.

She wheels her chair up to the four stone statues that look over the inner courtyard. The fabric of her nightgown is decorated with all kinds of animals.

She isn't cold.

She looks up at the sky. It's cloudless, softened by the white halo around the moon. The seven stars of Ursa Major sparkle overhead, standing perfectly still.

"We stare at you and you stare at us . . . ," Irene whispers. "Although our gazes rarely meet."

She leans all her weight against the wheelchair's armrests. "What do I do now?" she asks the moonlit night. "Was I wrong to choose my own niece? Alfred was killed. And now there are only three of us left. That shouldn't have happened. It's never happened before."

Her wrists trembling from the strain, Irene slowly pulls herself forward in the wheelchair.

"They kidnapped Mistral. And they're also prepared to kill. That wasn't part of the deal. How could it be, after all the effort we put into finding the kids? How could they go to such extremes?"

Irene rests her feet on the ground. Then she starts pushing herself up on her fragile legs.

"Tell me, Nature, can I still hope for the Pact to continue? In the shelter, we said it would begin in Rome. And so it was. The Ring of Fire was unearthed. The Maiden of the Cosmos beheld her own reflection. The summons of light was sent out. And the first step has been accomplished. Did you see it in New York? And in Shanghai? Did you see what a perfectly bright light our star had? It was hidden below and hidden above. Search below and you shall find it above. That's what was written, and that's what happened. In small reflections you shall see large reflections. But it was also written that the children wouldn't be harmed. Who changed the rules?"

Irene trembles, but her will is stronger than her age.

She remains standing firmly on her own two feet.

"Answer me, Nature . . . ," she asks once again, her teeth clenched from the effort. She raises a trembling hand toward the starry sky and pleads, "Answer me! Answer me! What do I have to do?"

She frowns, lost in thought. Her ears await the imperceptible reply.

When the answer arrives, the elderly woman listens to it with a sigh, letting it embrace her gently, and falls back into her wheelchair, exhausted.

She closes her eyes. And she smiles.

High above her, overhead, the stars of Ursa Major shine in the sky, perfectly still. But shining among them now is a new star, one invisible to telescopes and astronomers' eyes. It's a star that darts furiously through space with a long tail of fiery ice.

It's a comet. It's been summoned by the Ring of Fire.

And it's heading toward Earth.

ACKNOWLEDGMENTS

I stole many months of your time to think over and write this first episode. I normally don't care much for acknowledgments pages, but this time it's different. And you know why.

As always, Marcella was the first one to know what was going on, and she waited for me patiently. We talked over the plot of Century a few years ago, when we decided we liked the idea of writing a story set in Italy, in Rome, a Rome that was as true to life as possible and, therefore, particular. And I think we succeeded in doing just that.

I need to thank Clare because she's the most romantic, most stubborn-headed editor you could ever meet. She's the only person who knows how to track me down on my cell phone even when it's switched off. Thanks to Iacopo and Francesca for how they managed to see what I was writing before I even wrote it. Among my friends, special thanks go out to the two Beatrices. One will recognize herself in these pages and the other provided me with a fantastic business card. Thank you for your help, Alessandro, Walter, Tommy, Andrea and Franco. And, as always, thanks to Mom and Dad. Your critical (very critical) eye and illuminating (very illuminating) advice are truly irreplaceable.

Some of the characters in this first episode are based on real live people. Dr. Tito suggested the teeth to me, Elena suggested Elettra's character, and Professor Gianni Collu, with his incalculable number of books, provided inspiration for the character of Alfred. Linda Melodia, actually called Laura, is a wonderful person.

See you in New York!

293